H. A. McHugh loves family, reading, storytelling, travelling, socialising and golf. Writing has been a lifelong interest and ambition. *'Jinxed'* set initially in Achill, island of dreams, is her second novel. *'Inheritance: Gift or Burden'* was published in 2015.

The author lives in County Clare.

Dedication

This book is dedicated to Nóirín Williams Mooney, inspiring teacher and treasured friend. Thank you, Nóirín, for preparing the ground, sowing the seeds and cultivating whatever creativity and storytelling I may have.

H.A. McHugh

JINXED

AUSTIN MACAULEY PUBLISHERS™

LONDON • CAMBRIDGE • NEW YORK • SHARJAH

A CIP catalogue record for this title is available from the British Library.

ISBN 9781787108523 (Paperback)
ISBN 9781787108530 (E-Book)

www.austinmacauley.com

First Published (2018)
Austin Macaulay Publishers Ltd.
25 Canada Square
Canary Wharf
London
E14 5LQ

Acknowledgements

Anyone who has ever attempted to write a novel understands the debt owed to a large number of people for their inspiration and support throughout the long and painful process.

First I wish to thank my extended family for their inspiring stories. Sincere thanks to my editorial team at Austin Macauley for invaluable advice and assistance. A huge thank you to Jana, Niamh, Angela, Enda, Dermot, Ann and Maureen, my early readers, for their helpful comments and encouragement. I would like to thank my daughter Jana and my sons Kevin, John and Colm, for their faith and support. Thanks to my husband, Jackie, for endless cups of tea, fabulous dinners and being always in my corner.

Finally thanks to you, the readers. I hope you enjoyed travelling through the tale and can forgive me for any errors and whatever bits you didn't like.

Many of the place names used in this book are real but most are purely imaginative especially those closely associated with my fictional characters.

Prologue
1918–1931

Redmond was born in Dugort on Achill Island on December 27th, 1918, to Paddy and Bridie Gilraine. Paddy, like most Achill men in those days, worked in England for the bulk of the year, returning to his island home from Christmas until the following Easter. Redmond helped his mother Bridie with the jobs around the place and looked after his sisters Rose and Breda and baby brother Brendan. From an early age he loved spending hours on the hill, on the bog, climbing behind the house, helping with the myriad and endless tasks of a small island farm. When he enrolled at the local school, he quickly acquired the nickname Red because of his striking hair colour and also as a mark of affection. For the rest of his life, only his mother continued to call him by his given name.

Apart from the outdoors his greatest love was storytelling. The best house for stories was Kate's and the best night in Kate's was Wednesday. Kate's was a 'cuarding' or visiting house and had been for as far back as the oldest inhabitant of the village could remember and that was as close as dammit to a hundred years. Red loved going to Kate's and his mother didn't seem to mind his going. If he got there early, before the crowd gathered, Kate would slip him a well-buttered slice or two of her still-warm currant bread and he would settle down in a quiet corner where he could listen undetected and undisturbed. The adults all knew he was there but no one let on. Red was a well behaved young lad and the women made a pet of him, rubbing his head of ginger curls and calling him 'Young Red'. The men nodded conspiratorially and pretended to ignore his presence.

What he didn't want any of them to know was that the main reason he came so early was so that he could get past Abha Na Sí (the fairies' river) in daylight on his way over and would only have to face the terrors of the dark on his way back home. He couldn't share this fear with anyone, they'd only laugh at him and say he was silly to be afraid of his own little river and it practically on his doorstep. They didn't know its terrible voice in the dark stillness nor all the goblins and púcas and other horrors it could call upon to terrify a young fellow, especially on a dark moonless night in wintertime. His love of stories always won out in the end and every Wednesday night saw him heading for Kate's and trying to ignore his fear and trepidation until the time came for him to hurry back home. The stories were always worth it.

Usually they were just snippets of news and sometimes he just knew that the real juicy gossipy bits were being put on hold until after he had left. On certain nights, he could sense this from the frisson of excitement and ill-disguised impatience at Kate's mild suggestion that it was time for him to be going home. On other nights, events from local history were rehashed. By far, the best nights were the ones when the really old stories were retold in hushed tones, the ones about the prophecies. These were often told in sequence, one leading naturally to another over a number of evenings. The series would always begin with reference to Olde Moore's Almanac, leading to some discussion of the power of the second sight and which families were blessed or otherwise with the gift. Soon someone would bring up the name of Nostradamus and the wonders that had come about in the world directly as he had foretold. Inevitably and inexorably, the time came around to what everyone was eagerly awaiting, the local prophecies. Brian Rua Ó Bairéad had made a number of very detailed local prophecies in the 1750s.

It was here that Red first heard the story of the martyrdom of Father Magnus Sweeney, of how the priest had died defending his Roman Catholic faith in Penal times and of the shameful way in which he had been betrayed by a parishioner and neighbour. What stuck in Red's memory was the vividness of the description of what had been said of the British soldier who had passed a mocking comment at the scene of Father Magnus's hanging in Newport. "You'll not profit from this night's evil work. Before the year is out the dogs will drag your bones through the village of Tonragee." In the depths of the following winter, wild dogs were heard howling in the village. They had come down from the mountain carrying in their jaws human bones.

There were stories too about banshees and other harbingers of death. There were versions pertaining to different local families. The hair would stand on the back of Red's neck when someone would come in and say, "I wonder which of the Gilraines is dying. I heard the 'crying' last night. Did anyone else hear it?" This was chilling news for him as the Gilraines were his father's people. And next day, as sure as the sun sets, he'd hear in the schoolyard that one of the Gilraines had passed away during the night. Then there were the stories of sightings of ghostly funeral corteges being seen in unusual places such as on the famine path or coming around the base of the cliff from the seaward side where no houses stood, signifying some tragedy or death by drowning. Such sightings were invariably followed by bad tidings for some local family.

Brian Rua had also foretold drownings at various landmarks in Achill that came to pass during Red's own lifetime. He had prophesied that a young man would be found dead among the rocks near the pier at Dugort on Christmas day.

Red remembered hearing the prophecy in Kate's and decades later he attended the funeral of the victim, a young short-sighted man in his twenties who had taken a wrong turning on his way home and stumbled into the tide. That's where he was found sitting up facing the sea early on Christmas morning.

Another well-known prophecy scared Bridie for years on end as it foretold the drowning of a young man at the bridge in the valley that was on the route from Dugort East to the local school. She often watched anxiously through binoculars (always referred to locally as spying glasses) until her own children and their friends had passed safely over the bridge. She worried, heart in mouth, on the days when they chose, despite her repeated warnings, to delay at the spot gazing into the treacherous waters beneath. It had been foretold that a man wearing a red coat would discover the body of the young man. Many people pooh-poohed this particular prophecy in the belief that its time had already passed. Surely the reference to the man in the red coat must be to the long gone British Army uniform, for what man in mid twentieth century rural Ireland would be seen in public wearing a red coat?

In the early nineteen seventies, Red got word from his brother Brendan about a young neighbouring lad who had returned from working in England for the funeral of his father. He remained at home for a few weeks and having a car was extremely popular with the younger lads whom he happily transported to the pictures or wherever they wanted to go. He had confided in Brendan that he disliked driving the lonely valley road alone as he was terrified of the bridge and that was why he usually brought a passenger with him whenever he could. A few days later his body was found in the submerged car under the valley bridge. He had driven inside the left parapet of the bridge. He was alone. A neighbour going out for a day's shooting found him at sunrise. The man was wearing a red and black tartan hunting jacket sent to him by an uncle from Canada.

One other prophecy stayed rooted in Red's memory and haunted his dreams for years. It had to do with the search for the body of a young man at the bottom of a snow-filled ravine. It made no sense to him at the time as the only ravines, chasms or grikes in Achill were far too close to the sea to ever be snow-filled.

Part I
1931–1935

Chapter 1

Away from Home

Red loved every inch of his native island and his life farming the hillside farm. He loved the endless busyness of the farm work and the proximity to the sea. By the time he was twelve years old and had made his confirmation, Red knew that, like most of his island neighbours, he would have to emigrate to find work and make a decent living. His introduction to real work was in Scotland with a squad of local lads and lasses the summer he was thirteen. They walked to Cloghmore where at Darby's Point they boarded a hooker which brought them to Westport.

Here they transferred to the tender anchored in the bay. From Westport they sailed to Girvan in Scotland. On arrival there, the train brought them to the potato farms near Stirling. This is where they would stay for the season, sleeping in bothies and working all the daylight hours picking potatoes. After two stints at 'tatie hoking' over the summer seasons in Scotland, Red left school as soon as he turned fifteen. He spent the last week or two at home helping out on the family farm and encouraging young Brendan to take over the tasks he had undertaken up until then. In time-honoured tradition, he also lent a hand on neighbouring farms and smallholdings.

By the end of March, he was not only ready he was anxious to start full-time work in England. Both his parents were happy that he should go. After all, he was a strapping lad, healthy and strong, and there were no prospects in Achill for anyone in the hungry thirties. Worse still, men were now coming back from the United States having failed to find secure jobs there. So when Paddy was ready to head for England it was no surprise to anyone that Red accompanied him, leaving behind Bridie and her two young daughters with only young Brendan to look out for them.

Early in the morning of April 1st, 1933, they set off with a few neighbouring men on the nine mile walk from Dugort East to the station at Achill Sound. Like the others they were wearing their best clothes and Sunday boots. The rest of their gear in a variety of suitcases and bundles was piled onto a cart. Everyone appeared to be in good spirits, the younger ones enjoying the excitement of the new venture and the older men, knowing the hardship they were facing, playing along so as not to discourage them. All the goodbyes had been said already in the privacy of their homes so there would be no tearful farewells at the station. As they trudged along in the early morning sunshine, someone began to sing 'It's a long way to Tipperary' and soon others joined in. As they approached the next village, the singing petered out. More men joined them as they turned on to the main road. Red was looking around him taking note of the spring growth and the bog cotton like a fleecy blanket stretching away to his left. He was beginning to feel a little lonely already and was wondering when next he'd walk this way again and what changes to his beloved Achill might occur in his absence.

As they continued in silence, he watched the other first timers for signs of sadness. At last, they arrived at Achill Sound. Here people came out of their houses to watch them pass. Greetings were exchanged and they were wished a safe journey and the best of luck until their return. They boarded the train, piling into the front three carriages for the first leg of the journey. Once aboard, they sat opposite each other on two long wooden seats with their cases and bundles on racks overhead. The carriages were self-contained compartments with doors on either side, so for the duration of the journey passengers were confined to their allotted seats and also to the company of their fellow travellers. To get to Dublin took over five hours.

For the first few hours, Red enjoyed the views of passing scenery and the various conversations going on around him. Eventually, things quietened down and he found himself with little to relieve the monotony but his own thoughts. Some of the other men were already sound asleep and snoring, others were drowsily snoozing and a few of the younger ones like himself were staring into space. From the looks of them he suspected that he was not the only one already missing home. On their arrival in Dublin in the early afternoon, the bulk of the men set off up the quays, carrying their luggage, in search of a public house close to the North Wall where they would while away the long hours until the B and I ferry was due to leave at eight o' clock that night. Red and his dad took a taxi to St Margaret's Nursing Home in the Phoenix Park to visit Paddy's niece. Nano was the only daughter of Paddy's brother Joe and his wife Sally. She had been in residence in St Margaret's for over ten years. Nano had been born with some congenital abnormality and was not expected to live very long. Against all the odds the little girl survived and remained at home, lovingly cared for by her doting parents until her mother Sally's untimely death when Nano was a little over eleven years old. She had always needed full-time care as she was both physically as well as mentally handicapped. Sally and Nano had established a method of communication comprehensible only to themselves and to a lesser extent to Nano's dad. The trauma of her mother's death so badly affected her that she failed thereafter to recover her limited attempts at speech. Joe had always worked for spells on the buildings in England, earning enough cash to support his little family adequately if not lavishly. Unlike most of his neighbours Joe worked for

19

short stints, returning home after six to eight weeks for a month or so to be with his wife and much loved daughter.

After Sally's death he had had no option but to put Nano into a full-time care facility. This, on top of the loss of his lovely Sally, broke poor Joe's heart. After a good deal of searching, he eventually found St Margaret's and here Nano took up residence in the autumn of 1922. Joe visited her very frequently, always on his way to and from Achill as well as making the crossing to Dublin for special occasions and faithfully for her birthday every year. For the first couple of months in her new environment, Nano was very disoriented and had withdrawn deep inside herself. Joe found his initial visits extremely upsetting. Nano seemed now to inhabit a strange, sad world which had no place for him. He did not know whether she recognised him and was actively ignoring him or whether in fact she no longer knew who he was. After about nine months, on his fifth visit, he was requested to wait in one of the reception rooms. On all previous occasions, he had been shown straight to her cell-like room, so now he was more than a little concerned at the change in routine. He was pacing up and down when the door opened and Nano was wheeled in by a nurse who greeted him cheerfully.

"Nice to see you again, Mr Gilraine." Then, turning to face a smiling Nano, she said, "Isn't it great that your dad is here to see you on your birthday, Nano? Look, he even has a present for you and a card if I'm not mistaken." On her way out, she suggested that Joe ring the bell whenever he was ready to leave. He was delighted to see that this time Nano seemed in much better form. She even smiled tentatively at him when he bent to kiss her cheek. He was convinced that she recognised him and smiled happily in return. He drew up a chair and sat close to her, telling her all about his work and what had happened since his last visit.

This time he felt that she was actually heeding as well as hearing what he said. After a while she grew tired and, her eyes glazing over, she returned to the catatonic state which typified her condition on his earlier visits. He left his gift and birthday card on her lap and rang the bell for attention. When the nurse returned, Joe asked, "Is Nano improving or is it just wishful thinking on my part?"

"She certainly seems in better form of late. Not knowing what she was like before she came here, it's hard for us to judge really. Used she be able to talk?"

"Well, not talk exactly, she and her mother, God rest her, used to be able to communicate quite well with a combination of sounds and signs. A lot of the time I could understand her too. Sadly, since Sally died all that has disappeared."

"So far we've seen no sign of speech but Nano has been responding to us better in recent weeks. She smiles much more and responds to 'yes' and 'no' questions with nods and shakes of the head. On occasion, she gestures her needs or points out things of interest to her. So on the whole I would agree that Nano has turned a corner."

Joe left St Margaret's feeling much better about the future. Unfortunately his optimism was to be short-lived as on his next visit Nano had again reverted to a trance-like state. In fact, Joe doubted if she even recognised him. This kind of see-sawing from good to bad became the pattern of his visits over the next several years. Then one warm August night, in the summer of 1932, Nano became extremely restless. When the night nurse checked on her, she found that Nano was running a very high temperature. By morning, Nano had to be removed to hospital. She was brought by ambulance to Jervis Street Hospital where it was confirmed that she had suffered a severe stroke.

Joe was alerted when the site foreman asked him to step into the office where he handed him a telegram which read: 'JOE STOP NANO IN JERVIS STREET HOSPITAL STOP COME QUICKLY STOP'. Joe got the first available train from Euston station and arrived at Jervis Street Hospital early on the following morning. Nano did not know him. He sat quietly by her bedside for several days and then stayed a few extra days once she returned to St Margaret's. During all this time Nano showed no sign at all of recognising Joe or even knowing that he was there. In the months from then until Paddy and Red visited in early April 1933, there was no apparent change in Nano's condition. Though it was disappointing for them that she did not know who they were, it was of no great surprise to Nano's carers. They sat by her bedside and Paddy talked away in quiet tones for a long time, relating all the Achill news to a largely unresponsive Nano. When he stopped his monologue, she registered discomfort. So he resumed, trying hard to make his anecdotes as interesting as he could. Nano appeared to be listening at times but for the most part she either looked from one to the other of them with a puzzled expression or else she fidgeted agitatedly, wringing her hands and twisting her fingers. After an hour or two a nurse came to check on Nano and offered the visitors a cup of tea which they gratefully accepted.

To give Paddy a break, Red took over for a while, talking about the leave-taking that morning and describing the train journey and all the sights he'd seen on the way to Dublin. Late in the afternoon they took their leave. Paddy bent to kiss his niece on the forehead and Red shook her awkwardly by the hand. On their way out, they met a young woman on her way in to visit Nano. Paddy stopped to exchange greetings. "Who is the pretty girl and why is she visiting Nano?" Red enquired. Paddy explained that Alice Sweetman, who was studying to become a nurse in Dublin, was related to Nano on her mother's side and was in fact from Achill.

"Do you not remember her? She was often in our house with her parents Maud and Danny when ye were little."

"Oh my God, was that Alice? I'd never have recognised her. Why didn't you tell me?"

"Sure. I didn't want to embarrass you, Son. Anyway, what harm is done? You're bound to run into her again around Achill in the summer."

After leaving St Margaret's that evening Paddy and Red headed back to the city. They got dropped off in O'Connell Street and walked around the corner to a hostelry on Abbey Street where they had a good dinner. Paddy kept looking about him, aware that they were attracting attention from other diners, especially the women. Red was far too hungry to focus on anything other than the tasty food in front of him. Later, to his extreme embarrassment, he overheard his dad telling his friends about the incident and saying how proud he was to be seen with his good-looking son. "Just look at him, he's tall and broad-shouldered, over six feet two in his stockinged feet and with the bearing of a confident young man. His ginger curls framing his chiselled features emphasise his strong jaw and his deep-set eyes the grey of storm clouds." Tommy Malone agreed that anyone would be proud to be seen with such a son before reminding Paddy that to every parent their ugly duckling is a beautiful swan. "You are right, Tommy, I'm just a foolish old man but I can't help thanking God that Red has taken the best traits from both sides of the family."

All too soon it was time to head off for the North Wall and the cattle boat. Here they joined up with the rest of the Achill men, some of whom were already somewhat the worse for wear having been drowning their sorrows since early in the afternoon. Others, like themselves, had used the intervening hours to visit relatives and the remainder had taken the opportunity to take a walk about and explore the city. By the time they had got aboard, it was past eight o'clock and they were beginning to feel tired. It was hard to find anywhere comfortable to sit in the crowded accommodation below decks so Red opted to stay on deck with a crowd of younger men. Paddy, knowing how cold the night would get later on as the boat reached open waters, settled for a seat in the stuffy and packed saloon. He found himself in the company of two neighbours and a couple of County Roscommon men on their way also to 'the gardens' in Cheshire. At first, they didn't have much to say to each other as they read their newspapers or just kept their thoughts to themselves.

After a while they got into chat and began to share experiences of working the big farms in Cheshire. They discovered that over the years each of them had worked for the Millers and on the Williams' farm but never at the same time, so they whiled away an hour or more in sharing memories and telling yarns. Before the night was out they had established that one of the Roscommon men, Jack Flatley, who was now the gaffer for the Millers. Because he liked Paddy and was aware of his reputation as a hard worker, he offered to take on both father and son. This was good news for the Gilraines as the Millers were known to be good employers and usually paid a bit over the odds. Best of all it meant that Paddy didn't have to wait for his pompous neighbour Paudie Flynn to finally get around to offering him work on the Williams' farm. Paudie was an arrogant individual who liked to lord it over others and ever since he had secured the position of gaffer liked to throw his weight about. He enjoyed leaving things to the last minute so that his fellow Achill men never knew from season to season whether or not they were on his team. Paudie and loyalty were strangers and although he was in fact related to the Gilraines he took pleasure in keeping Paddy in the dark. If in fact he had intended to take on Paddy, there was no way he would have taken Red on as well without exacting a price. He would either have refused to take him on at all or else would have underpaid him, pocketing the difference for himself.

The boat docked in Liverpool at about five o'clock in the morning after first unloading the cattle at Birkenhead. Having disembarked, the men made their way to Lime Street station to catch the six o'clock train to Cheshire. On arrival at Hoylake, Mr Flatley's gang, including his two latest recruits, got off and headed for a couple of Miller trucks which would take them on the last leg of their journey. Paudie Flynn stood open-mouthed, glaring balefully at the Gilraines surrounded by a knot of Achill men only some of whom he intended to have in his gang. To avoid public rejection some of the men opted to remain on the train and take their chances by presenting themselves personally at the farms.

Chapter 2
Cheshire

When they got off the trucks in the Millers' yard, Red was surprised at the speed with which everything happened. The men were immediately divided up into work gangs and shown to their accommodation. Each working group consisted of four men with five groups in each gang. They were all housed in corrugated steel structures in the shape of a half cylinder. The huts were boiling hot in summer and freezing cold in winter. On this fresh early April morning as a first timer, Red was blissfully unaware of this. Here they would all sleep and eat and spend what little free waking time they had. The upper end of each hut was where the cooking and eating took place and the beds were laid out in two long rows on either side. Orange boxes on their ends as bedside lockers were placed to the right of each bed. Paddy and the rest of his gang, including his son, were shown to their hut and directed to select a bed and leave their gear. They had only five minutes to change into working gear and report for work. By now, it was a little after 8.00 a.m. and, because this was their first day, they were offered mugs of tea and slices of homemade bread. By 8.30 a.m. they were all aboard the trucks again and heading for the fields. The work was tedious and backbreaking, the conditions freezing and wet. First they had to dig and aerate the recently ploughed muddy fields and turn the mess of cloddy soil into endless even rows of drills. Initially Red couldn't get over where all the stones had come from. Day after day they dug and gathered the stones into heaps which then had to be hauled to the headlands. Then they spent weeks on end sowing seeds and setting vegetables. And just when they thought that it looked like they were feeling a sense of achievement they realised that all those acres and acres of crops had to be kept weed free.

As the weather improved, the sun beat down on their bent backs and now they cast their minds back with longing to the coolness of early spring. Despite the long days of agonising work, the improving weather cheered them up and, as their muscles developed and they got more used to the physical challenges of the labour, their spirits lifted and they learned to pace themselves better. It wasn't long until they had established smoother rhythms of stooping and bending while moving on relentlessly up and down the drills. Soon the younger fellows in particular began to enjoy themselves. A certain level of high jinks was tolerated so long as it didn't interfere over much with productivity and many a trick was played and joke was made at the expense of some unfortunate or other. All this was carried out in the spirit of good fun and companionship and in the knowledge that more entertainment would be gleaned from these episodes in the telling and retelling in the darkening evenings of the following autumn and winter.

For now there was the enjoyment of the wonderful sight of neatly set crops, busily growing to fruition in the well-tilled soil of Cheshire. This enjoyment was underscored by the satisfaction of a job well done and the anticipation of excellent yields and correspondingly good earnings. After all, the better the crop the greater the yield, and the greater the profit for the farmer, the better the potential earnings for the men. Payment would depend on the fulfilling of quotas when the harvesting was done. By the end of November, as the season was drawing to a close, Paddy and Red were looking forward to the prospect of being home in Achill for Christmas. Red was feeling fit and healthy and largely unaware of the changes that nine months of hard physical labour had wrought on his appearance. He had gained a lot of muscle, his shoulders had broadened and the body of the boy had long since been overtaken by the physique of a powerful man. His hands had coarsened and spread and were now considerably bigger and broader than when he arrived in Cheshire. Most significantly he had gained more than three inches in height and now towered over his father. Paddy maintained that if Red were to return home alone neither his mother nor his siblings would recognise him. And it was not just physically that he had developed and matured since leaving home. Gone forever was the sweet-faced schoolboy who had left Achill, and although he was not quite sixteen he was returning to his family a working man. On their return to Dugort, in the days immediately prior to Christmas after the initial excitement of the family greetings, they learned the sad news of Nano's death. Paddy's heart went out to his brother in this, his hour of trauma and sorrow. He deeply regretted his decision to go directly home to Achill and berated himself for postponing his visit to Nano until the return journey. As it happened, he would not have been in time to have seen Nano alive and even if they had gone to St Margaret's on their way home they would still have missed the funeral by thirty-six hours. Nevertheless, Paddy was heart-sore and sorry that poor Joe had had to face this ordeal alone and without support.

Nano's death cast a shadow over the Christmas festivities for the Gilraines. For the young people, it meant that it put a dampener on Red's homecoming. He and his siblings and other close relatives could not be party to any of the social events, the local house dances, the Wren Boys' activities or even the parochial socials. All over Ireland of the 1930s this society-imposed ban on entertainment of any kind, either within the home or outside of it, was strictly observed for a period of twelve months following the death of a family member. This meant no card games, no alcohol consumption and most significantly no visitors. The ban on callers did not apply to members of the clergy, however. They were always welcomed and invariably well fed. For Bridie, nothing could quite spoil the return of her husband and eldest son at Christmas. There was nothing to stop her cooking the choicest of what food was available so she plied them with the best of home-grown traditional fare prepared with love and devotion. She had scope too for plenty of plain and fancy baking. Also, she could afford the odd shop-bought treat of baker's bread, biscuits and preserves. She couldn't help thanking God for the blessing of the safe return of her men and secretly she was pleased to have them all to herself under her own roof, with no outside distractions, for the entire length of their stay.

Christmas came and went and one week flowed smoothly into the next with Paddy and Red busying themselves around the house and farm. They were mostly involved in doing running repairs, painting and decorating within, fencing and rebuilding stonewalls outside. They knew that as soon as the weather was at all suitable they would be very busy indeed. The turf would have to be cut and the vegetable and potato plots dug and ready before their return to 'the gardens' at the end of March. When the time came, Red was surprised at how eager he was to return to the life of work and companionship and the satisfaction of earning good money. This time the journey held no surprises for him and he fitted easily into the all-male world of returning immigrants. When they arrived at the farm, they slipped back into the rhythms of the work and, being more experienced, stronger and fitter, he found that he was not as exhausted at the end of day. Now he was far less inclined to collapse into his bunk as soon as he had eaten. He used the time to read and visit the local hostelries in the company of the younger men or even occasionally to go to the cinema. At weekends, he often went to Birkenhead or into Liverpool to the dances. He tended to keep the details of his social activities to himself as he did not want to further distress his dad who was still observing the year of mourning for Nano. At the dances, he met up with lots of his fellow countrymen and women. Every county in Ireland, north and south, was represented especially at the events in the Irish Club. Inevitably where he found himself most at home was at the dances, concerts and events organised by the Mayomen's Association. Here he met lads and lassies from all over his native county, especially those from his home place, Achill. And, as young people did then, they made arrangements to meet up in smaller and larger groups for picnics, barn dances and other outings all through the long summer evenings when work was done.

After a while he began to notice that some of the young men were far more attractive to the young women for a variety of reasons, chief of which was their sense of fashion and their stylish attire. It didn't take him long to figure out that these were the guys who were working in construction. They appeared to have much shorter working days than he and his ilk did. And undoubtedly they were earning far more money. Better still, they tended to work only a short day on Saturdays so, unlike the land labourers, they had time to go shopping. It wasn't long before his initial envy turned into a resolve to better himself and so by the time he finished work the following November he had made up his mind that he would not be returning to the backbreaking slavery of work in the gardens.

He had become particularly friendly with Frank O Neill, a lad from Kerry who worked on the buildings in Liverpool. Frank was a big raw-boned, fair-haired, happy-go-lucky kind of fellow who had been working with an uncle and several cousins for the past three years. He was now twenty years old and as soon as he had reached twenty-one he planned to leave the family firm and head for London where he would make his fortune and achieve independence. He and Red got on very well together; they had similar interests and were of like mind on a lot of issues. In particular, they both burned with an ambition to become self-sufficient and masters of their own destiny. They were both beginning to find the yoke of working for others irksome. While they were at home with their families over the Christmas period they had kept in touch by letter. Frank came to Achill for a few days immediately prior to Christmas and Red went to visit the O Neills in Killduff outside Killarney in Kerry for the New Year celebrations.

Chapter 3

London

Immediately after the festivities were over, in the first days of 1935, Red and Frank set off for London. This time there were no emotional farewell scenes at all. Frank's mother Daisy had died when he was only nine years old and as far as Bridie knew Red had only left Achill to visit with his best friend's family. By the time he was due back home, he would have sent his parents a letter from London where he was confident he'd already have secured a job and decent accommodation for himself. He had chosen to do it this way, not because he was taking the coward's way out, but because he knew that in the long run this was the kindest course of action. Had he waited until his father was due to return to Cheshire he would have felt guilty about not returning with him. Furthermore, his mother would have been distressed at what she would inevitably construe as his betrayal of and abandonment of his dad. This way his parents would have time to adjust to his decision and accept that it was probably all for the best. In their hearts, they would understand his need for independence and also approve of his plans to better himself.

So it was with light hearts and a great deal of excitement that the lads set off on the train from Killarney to Dublin, then by boat to Liverpool and from there again by train to London. They were young and free and mad keen to experience the freedom and independence waiting for them in the city of their dreams. Their minds were filled with notions of unlimited opportunities and streets paved with gold. London was the place where all men were equal and where hard work and dedication would make you your fortune. All you needed to be successful in London was a cool head, determination to work hard and belief in your dreams and Lady Luck would smile on you. Hadn't they both relations who had become very successful in the building industry in London? Red's own cousin Paul was a sub-contractor who had done very well for himself and was now living high on the hog having married a rich heiress. He was currently living in a wonderful house set in its own grounds in Surrey. Frank's uncle, Mike, had worked his way up from laying bricks to studying at night and was now a civil engineer with his own very successful company employing more than seventy men. He too had married well. His bride was a posh English Rose whose grandfather had emigrated from North Kerry in the latter part of the nineteenth century. To hear Dawn's cut glass vowels and her bell-clear articulation, not to mention her Sloane Square accent, one would never have guessed that she was only two short generations from a humble overcrowded cottage outside of Listowel. These then, were the models that Red and Frank had set for themselves.

Of course, they hadn't the remotest idea of how these men had achieved their success. They had never heard the term 'on the lump' and no one was about to tell them that this practice, the single greatest example of the Irish exploiting their own was more than likely a factor in the success of their idols. Later on they were to learn that working on the lump meant being paid by the job or for the contract. What usually happened was that the contract went to the under-bidder who, more often than not, was either un-insured or under-insured to save costs. It could also mean working for a daily rate without insurance cover or welfare benefits and with no security of tenure. The work itself was arduous and dangerous and almost invariably involved digging. Worse still, such workers would have to go to the pub in the evening in order to be paid which contributed to many a man becoming addicted to drink. Nor had they ever heard any detail of the struggles that these men had faced in their own early years in London. All they knew was what stories they had been told of the fine lifestyles these successful men now enjoyed.

They arrived in London full of hope and enthusiasm, confident in themselves and each other and utterly convinced that success was only just around the corner. Luckily they had some money saved so they had a little security while they searched for work. Not wanting to be beholden to relatives, they first attempted to find work for themselves. Despite huge amounts of construction work underway in the capital, road works, bridge building, tunnelling for the Underground as well as the ever-increasing need for commercial premises and houses and flats, Frank and Red failed to secure employment in the first two weeks of their endeavours.

Disappointed and disgruntled, they had to reconsider their position so over the weekend they had a discussion about what to do next. In the end, they decided that as their funds were fast diminishing they ought to swallow their pride and seek help from their relatives in the trade. First they drew up individual lists of whom they should approach. Starting on the Monday they would take turns at calling on the likeliest prospects in turn. While Frank went off to call on his relations, Red found himself at a loose end, so he took a stroll around central London. Having walked for quite a while, he grew cold and miserable and decided to take shelter in a betting shop. Here he put a few bob on some races and found the environment warm, the atmosphere friendly and the clientele congenial. Soon he was in pleasant conversation with a number of punters as they were continually up and down to the counter laying bets and collecting their winnings. Eventually, as the afternoon wore on, people began to drift away to get something to eat or to celebrate their winnings or drown their sorrows in nearby hostelries.

Red had been in the company of a well-dressed well-spoken man in his forties for some hours by now and when, after introducing himself as Jack Jones, he invited him to join him for a drink, Red agreed. They left the warmth of the betting shop and found themselves braving the elements. The wind had risen and the squally showers were now sleet laden and hail filled. Now Mr Jones suggested that rather than walking on to find a public house they should perhaps go to a nearby hotel where he was staying. This they did. Jack Jones went straight to the reception desk and asked for his key, whereupon the concierge, glaring at Red for some reason declared in an overly-loud voice, "I'm afraid, Mr Jones, that you cannot access your room just now as it is being cleaned as we speak."

Jack glanced impatiently at his watch and answered in a most irritated tone, "What kind of time is this to be cleaning rooms?"

Then he demanded a tray of tea and sandwiches for himself and guest to be served in the foyer. Red sat himself down gratefully by the fire, looking forward eagerly to the tea and food. After a while he asked Jack where the toilets were to be told peremptorily that he'd be as well to wait until the room was ready when he could use the bathroom there. Red was a little taken aback at the suggestion, probably more so at the tetchy tone. Despite this, he did as he was told and waited. Next thing he noticed was the concierge making urgent signs to him. It looked like the man was trying to shoo him off the premises. When Jack turned around to see what he was looking at, the concierge immediately adopted an attitude of deferential busyness. As soon as he turned back, the gesticulating began again. Red decided to just ignore it as they waited for the sandwiches in desultory conversation. Then the concierge approached. "Excuse me, Mr Jones, you have a phone call, please take it at the desk."

Jack appeared startled and, in a puzzled tone, asked, "Who could be calling me here?"

"Sorry, sir, he didn't leave his name."

"Who could it be? No one knows I'm here. And by the way I'm not at all impressed with the service, young man. Did no one ever teach you to take a name and message?"

When Jack reluctantly got up to make his way to the desk, the concierge, through gritted teeth, hissed at Red, "Are you a rent boy or just a stupid kid? Get the hell out of here if you know what's good for you."

With that a disgruntled Jack Jones returned, muttering, "There was no one on the other end of the line."

"Maybe they got impatient and hung up, sir."

"Or maybe, young man, there was no phone call to begin with."

A few minutes later the tea and sandwiches arrived and Red took the opportunity to excuse himself and ask the waiter where the gentlemen's toilets were. As he made his way there, he was immediately joined by the concierge who followed him into the restrooms. "Before you start again, what's a rent boy?"

"Oh God, preserve me from innocent young fellows! You really don't have a clue, do you? You're Irish, aren't you? Bear with me for a second. I don't know where you met that Jones character. You need to wise up, young man. Why do you think he's brought you back here?"

"We're hungry and he offered to buy me a sandwich. What's wrong with that?"

"Think, lad, think. Did he bring you to the Lyons Tea House on the corner? Did he even order tea and sandwiches when he came in here? No, he came in and asked for the key to his room. He's not interested in feeding you or even talking to you, you silly boy. He's after your body. Now if you have the sense you were born with you'll make good your escape before he comes sneaking in here looking for you. When you're ready, come out and turn right rather than left and follow the corridor to the end and go out through the bar door directly onto Regent Street. And by the way, good luck and watch yourself." Red did as he had been instructed and made his way back to the hostel where he told Frank about his day. Frank was horrified at how close Red had come to disaster and was astonished at how easily he could have been led astray. For his part, Red had learned a valuable lesson and was relieved that his beloved parents would never need to hear of it.

Over the next couple of weeks they forgot all about it as they were both working so hard. Red's cousin Paul had come up trumps and offered to take on both of them immediately. He had lots of work on and was in fact handling subcontracting work on three different sites at the time. So Red and Frank started work the following Monday on a very large housing project in Shepherd's Bush. They worked hard from dawn till dusk. They were collected by truck at 6.30 a.m. Very quickly they learned that if they weren't at the appointed place at 6.30 a.m. on the dot there was no way the truck would wait for them. So they'd miss the day's work and of course the day's wages, if they were lucky and didn't get the sack altogether. It only happened once, they'd made sure they were on time after that. They'd be on site by seven or a little after it and have just enough time for a quick brew up before starting work at 7.30 a.m.

Frank had experience at block-laying so they saw little of each other during the working day. Because Red was only starting out he was assigned to a shuttering team as this was semi-skilled labour as opposed to the skilled work Frank was engaged in. The work was physically demanding and at first very tiring. It didn't take long for him to get into the rhythm of it and soon he was working well with the other members of the team. By mid-summer, he was well into his stride and finding that even after working eight to ten hour days five days a week and a half day on Saturday, he still had enough energy left to enjoy a social life, especially at weekends. He loved the music sessions in the local pub on Friday nights where he was always willing to join in the singsongs. Saturday nights were happily spent at concerts in venues anywhere in London or dancing the night away in the Slievemore Ballroom in Cricklewood. Sometimes they would manage both a concert and a dance on the same evening. By the time the summer was over, the Shepherd's Bush housing development was also complete so it was time for the lads to move on again. Over the previous seven months they had proven themselves reliable and hardworking employees and Paul Gilraine was more than happy to extend their contracts. It was now the middle of August and there would be no new job starting until September at the earliest, so for now they were free to enjoy a well-earned break. "Well, Red, where will we go for our three week break? Any ideas, mate?"

"I don't know about you but the only place I'll ever want to be in summertime is Achill."

"Oh, you old 'stick-in-the-mud'. Or maybe you're just a mammy's boy."

"I don't care what you call me, you big Kerry galoot. You wouldn't recognise great scenery if it jumped up and hit you in the face. You've only seen Achill in winter. I tell you, there's no finer place on earth to be in August."

"What do think you're saying about scenery to a man raised within spitting distance of Killarney? You mad yokel."

"You have no idea how beautiful Achill is on a fine summer's day."

"Okay! Okay! Okay! Red, you win. Are you really sure you wouldn't prefer to go someplace new?" Asked Frank, making one last ditch effort to make him change his mind.

Chapter 4

A Visit to Achill

In August, Red and Frank headed for Achill to visit with Red's family. Here they were welcomed to stay a while to be spoiled by Bridie. They were both looking forward to enjoying all that Red's beloved island had to offer to summer visitors. There would be swimming and hill-walking by day as well as boating and fishing. They could take the currach across to Inishbiggle for the day or follow the mackerel to Clare Island. They might even go shark fishing for the fun of it if they could persuade someone to take them on for a day or two. Certainly, they must take a trip from Dugort Pier to see the seals. And at night there would be wonderful singsongs and traditional music in the pubs in all the different villages. Best of all there would be beach parties and bonfires and harvest dances. They would be sure to enjoy the outdoor dancing in the Deserted Village in Slievemore where the youngsters gathered of an evening throughout the summer for the boleying.

'Boleying' was the term used for the tradition of moving the cattle from their home-farm winter quarters to summer pastures on the lush lower slopes of Slievemore. These pastures were commonage, in other words all the families were equally entitled to grazing rights there. So the younger members of each family in turn were charged with supervising the grazing cattle. At nights, outdoor dances were organised where local musicians gathered and set dances as well as traditional Irish and old time waltzes were enjoyed into the small hours. Young and old walked long distances to partake in these 'boley' dances. From the very first night Frank was hooked. He loved the grace and beauty of the music, the physicality of the movements, the energy required and the sheer excitement of the atmosphere. The balmy evenings and the outdoor setting were just an added bonus. Also he was very taken with the local girls and their rosy-cheeked enthusiasm. Night after night he persuaded Red to return to the scene of all this jolly frivolity. He also loved the old stories told and retold around the fire late at night. Many of these he had heard already from Red. They were so much more real when told by the older men and women to an attentive audience of entranced youngsters huddled around a bonfire on a warm summer night. It was only on this visit home after almost two years since he had set off for London that Red realised how much his departure had hurt his parents, particularly his dad. With the selfishness of youth he had gone without considering the effect on the older generation. Typically not a word of censure or complaint was spoken but Red noticed that his relationship with Bridie was strained for the first time in his life. Worse still, Paddy seemed to have aged prematurely. Physically he appeared to have shrunk and the light had faded from his eyes. Red vowed that he would keep in touch by letter with his parents regularly from now on.

By the end of their two week stay in Achill, it was obvious that Frank had fallen head over heels in love with lovely Nora Sweetman, the sixteen-year-old neighbour of the Gilraines in Dugort. She was a gorgeous blue-eyed girl with the face of an angel and a mane of long dark hair falling to her waist. She was tall and elegant and had a sparkling wit and a bubbly personality. It was easy to understand why Frank was bewitched by her. Nora was equally besotted with the devil-may-care Kerry man who could charm woodland creatures from their lairs.

When the time came for them to spend a few days with the O Neills in Killduff, Frank had to be almost forcibly dragged away from Achill. The night before their departure was spent with Nora and Frank sitting a little apart from the rest of the crowd at the edge of the bonfire. They were by turns smiling and happily chatting to each other and then morosely sitting in silence, gazing into the embers with woebegone expressions. Sometimes they were seen to be holding hands and later Frank was comforting an obviously distressed and weeping Nora in his arms. Around dawn Nora's cousin Alice Sweetman and Red decided to intrude on the pathetic scene and persuade the lovesick pair to part company. Alice escorted her younger cousin homeward and Red tried to hurry Frank along to prepare for the long journey to Kerry next day. The few days spent in Killduff were a damp squib after the excitement of the holiday spent on Achill. Frank's heart just wasn't in it. He spent the days mooning about like a lovesick calf. Red had to agree with the O Neills that he was useless company and about as interesting to be with as a bowl of cold porridge. It was almost a relief to be heading back to London and to work.

As soon as they returned to London, their first port of call was Frank's uncle Mike's house in Richmond. His wife Dawn invited them in and offered them a bite to eat in the kitchen where Florrie, the warm and welcoming housekeeper, fed them like fighting cocks. Later they were interviewed by Uncle Mike in his book-lined and heavily furnished study. After they had been assigned to one of his work teams on a construction site in Tooting starting the following Monday morning, Mike O Neill showed them hurriedly off the premises without even enquiring if they had accommodation for the night.

Although it was late, Red and Frank hoisted their bags onto their shoulders and caught the train back to central London where they cheerfully booked into a workman's hostel for the night. Here they slept uneasily for a few hours, taking it in turns to keep an eye on their meagre belongings. They knew enough to keep their money close to their persons before seeking rest. The following morning they were up early for Sunday Mass before setting off for Tooting where they expected to find other construction workers in either of two pubs, The Queen's Arms or The Magpie's Nest. Their hunch paid off, so when they walked into The Queen's in the early afternoon they found a large crowd of mostly Irish construction workers having a good time, playing darts and drinking pints. In one corner, a singsong was already underway. A knot of men of all ages was gathered around an elderly, neatly-dressed, if somewhat careworn, down-at-heel man. The old man was leaning against the bar with eyes closed singing 'Danny Boy' in a melodious voice with such intensity and feeling that the assembled men were listening with rapt attention in respectful silence. When the song drew to its haunting climax, there was a moment or two of absolute silence before everyone in the pub clapped in thunderous applause. Then the old man said, "I suppose I'm still entitled to the noble call, am I? And if I am, I'd like to propose a change of tone. We've had enough of sadness and nostalgia, so let's have a new song, a young voice and something lively now. I call on the cheerful looking redhead who just came in with his lovesick friend and their bags. Come on, Ginger, give us a song. Shh, Now, all of you. Silence for the singer."

With all eyes now on him, Red had no option but to do as requested. So he cleared his throat and launched into a lively rendition of Percy French's 'Are you right there, Michael, are you right?' When he finished, to enthusiastic applause, he discovered that the old man had been absolutely right, the atmosphere in the pub had completely changed and now all the younger fellows were happily putting themselves forward to sing lively songs. He looked around to find the old man. When he enquired, he was told that, with quiet dignity, he had already

42

slipped unobtrusively away. Red wondered if their paths would ever cross again. In the course of the evening, he and Frank chatted with lots of the construction workers. Among other useful pieces of information they found out exactly where the meeting point was for the following morning. At some point, they were introduced to the landlord who was able to recommend good digs for them close by. Later they deposited their baggage there with the intention of going out to find somewhere they might get a bite to eat. Their new landlady, Mrs Bolster, wouldn't hear of it and insisted that they go and freshen up and join herself and her husband for dinner in a quarter of an hour. Exactly fifteen minutes later they presented themselves changed and freshly shaven at the kitchen door.

They were invited to be seated at the kitchen table before a spread of home-cooked food fit for a king. Mrs Bolster proved to be a fine cook as well as a most generous and big-hearted hostess. Her husband was a tall, spare, taciturn individual who ate large quantities of food efficiently and methodically in almost complete silence. He was as quiet and dour as his wife was smiling and talkative. During the meal Mrs Bolster kept up a constant stream of chatter, a mixture of comment on current affairs, the weather and local news interspersed with what appeared to be casual and harmless questioning. It was only much later that the lads realised that they had been subjected to a thorough and searching interrogation worthy of one of the best of MI5's agents.

Mrs Bolster, whose given name was never divulged, gloried in the title of 'Queenie' to her family and those closest to her. The speed with which they were invited to use this familiar form of address was a measurable token of the esteem in which she held her friends. Thus the other residents of the establishment were very impressed, if somewhat surprised, that both Red and Frank had been granted this privilege on their very first night. As the days wore on, turning into weeks and then months, neither of them gave a thought to moving out and, to be honest, Queenie never gave any hint that they were not more than welcome to stay on indefinitely. By Halloween, Bolsters' had become the nearest thing to home for both of them and Queenie was quite happy to treat them like adopted sons. Her husband, George, accepted this state of affairs without quibble or comment.

Since their departure from Achill in late August, Frank had been carrying on a steady correspondence with his beloved Nora. Letters flew back and forth between Achill and Tooting with frenetic frequency. Seldom did a week pass that Frank was not the recipient of at least one letter from Nora and vice versa. Occasionally, Alice called at the Bolsters' too, bearing small tokens of affection from her cousin to Frank. These would have arrived in the weekly package from the Sweetman home or, alternatively, they might come via one of the many returning Achill emigrants to London. Alice was a nurse in Guy's Hospital and lived in the nurses' residence attached to the hospital. At first, no one took too much notice of how frequently she called and, as she became friendlier with Queenie, it took Red a while to notice just how often Alice seemed to be about, especially if she were free at weekends. Soon it was part of the weekend routine for Alice to accompany himself and Frank to their local haunts or further afield to pubs and concerts.

After a while she too was invited to the dances with them until eventually she and Red appeared to have become, by default, a couple. Inevitably they spent a lot of their time discussing the great love affair being carried on at a distance between Alice's cousin and Red's best friend. Plans were soon afoot for Christmas. Given that they, and particularly Alice, only had a few days off, it was eventually decided that it would make more sense for Nora to travel to England rather than for Frank to go to Achill for the holidays. First, arrangements had to be put in place to ensure that she would be safe and chaperoned suitably at all times. It was absolutely imperative

44

that no suggestion of impropriety would attach to a single girl's visit to London. In the end, through Queenie's good offices, a solution was found. Father Reynolds, the curate in the Tooting parish of Saint Boniface, was put in touch with Father McNamara, the parish priest in Achill. Nora would stay in the Catholic Hostel for Young Women attached to the Presentation convent in Tooting, where she would be well looked after for her week-long stay. Her parents, thus reassured, saw an excited Nora off on the train from Westport, and Alice, accompanied by Frank and Red, met her early the following morning off the train at Euston Station.

Chapter 5

Christmas in London

The four young people were delighted at the prospect of several free days stretching ahead of them. There was no work for the lads from Christmas Eve until January 2nd. Nora was on her holidays from her final year in school and Alice had managed to organise her annual leave to coincide with her cousin's stay in London. So, as soon as Nora had deposited her luggage at the convent, they all hurried into the city centre for some last minute Christmas shopping. A good deal of time was spent in making sure that purchases were made and gift wrapped without the intended recipients' knowledge. There were some very sticky moments as they did their best to keep each other distracted, all of which added to the fun and excitement.

As Nora had to return to the convent before eight o'clock and would not be allowed to leave again until the following morning, there was a degree of panic in ensuring that all of them had a bite to eat before curfew. Nora would attend the midnight Mass in the convent and Alice would return to attend Mass near the hospital with the other nurses. Frank and Red intended to join the landlady and her other guests at Mass in Tooting. All four of them had been invited to celebrate Christmas 1937 at the Bolsters'.

Over the years Queenie and George had established a routine of entertaining their guests and neighbours to mulled ale and mince pies at 11.30 a.m. on Christmas day. The plan was that Red, Frank and the two girls would join them this year. After the neighbours had departed presents were exchanged and unwrapped in the living room where a huge Christmas tree laden with decorations and lights filled one corner. Frank and Red had pooled their resources to purchase a heavy gold bracelet for Queenie as a token of their appreciation for her kindness to them and also her welcoming of the Sweetman girls on this most important of family days. For Mr Bolster, they had bought a meerschaum pipe and a supply of his favourite tobacco. Queenie was overjoyed and hugged and kissed the two young men by way of thanks and her husband volunteered a nod and smile before immediately trying out his new pipe. Frank had bought a dainty heart-shaped eighteen carat gold pendant on a delicate chain for Nora who was understandably thrilled with it. She in turn had knitted an Aran sweater for Frank who wore it with great pride for years afterwards. Red had played it safe by getting boxed sets of soaps and lotions for both girls and Alice had got a fancy tie for Frank as well as one for Red. The girls had already exchanged gifts earlier when together they had opened the parcels from Achill.

Now it was time to tuck into the feast that Queenie had placed before them. All the traditional fare, cooked to perfection and beautifully presented, proved only a minor challenge to the appetites of young and old. Twelve people sat around the dining table at one o'clock and started to work their way through course after course. The food was excellent and the company congenial. Dinner lasted several hours and it was late afternoon before they all retired to the sitting room. After they had listened to the new king's speech and enjoyed their cups of tea, it was time for entertainment. The choice was between board games or charades. This called for a vote and the majority opinion was for charades. First the teams were made up of residents versus visitors, but when impasse had been reached for the umpteenth time they changed to girls against boys. This proved to be a much better idea as the games moved much more quickly with the improved age balance on the teams. Soon they were all falling about with laughter and no one felt the time slipping by. Nora's curfew applied even on Christmas day so Queenie had to ask her neighbour to drive Nora and Alice home. It was in a flurry of excitement, then, that the cousins had to rush off. After the girls had left, the tone of the evening changed. Queenie wandered off to the kitchen with her cook and companion Eliza, leaving the menfolk to chat among themselves.

On their return, the women carried in trays of turkey and ham sandwiches, mince pies and biscuits and a large pot of punch. Eventually, sated and happy as midnight approached, they all drifted off to their beds.

Early the following morning Alice presented herself at the convent to collect Nora. They were to meet up with Frank and Red in central London. On their way they chatted away, reminiscing about how they had celebrated this day in previous years in Achill. If at home now, they would all be up early and, rain or shine, sleet or snow, mild or stormy, they would be setting off for a day of thrills and spills, music, dancing and roistering from village to village with the Wren Boys. They'd all congregate at Dugort School, the agreed meeting point close to Red's family home. They'd be dressed from head to foot in sheets and old clothes. Their faces would be masked or painted or else they'd be wearing on their heads straw bonnets which concealed their faces. The revellers, called Wren Boys, Straw Boys or Clamairí depending on the locality, would be involved in similar activities. The tradition stretched back hundreds of years and celebrated the legend of St Stephen. The story goes that when being pursued by Roman soldiers he took refuge in a bush. Unknowingly he disturbed a wren, which flew off, alerting the soldiers who captured St Stephen and stoned him to death. Ever since, on December 26th, Irish youngsters paraded from house to house collecting money to symbolically 'bury the wren'. Householders, according to tradition, demanded some kind of entertainment in exchange for the donation. So the troupe played music, sang songs or danced set dances or perhaps even enacted sketches. As the identities of the performers were concealed, the humour and lampooning were often very close to the bone.

Things were very different in London where the day was even referred to by a different name. Here it was called Boxing Day due to the tradition of bestowing Christmas boxes on servants and estate workers in the big houses of the gentry. One major aspect of the day was common to both countries and that was the tradition of family time and pursuits, preferably outdoors. Hunting and horse racing meetings featured strongly on both sides of the Irish Sea. In Ireland, those who were not interested in or involved with Wren Boys would happily spend the day hill walking, visiting friends and family, following the hunt, beagling or going to local races. In the towns and cities, children were sent off to visit the churches and see the cribs or maybe watch matinee films at the cinema. Nora was curious to see what outdoor activities London might have to offer. So, when the four of them met under the statue of Eros in Trafalgar Square, she was eagerly anticipating what had been planned for the day's entertainment. Following Red's instructions, they were all clad warmly for the chilly weather, complete with woolly hats and gloves and wearing their strongest walking boots or shoes. It was just as well that they had heeded him as they awoke that morning to a crisp, white world. Overnight snow had fallen and now a two inch thick layer blanketed every surface. Everything looked magically new minted, clean and shiny in the early morning sun. In the run up to Christmas, Red had arranged with a friend to borrow ice skates in the hope that the weather would be sufficiently cold to ensure that the lake in the park would be frozen over for the holiday period. Already he had spotted several people carrying skates in the city centre so he was happy that his planning had paid off.

Though neither Frank nor Red was expert, they had a little experience gleaned from the previous January and furthermore they had both thoroughly enjoyed the experience. They sincerely hoped that the girls would also enjoy the exhilaration of outdoor skating. Red had planned to surprise them all so he'd arranged to meet his friend at Speakers' Corner where he would hand over the bag of borrowed skating boots.

When they arrived, they hung about listening to the various orators for quite some time. Red managed to slip away unnoticed to pick up the bag of skates and then stood nonchalantly by as the others became increasingly restless and impatient. Eventually, Frank cracked and, turning to Red, said, "I'm not too sure about this for entertainment. I have a feeling that the girls are bored witless. If this is all you've planned, I suggest we think of something quick before we're dragged around the city window shopping."

Red laughed at his friend's discomfiture and then turning to the girls said, "Okay, okay, you've suffered long enough. Follow me; we've a little bit of walking to do first. Then I promise you a new experience which I hope you will enjoy."

They made their way across the park to the frozen lake where hundreds of spectators had gathered to watch their more intrepid friends and family take to the ice. Many of the skaters were comfortably moving gracefully across the icy surface while others took more tentative steps around the firmer edges. Everyone was in great form, rosy cheeked, smiling and happy. The skaters were flushed with exhilaration and the excitement seemed to have spread to the crowd who were admiring the more balletic movers while actively encouraging the more timid stragglers. Frank and Red, having donned their own skates, helped Alice and Nora into theirs and then led them carefully onto the ice. For the first ten minutes or so, they guided the girls cautiously around the edge before attempting some more ambitious moves of their own. Soon they were speeding skilfully to and fro and making smooth turns and circles. It didn't take the girls long to find their balance and soon they too were making their way smoothly and confidently in circles around the lake. Nora in particular seemed to be making excellent progress and was obviously thoroughly enjoying herself, careening merrily ahead while waving to Alice, who was moving more circumspectly around the perimeter at a much more sedate pace. Emboldened by her progress, Nora continued at an increasingly hectic rate until inevitably disaster struck. While trying to avoid a slower skater, she ran out of space for her turn and ended up hitting the grassy verge which brought her to a sudden and painful halt, toppling head over heels into the crowd.

By the time the others reached her, she was sitting in the centre of a sympathetic group with one of her boots removed and tears running down her face. Her bared ankle was already swelling visibly. Her tears proved not to be from pain but rather from humiliation. Frank felt the ankle and, having established that it was only a minor sprain, packed some snow around it to bring down the swelling. After a few minutes she was ready to be helped to hobble the few yards to where a taxi could be hailed. Their skating adventure thus cut short, they returned with Nora to the convent so she could rest her ankle. Red, Frank and Alice then went to the cinema to while away the evening hours.

The agreement made earlier the previous day was that they'd meet up the following day at the ungodly hour of 08.00 a.m. Alice was the one who had most experience of Christmas in London. The others were curious to see what she had planned for the day. They worried whether Nora would be able for the planned activities. On arrival at the convent, they found her with her ankle professionally strapped. She declared herself ready for action and in her own words 'rarin' to go'. They headed off immediately after Alice, who set a cracking pace towards the 'hop on hop off' buses. She had booked the original London Tour at 08.30 a.m. so that accounted for the hurry.

Alice's itinerary suggested that their first stop would be Madame Tussauds. After they had taken the guided tour of the famous waxworks they went on to the Tower of London and from there to Sir Christopher Wren's architectural masterpiece, St Paul's Cathedral. After lunch they strolled around the city's golden mile before heading down to the river to take the Thames tour to Greenwich. On their return from Greenwich, if Nora were fit enough, they planned to do the guided tour of Kensington Palace before calling it a day and getting Nora back to Tooting.

On their way upriver, Red joshed Alice gently about her obsession with her 17th century boyfriend, Christopher Wren. They had gone from St Paul's to the Greenwich Observatory, passed by Greenwich Palace and on to Kensington Palace, all designed by Wren. In the course of their very busy day in London, they had had a chance to make plans for the next few days and before parting had agreed to meet up at eleven o'clock the following morning. Next day's activities were to be Frank's treat and he planned to do something completely different.

First he wanted to give the girls some time to themselves to have a look around the shops, so he presented them with vouchers for lunch in Lyons Tearooms in Piccadilly. He and Red were to meet up with them later for a pre-theatre supper before going on to see Noel Coward's new comedy 'Hands Across the Sea' at the Phoenix Theatre, for which Frank had already reserved tickets. Nora, who had never been to a live performance, was utterly enthralled and the others thoroughly enjoyed the experience. Afterwards, as they made their way home, they agreed that these days, because of the intensity of their shared experience, had left an indelible mark on each of them. They would all, in their different ways, remember this amazing week, jam-packed as it was with such a variety of new experiences. Years later they would look back fondly at this magical time and the burgeoning of their parallel love affairs. By the time Nora was ready to return to home and school, an understanding between Frank and herself had been reached and they both knew that they would spend the rest of their lives together. They also agreed that they would have to wait some time before they would be able to realise their dreams of happy-ever-after romance and marriage. The high octane burn of their love seemed to have rubbed off on Red and Alice. Basking in the shadow of Frank and Nora's love, they had slowly come to the realisation that the feelings they had been developing for each other over the previous eighteen months had now blossomed into an interdependent love affair. Furthermore, there was nothing to stop them planning for marriage in the not-too-distant future. Alice, having completed her nursing training in Dublin, had already established herself in well-paid employment in Guy's Hospital.

Chapter 6

Marriage and Rumours of War

Red was by now a skilled builder with a good head on his shoulders, strong in physique, intelligent and independent in spirit. Young as they were, they were confident that they were ready to take on the responsibilities of married life. So, while the rest of their London co-workers and friends were worrying about the imminence of war, Alice and Red were happily planning their wedding. The date they had selected was Alice's twentieth birthday, on June 9th, 1939. Red had turned twenty-one at Christmas and over the past few years had been putting away quite a lot of his earnings. Alice had already managed to accumulate some savings too. Furthermore, being a talented seamstress, she had a sizeable amount of lace and linens gathered for her bottom drawer. They were both looking forward to setting up home together and were planning a rather fancy wedding with all the trimmings. The Roman Catholic Church of Saint Boniface had been booked and Father Reynolds had already agreed to perform the ceremony. The reception would be held in the adjoining parochial hall and Alice was currently trying to choose between two caterers. The decoration of the parochial hall had been carefully planned and would be executed on the eve of the wedding under Red's supervision by his workmates and friends. While all this was underway the bride and her friends would be decorating the church with flowers.

All was now in readiness for the nuptials. They had issued invitations for their big day four weeks earlier. Alice was thrilled that Red had managed to persuade his mother, Bridie, to attend the wedding. She was perhaps even more pleased that her own mother, Maud, her aunt Aggie and her cousin Nora were to travel the long journey from Achill to London for the special occasion. Neither she nor her parents felt it appropriate that her younger siblings would attend even if they could afford the expense of the travel. In the times that were in it, no one expected the dads to undertake this journey.

June 9th dawned sunny and bright and the forecast promised a typical English summer day with cloudless skies and the lightest of balmy breezes well into late evening. As was traditional for Achill weddings, invitations had been sent to any and every relative of either bride or groom who happened to be living in the greater London area at the time. A few close friends, including the Bolsters and the small family party travelling from the village of Dugort East in Achill, made up the rest of the wedding guests. All gathered in the church coming up to eleven o' clock for the nuptial Mass. Red stood at the altar in a lather of sweat beside Frank, nervously awaiting the arrival of his bride with her bridesmaid Nora. In the absence of Danny, Alice's beloved dad, George Bolster, had been inveigled into giving the bride away and now he stood quaking with trepidation and bursting with pride in the church doorway, prepared to walk the beautiful young bride down the aisle. For her part, Alice, all four feet ten inches of her, stood for a moment serenely looking towards the altar and then, with quiet self-possession, made her stately way on George's arm towards her welcome future. Despite her tiny stature, she looked stunningly elegant in her full length taffeta wedding gown with its four foot train and high stand up collar. Her bouquet of white roses trailed to within a few inches of the ground and her long veil fell from a single white rose worn atop her piled up blonde curls. Standing stiffly at the altar, Red could hear the gasps of appreciation as the bridal party processed up the long aisle. Nothing had prepared him for the vision that now stood beside him. As George handed Alice over to him, Red couldn't help gaping in amazement at how she looked before his face burst into an enormous grin of pride and happiness. The church ceremony went off without a hitch, as did the reception, and all too soon it was time for Mr and Mrs Redmond Gilraine to set off on their honeymoon. It was about seven o'clock when they departed in a taxi, heading back to the little flat in East Acton where they would spend the early years of their married life. As soon as the happy couple had gone, the singsong petered out and within half an hour the large crowd had dispersed completely. The women made their way homewards and the men adjourned to the local pubs, the former to relive the highlights of the day over endless cups of tea and the latter to finish the process, begun at the reception, of getting thoroughly inebriated. As newlyweds, Red and Alice had a week off work and were intending to spend their honeymoon in their new flat. They had lots of ideas on making it more homely and were looking forward to these leisurely days together wandering around the city, shopping for bits and bobs, doing odd jobs and getting to know each other. The weather was wonderfully bright, sunny and warm when they awoke on Sunday morning. They set off fasting to the ten o'clock Mass in their local parish, Church of Our Lady of Lourdes.

After Mass they joined the rest of the congregation for tea and biscuits in the parish hall where they were met by the parish priest who introduced them to members of the parish council and also to their next door neighbours Bill and Lizzie Baldwin. Coincidentally, Lizzie was from Achill Island too. She had spent the last forty years of her life living in East Acton. She and her English husband, Bill, loved going 'home' to Achill Sound every summer. Red and Alice were immediately invited round to the Baldwins' for tea that very evening. Before that, on this the first day of their married life, they were treating themselves to an early lunch in central London followed by a long and leisurely walk in Hyde Park. By late afternoon, they were footsore and exhausted as they headed back home. They decided to have a little lie down before heading next door for tea at seven o'clock. At first, they lay companionably side by side on top of the clothes on the narrow bed, resting and chatting. After a while they began cuddling and then kissing and soon, one thing leading to another, they found themselves making love once again. Next thing they knew it was five minutes to seven and they were under enormous pressure to make themselves presentable and not to be too late going next door.

If Bill and Lizzie had their suspicions about what their young neighbours had been up to, they gave no sign, just welcomed them into the warmth of their family and home. First, all five of the Baldwin children were introduced to Red and Alice. Soon they were all happily seated around the kitchen table together. Bill sat at the head with Lizzie to his right and Red next to her. Alice was seated to Bill's left next to fifteen-year-old William. Catherine, aged thirteen, sat with four-year-old Mollie, and eleven-year-old Fred and his twin brother, Tim, were at the lower end. Lizzie had been busy since morning and the laden table bore witness to her industry. Plates of homemade brown bread and railway cake sat cheek by jowl with fruit scones. In pride of place, in the centre of the table sat an enormous dish containing a squat and juicy apple cake. Dainty dishes of butter and homemade jams dotted the spaces between and a large glass bowl full of whipped double cream sat beside the steaming apple cake. "Don't be shy," directed Lizzie. "Help yourselves, it may not be very fancy but it's all healthy and fresh."

The conversation flowed, and everyone was curious to learn more about their new neighbours. Even the youngest of the children had questions to ask. Alice and Red answered whatever they were asked and they were both a big hit with Lizzie as they sampled all her baking in turn and appeared to enjoy everything on offer. In fact, if she had been a little more observant she might have noticed Red had put away seconds of both the scones and the apple cake. Soon it was bedtime for the younger children as the evening was drawing in. Bill suggested that he and Red should go for a quick pint while Lizzie and Alice got a chance to get to know each other better. Lizzie immediately protested. "You're an awful man, Bill Baldwin, keeping a young couple apart on their honeymoon, you and your quick pint. There will be time enough for that kind of thing in the future; that is, if you don't drive our lovely new neighbours away with your nonsense. Now, Red, I suggest that you take your lovely bride home. The four of us could go to the Irish club next Saturday night instead, where we can enjoy a nice evening of conversation, music, a dance or two and where these husbands of ours can have as many pints as they want." Goodnights were exchanged and Alice and Red thanked their hosts for a lovely evening and, having agreed to the arrangements for the weekend, set off next door to what was already beginning to feel like home.

All that long, glorious summer they went about their daily lives barely conscious of the rumours of war. Like most people they would clearly remember for the rest of their lives Prime Minister Neville Chamberlain saying on the wireless that war had been declared. They had all been issued with gas masks and for the first few days after the announcement people were very good at obeying the strict instructions not to leave home without them. Children had to carry theirs in little boxes with a long string attached over their shoulders along with their satchels on their way to school. They were terrified to go without them. After a long autumn and winter of fearful anticipation as nothing happened, people became more relaxed and for the most part were ignoring even the air raid shelter drills. The Gilraines and the Baldwins became good friends as well as good neighbours for the duration of the war and the subsequent almost three years that they lived next door to each other in East Acton. World War II was officially more than a year old when the conflict everyone had been dreading finally began in earnest. On August 24th, 1940, the Luftwaffe offloaded seven or eight bombs over London. The new Prime Minister, Winston Churchill, ordered raids on Berlin and the retaliation was brutal. On September 7th, in the middle of a glorious sunny afternoon, swarms of German bombers dropped their deadly loads on the London Docks area. The first bombs fell on the Ford works in Dagenham and on Beckton gasworks, the largest in Europe. Within the hour, the entire East End was in flames. When the 'all clear' siren sounded, Eastenders emerged from their homes and shelters to be greeted for the first time with the horrific sight of raging fires, destroyed and damaged houses, tons of debris, piles of bricks and broken glass and death and devastation everywhere.

For the next eight months of vicious bombardment known as the blitz, these sights became commonplace for the residents of East Acton in West London, which was close to the Rolls Royce factory. Amazingly, families adjusted to this terrible reality and remained where they were. Though never inured to the loss of family members and neighbours, the famed 'spirit of the blitz' saw them through the worst of the trauma. A neighbour, Phyllis Warner, who was a teacher, described it some days after the first bombings: "One of the oddest things about our everyday life is its ruthless horror and everyday routine."

Red said one day to Bill, "I know it's mad to stay in Acton with bombs falling and flattening all around us every night, but Alice and I feel if others can stand it then so can we." Like lots of their neighbours, the Baldwins had an Anderson shelter in their garden which the Gilraines were welcome to share. The shelter was dreadfully damp and, after a few experiences of screaming women and children as furry creatures ran across their bodies, both Red and Alice took to sleeping under the big oak table in their living room. When the air raid sirens went off, they'd just ignore them and continue what they were doing until they heard the 'Jerries' getting closer and then they would dive under the table for shelter. Life continued as normally as possible for housewives and children in Acton. Mothers shopped and, despite rationing, made the best and most nourishing meals they could for their families. Children attended school and played among the ruined houses and on the bomb sites. The men went to work on construction and clearance work. And they volunteered as fire and air raid shelter wardens and ambulance drivers. The Baldwin children attended the local school on Long Drive close to Taylor's Green in East Acton. John Perryn School remained in operation throughout the war.

The Gilraines and the Baldwins celebrated the happy events of each other's lives together and consoled each other in times of sorrow and were always on hand to support each other in times of trouble. Alice and Red were there to celebrate the births of another two Baldwin children, baby Bob in 1940 and the following year little Elizabeth, named after her mother Lizzie. Within a week of her birth, she was to become known as Liza. Meanwhile, Lizzie was a rock of strength and loving comfort for Alice through three miscarriages in these same years, the first of their marriage.

Alice, in turn, helped Lizzie through a late and difficult pregnancy in 1944, resulting in the birth of her eighth child when Lizzie was forty-five. They all welcomed, loved and cared for little James who had Down's Syndrome, giving him the stability to develop his warm personality which made him a firm favourite with all he came in contact with for the rest of his life. Miraculously, both the Baldwins and the Gilraines had survived six years of hell without losing any immediate family member. In the latter days of 'the war to end all wars', young

William Baldwin went missing in action in France. Lizzie had come to depend on her and found Alice's quiet strength a great support as she tried to keep her own grief hidden while she helped William's devastated siblings and his shattered dad to cope with the trauma of his disappearance and the subsequent awful news seven weeks later that he had been killed in action.

Chapter 7

New Beginnings

Around this time Alice was pregnant again and coming up to Christmas everyone was looking forward to some good news at last. The morning of December 23rd, 1945, dawned crisp and cold and as the two families were getting ready for the ten o'clock Mass, Alice went into labour. Lizzie packed all of them, including Red, off to Mass while she hurried next door to attend to Alice. She sat with Alice throughout the morning, chatting and setting her at ease as she mopped her brow and held her hand through the early contractions, only leaving her briefly when Red returned. Then she rushed home to check on the progress of the day's dinner and the preparations for Christmas, rattling off instructions, orders and advisory comments in an endless stream, until her own family were glad to see the back of her as she returned next door. Catherine, who was home for Christmas with her new husband Tom, reassured her mother that everything was under control and that she could cope.

"Please, Mam, will you get back to Alice? She needs you now. Honestly, I can manage. I'll serve up here and bring yours and Alice's over. Red should come and eat with us lot here, 'twill take his mind off things for a while." So Lizzie went back to Alice with a clear conscience, knowing that Catherine could and would cope. She could now concentrate on doing what needed to be done for her friend and confidante. She plastered a smile back onto her face and re-entered the house next door via the back door to relieve Red at Alice's bedside. To tell the truth, he was over anxious and pretty useless to Alice at this point. As the hours passed and labour continued, it became increasingly obvious to Lizzie that they were in for a long and slow time of it. By nightfall, the contractions, though painful and debilitating for the mother, were still coming at uneven intervals and Lizzie feared that the birth was still a long way off. After midnight the contractions seemed to ease a little and Alice managed to snatch short bouts of sleep. Lizzie and Red kept vigil with her and at about dawn things began to speed up again. By ten o' clock on the morning of Christmas Eve, the contractions were coming at regular five minute intervals and an exhausted Alice was in great pain. Lizzie and Red agreed that it was time to send for the midwife. Nurse Holloway arrived within the hour, all hustle and bustle and self-important efficiency. She immediately examined Alice and, turning to Lizzie, said, "Mrs Baldwin, I am surprised at you with all your experience sendin' for me at this early juncture. Isn't it obvious that the birth is hours and hours off? If you ask me, it'll be mornin' before this one puts in an appearance. I'll be off now, call me when I'm needed. Tut! Tut! Tut!"

Lizzie hurried after her. "Hold on a sec, Nurse Holloway. I know that Alice's contractions are still not close enough and she has been in labour now for over twenty-four hours. She's exhausted and in considerable pain. I'm concerned that there may be complications. She's also very tiny and I think it may be a breech presentation. I'm sorry if you think I'm wasting your time but I can't help worrying about her. You know she's already had three miscarriages and I don't know how she'd cope if anything were to go wrong at this late stage of her pregnancy." Immediately Nurse Holloway halted in her tracks. Then she went into overdrive.

"Why didn't you say so sooner? What makes you think it's a breech presentation? Why did you not send for the doctor? Get out of my way, Lizzie, and let me have another look at her."

After she'd had a chance to do an internal examination of the patient, Nurse Holloway decided that the doctor should be called as it was indeed a breech presentation. She explained to Lizzie that the baby needed to be turned. She instructed that while she was gone to find the doctor Lizzie should remain with Alice to reassure her and try to make her as comfortable as possible.

By the time Nurse Holloway returned, Alice was in considerable distress and excruciating pain. Lizzie was mopping her brow and pleading with her not to bear down as the contractions reached their peak. Nurse Holloway took over and soothed the worried mother-to-be and explained that the baby needed to be manipulated into a more appropriate position before Alice could give birth. As it was, the baby was presenting feet first and the doctor would attempt to turn it so that the head could engage first and thus have ease of passage through the birth canal and the mother's pelvis. Thus reassured, she understood now the importance of not pushing until the baby had been turned. Nurse Holloway suggested that it might be easier on her were she to walk about for a bit, so Lizzie helped her to her feet and they walked about the bedroom for quite some time until the arrival of the doctor. Dr Patrick Thornton had made his way as quickly as he could from the local hospital and, assisting Alice back to her bed, managed to reposition the baby as gently as he could. This was not easily achieved and took longer than anyone expected. The manoeuvre also resulted in temporarily halting the contractions. The doctor remained for a while to ensure that things had settled down and then left the mother-to-be in the care of the nurse and Lizzie. Before he left he said that the birth was unlikely to occur before morning and should now be trouble free. If they were worried, he would be happy to return to assist. On his way out, he had a quick, kind word with the anxious father to be. "Don't worry, everything is fine now but it may still take some time. If either of the good ladies above has any concerns, just come and get me. Here is my address and I'll be home by eleven o'clock. It doesn't matter what time; call me if I'm needed. Good luck now, I must get back to the hospital."

It was now almost five o'clock and already dark. Lizzie was again seated by Alice's bedside administering to her needs and trying to keep her distracted with yarns and stories. It was important that she now remain as still as possible until labour resumed, thus ensuring that the baby's head remained engaged. At last, coming up to seven o'clock, the contractions started again. Over the following few hours they increased in frequency and strength. Nurse Holloway proved to be very competent and efficient as well as kindly and understanding. She checked regularly to see how the dilation was progressing and somewhere near ten o' clock she decided that she could cope alone and that there was no need to bother Dr Thornton. After so many hours of labour Alice was thoroughly exhausted. She felt resigned now and comforted by the presence of the midwife who kept reiterating that all was well and a normal birth imminent.

When, a little after midnight, Nurse Holloway finally uttered the time honoured phrase, "I want you to give one last push," she summoned the last remnants of her strength and pushed as hard as she possibly could. She was rewarded with the relief of the final gush as the baby emerged at last into the world. As she lay panting from her exertions, she heard a tiny whimper and knew that her mission was accomplished.

"Tell me, Lizzie, is the baby all right? Its little cry sounds so weak and weary."

Nurse Holloway, having cleaned the little mite, placed it carefully in Alice's arms saying, "Congratulations, my dear. I wish you joy of your son," before hurriedly leaving the room.

First she sent Red in to meet his new-born son and congratulate his wife, telling him to be careful as the baby was very tiny. Then she set off to wake Dr Thornton and ask him to call on mother and child. By her calculation, the baby weighed no more than two pounds, maybe two and a half at the very most. She prayed that the little fellow would survive for his parents' sake but more than anything she pleaded with her God that the tiny baby had emerged into this cruel world undamaged.

Red entered the bedroom on tiptoe and, kissing Alice tenderly on the forehead, he got his first glimpse of the baby held protectively in the crook of his mother's arm. His initial reaction was one of profound shock; he had never in his life seen such a tiny scrap of humanity. He never admitted to Alice that his first thought was the baby looks more like a new-born marmoset than a human child. When Alice reached across to hand over their son, Red was immediately overcome with a mixture of love and an overwhelming desire to protect this tiny person from any possible harm. He was also absolutely terrified that he might somehow damage the tiny body he was holding so carefully. He couldn't help thinking the little mite would be safer lying cupped in the palm of one of his own large hands rather than being held precariously as he was in both.

The baby was swaddled in a terry cloth nappy as even the tiniest blanket would have completely swamped him. Red knew, as he looked at his little family, that life would never be the same again. He and Alice were no longer just a young couple in love; they were now parents to a little boy with all the responsibilities that this entailed. Red loved him fiercely and knew that whether the little fellow ever lived in Achill his dad would teach him about its beauty and its magic and share its stories and its history and his heritage as his gift to this blessed and most welcome child.

When Nurse Holloway arrived at the doctor's house a little after one o'clock on Christmas morning, she found he had not yet returned from the hospital, so the best she could do was leave a message asking him to call at the Gilraines' as soon as possible and stating the reasons for her concern. Then she returned to help the new mother with the business of feeding the baby. Like all new mothers she had a fair idea of what to expect but found that reality differed significantly from what she had imagined. By the time the nurse returned, the baby was howling and poor Alice was almost in tears with the frustration of continued failures to get the baby to latch on to her breast. Lizzie, who had never experienced any difficulty even with her first child, simply did not know what to do and was reluctant to make what might be considered unwelcome suggestions. She was therefore extremely relieved to see Nurse Holloway who immediately set about getting to the bottom of the difficulty. Alice had a condition known as 'inverted nipples'. This in itself was no deterrent to breastfeeding. Because her first attempts had been unsuccessful and her breasts were not just tender but were in fact very sore and somewhat inflamed, she worried that her problem with the feeding was a result of this condition. Nurse Holloway was able to reassure her and dismiss her worries as merely rooted in old wives' tales and idle gossip. She showed Alice how to position the baby better and help him to latch on successfully. She also produced a nipple shield from her 'bag of tricks' to ease the situation and to demonstrate that there was nothing particularly unusual or weird about the condition. By three o'clock, the baby had had a feed and was sleeping peacefully. Alice had been freshened up and was sitting up enjoying tea and toast with her husband. Lizzie and Nurse Holloway were sitting companionably in the kitchen enjoying a welcome pot of tea prior to their departure and return to their own responsibilities. Lizzie promised to keep a watchful eye on mother and baby and make sure that they were kept comfortable, warm and resting insofar as possible. The winter weather was harsh, cold and icy outside and not much better inside in the older houses in East Acton. True to her word, Lizzie was in and out of the Gilraines' bearing homemade bread, pots of stew and chicken broth and whatever delicacies she could lay her hands on to tempt Alice to eat. She kept the stove refuelled and the fire in the bedroom topped up. She also kept her spirits up with tales of the Baldwin children's antics and the excitement of Christmas Day.

It was late afternoon of St Stephen's day before Dr Thornton managed to put in an appearance. He had been busy at the hospital with the usual weather and alcohol related accidents common at Christmas time and also with the victims of a horrendous house fire in Churchfield Road. Of the twelve occupants of the house fire luckily all survived and only two were very badly burned. All needed attention and it was many hours before Dr Thornton could get away. On his way home for some much needed rest, he had made a point of calling on Alice and her new baby. He sat by the bedside for a minute talking to her when Lizzie appeared with a welcome cup of tea for him. Before he accepted it he stood up and, leaning over the cradle, gently touched the baby with his forefinger. The baby immediately grasped the extended finger and judging by the strength of the grip the doctor said, "Well done, Alice, he's a fine boy. There's no doubt he's small, in fact he's very tiny, but he's strong. Ignore everyone who comments on his size, he may be puny now but he's a battler. Continue feeding him and make sure to keep him warm. I've every faith that he'll be a great comfort to you in your old age. By the way, what are ye calling him?"

"He's to be called Patrick. Lizzie had panicked because he was so small and insisted on baptising him within minutes of his birth. We're naming him for Red's dad."

On his way out, the doctor had a word with Red. "My best wishes to young Patrick who may be named for his granddad, he has my name too. I've just been telling Alice not to worry, he's a survivor." Red thanked Dr Thornton. Despite reassurances to the contrary, both he and Alice were understandably worried about the survival of their tiny baby.

Dr Thornton proved to be correct and, with loving care and overseen by the doting Lizzie, surrounded by the love of all of the Baldwins, young Patrick thrived. He gained weight steadily and passed all the childhood milestones on time and with flying colours. By the time he was seven months old, Patrick was a big hit with Frank O Neill and his new bride Nora when they stayed in East Acton while on their honeymoon in the summer of 1946. Knowing how much his parents had worried about his health in the early days, Nora was both surprised and delighted to find such a happy and healthy little fellow to cuddle and spoil. Frank knew the lad quite well by now as he was a frequent visitor in the house. For Nora, it was her first meeting with her new cousin.

Frank had been doing rather well in construction in the aftermath of the turbulent years of the war. He had gone into business for himself some years earlier and had become quite successful. He was now employing over fifty men, including Red, and was more than comfortably off. His romance with Nora had survived the years and, seeing how serious they were about each other, Nora's parents had finally agreed to the marriage. They had imposed conditions. First, Nora must be allowed to study for her Leaving Certificate examinations without too much distraction from Frank and his relentlessly frequent letters. And as soon as that hurdle was jumped they insisted that she be allowed to accept her place in Teacher Training College in Dublin where she would study for two years. After that they could become engaged officially. In her parents' view, it would be better if Nora taught for a few years until she was fully probated and then she would be qualified to teach not only in Ireland but in the United Kingdom or even further afield if that was what she wanted to do.

Part II
1946–1962

Chapter 8
Australia

In 1946, Australia had signed an agreement to provide free or assisted passage for British ex-servicemen and their dependents, as well as for other selected British migrants, for example successful businessmen with proven skills. Red's friend and employer Frank O Neill recently married and, in search of greater challenges, had been invited to move to Australia to set up a construction company in Brisbane.

Brisbane was growing at a tremendous rate and skilled labour was at a premium. Now what this new country needed most was experienced builders and company directors to oversee the boom and keep an eye on standards. Frank was very anxious to go and he wanted to be absolutely sure that Nora was happy to make this courageous move. It was the main topic of conversation all that summer and by the time they had returned to Ireland the O Neills had made up their minds to move to Brisbane that September. By Christmas, they had settled happily in Emmingham, a new, rather upmarket suburb of Brisbane. Nora was very happy in her lovely new house, designed by Frank and built to exacting standards by his construction company 'O Neill's, the best builders in the business'. She loved her husband, her beautiful new home and especially the secret she had been hugging to herself for the past couple of weeks. She was looking forward to Christmas and to sharing her good news with her family and most especially with her cousin Alice. She had already written the Christmas cards and the letters she intended to enclose. She would post them on November 8th to be absolutely sure they would arrive in Ireland and in London in the immediate run up to Christmas. This would give her parents and family as well as the Gilraines and the O Neills the chance to pray for her at midnight Mass.

Nora knew that she would miss her family and friends at this very special time of year. She was pragmatic enough to realise that what she could not cure she must and would endure. Part of her, too, was looking forward to seeing how the Australians celebrated Christmas in the middle of summer. And besides, she had her wonderful Frank to enjoy the celebrations with and that was more than enough for her. Furthermore, she had the New Year to look forward to and the letters from home and London in early February followed (God willing) in late May or early June by the arrival of her baby. When she awoke each morning, the first thing she did was thank God for her good fortune in meeting Frank and for all the other blessings that the Lord had bestowed on her in the intervening years.

In the meantime, she was lucky to have a job she loved to go to each day. When she had arrived in Brisbane, in September, the academic year had already begun so the chances of getting a permanent teaching job were slim. So straight away, she applied for hours supply teaching in the locality. She was fortunate that there was a vacancy in the local school in Emmingham, a mere three minutes' walk from her new home. She was initially employed for a three week period, teaching four and five year olds. By the time September was out, she had a contract from October until the end of November. And after that she would have a job in the same school from December 1st, 1946, until mid-April, 1947. This arrangement suited Nora admirably as she herself would need time out to have her baby around that time anyway.

Nora's next teaching experience in Australia was with the equivalent of British and Irish fifth class primary schoolboys. She got on well with this group of ten and eleven years olds. She was also looking forward to teaching their older sisters in their final year of primary school from December onwards. In truth, Nora detected little difference in the curriculum from what was being taught in Irish schools, based, as both curricula were, on the British system. Apart from the content of the lessons in history and geography the single greatest difference she noted was the willingness of the school authorities to welcome parental input into the learning process for their children. Parents were welcomed as assistants in the classrooms, as fundraisers for the purchase of extra resources and also as role models and sources of information regarding their own careers and work experiences. She thoroughly enjoyed the challenges of teaching as well as the warmth of her interactions with her, albeit temporary, pupils.

Nora and Frank had settled in very well in Brisbane. They had already made very good friends among their neighbours and workmates. The pace of life in Brisbane was very different from what they had experienced in either rural Ireland or in London. So, too, the social mores were different. In Australia, society was much more egalitarian. Mixing with all types was very much the norm and the opportunities to meet people at social gatherings were myriad. Hardly an evening went by that there wasn't a barbecue or a dinner party to which they were invited. Perhaps it had something to do with the clemency of the weather. It's likely that it had more to do with post-war loosening of the bonds of convention. This was a new country, buzzing with the excitement of growth and development, where people were valued, not for where they came from or who they were descended from, but for themselves. Australians appreciated hard work and dedication and they had a healthy respect for individual success stories. Frank's business success and Nora's independent career made them very popular and the kind of couple who were admired and looked up to in Brisbane. They were also popular because they were genuinely lovely people who made friends easily and were loyal and non-judgmental. Their obvious love for each other surrounded them like an aura. As well as all that, they were good company and great fun to be with. They had the kind of easy rapport which drew others to them. They were the kind of people whose deep and loving relationship enhanced their personal friendships rather than threatened them. Any friend of either was automatically a friend of both. When Nora's letters arrived the week before Christmas, there was wild excitement in Achill, Kerry and London. The O Neills and the Sweetmans were thrilled to hear of the expected child and the Gilraines, especially Alice and Red in London, were absolutely delighted with the news. Since the birth of her son, Alice could think of no other blessing she could wish for her beloved cousin Nora than that she too would share the joys of motherhood. She couldn't wait to congratulate the happy couple on their news, so, before going to bed that night, she had penned a long, loving and enthusiastic letter which she posted to Brisbane the following morning. She calculated that with the very best of good fortune Alice might receive it within six weeks and were she to answer immediately in all likelihood her baby would already have arrived in Australia prior to the arrival of her next letter. For this reason, the women had taken to writing to each other every week. The downside of this was that their letters were more like diary entries than exchanges of current news. The upside was that the regularity of the correspondence made them feel closer.

Meanwhile back in London, Red was working away in the building trade and Alice was busy looking after young Patrick. By the time he was eighteen months old, it was hard to believe that this sturdy toddler had had such a precarious start in life.

He was already falling in love with Red's stories which had become an integral and deeply satisfying part of his bedtime ritual. At first, his dad told him Achill stories and those he remembered from his own school days. Later he shared some of his own early experiences. Patrick particularly loved to hear the one about the rearing of the pig. When Red was five, his mother Bridie decided to raise a pig for the table. The pig was duly bought and was minded more carefully than many a child was at the time. Over the next few weeks it was fattening satisfactorily and Bridie was following its progress with great attention and interest. She had even sought the advice of the inspector from the Department of Agriculture regarding the overall welfare of the said pig. The expert pronounced the pig fit and well and gaining weight at a satisfactory pace. He also warned of the dangers of heart failure in the breed should the pig get overweight too rapidly. Fearing that she could lose the pig after all her effort and that she might end up with neither profit nor pig, she asked for further advice. It would be a good thing, she was told, to give the pig some gentle exercise, perhaps to take it for a little walk every day. On Red's return from school each afternoon, he was given the task of walking the pig. He was delighted with the responsibility and every evening he set off dutifully up the hill with the pig on a lead. He'd walk the pig back as far as the sand pit where it would gladly take a rest while he played in the sand for a while and then they would head home again. This lost its novelty value pretty quickly and within a few days Red had grown thoroughly sick of the routine. He began to exercise his imagination and soon, of course, the pig was enrolled in his cast of imaginary characters. At first, all the action roles were Red's alone, with Pig playing semi-somnolent support. After a while he tired of this and Pig was encouraged to participate more actively. Soon Red had mastered the art of riding bareback on his trusty friend. It wasn't long thereafter that 'Silver' had to learn to wear a harness so as not to lose its cowboy rider. Around this time the radio crackled with daily accounts and commentaries of summer race meetings so Pig's repertoire of skills had to be broadened further. Now evenings were spent in training it to jog, trot and gallop, to complete a ready-made circuit, half of which was uphill through the heather. It was only after it had been successfully competing over jumps for a week or so that Bridie noticed one very fit Pig was looking rather sleek and rangy. She thought it was high time to kill it.

Red was broken-hearted at the loss of his daily companion so, by way of distraction, he was allowed to accompany his dad to the fair in Westport the following Saturday. While they were gone Pig mysteriously disappeared to be replaced by lashings of pork dinners, black puddings, rashers, flitches of salted bacon and all kinds of other delicacies. Interestingly, the much-vaunted home cured ham was mysteriously tough and stringy. Bridie was puzzled and Red kept mum. Now, many years later, it was Patrick who was the first to learn the secret.

Life was reasonably comfortable for the Gilraines in London even though they were not very well off. Although there was plenty of construction work available, there were also large numbers of demobbed soldiers queuing for it. Once Frank had emigrated, his place had been taken by Michael O Neill, a cousin who, unlike Frank, played favourites with his men. Perhaps it was because his dad had thought so highly of his nephew that Michael was jealous. He was delighted that Frank was out of the picture. However, he couldn't help venting his spleen on the friend Frank had left behind. Almost immediately he began to punish Red in subtle ways and as time went on more overt forms of bullying became the norm.

First it was little things like ensuring the transport left a critical two or three minutes early so Red got left behind. Then tools mysteriously disappeared or a lunchbox got filled with sand and surprise, surprise these 'accidents' invariably befell only Red. Not wishing to burden Nora and out of a sense of gratitude and loyalty to Mike Senior, he kept his own counsel

78

and suffered the indignities in silence. He and Alice continued to be best friends with the Baldwins, their close neighbours, so much so that both Bill and Lizzie had begun to worry.

Alice was completely absorbed in looking after young Patrick to the extent that she didn't seem to notice anything or anyone other than her precious son. Perceptive as ever, Lizzie had noticed that Red was losing weight and increasingly complaining of being too tired and dispirited to participate in any form of socialising. It wasn't that Alice had fallen out of love with him. She still told him that he was her best friend, her hero and the best provider she could have hoped for. Red couldn't help feeling that he was no longer the centre of her universe. That place had been taken by Patrick. Alice herself was unaware of this shift in her focus and while Red recognised it he also understood and accepted it without resentment. He did miss the easy companionship of their early marriage when his lovely wife hung on his every word and no detail of his day was too trivial or too insignificant to be shared. He appreciated Alice's unconditional love for their precious son and was proud of her total commitment to his well-being. He himself missed the sense of belonging. Frank and Nora's little girl arrived safely on May 31st, 1947. She was named Daisy in memory of Frank's mother. Alice and Red were to be the godparents, albeit by proxy. Needless to say, they were absolutely delighted to hear that news. It was strange to think that the christening had already taken place and that Daisy was already six weeks old before her godparents were aware of her arrival. Nonetheless, the occasion was celebrated in style in London. Alice invited the Baldwins to high tea and photographs were taken of the youngsters, the adults and even the cake. These snaps were treasured and carefully mounted in albums, their white scalloped edges standing out sharply from the charcoal pages. Copies were sent on to the O Neills in Brisbane where Nora also happily placed them in an album. The picture painted of life down under was one of blue skies, wonderful weather, good money, great opportunities and happy times. In marked contrast, life in London was increasingly one of dull drudgery. When things came to a head at work in late 1947, Red was finally forced into making a momentous decision. The evening of November 15th, he reluctantly sat down with Alice and explained to her that he could no longer continue to work at O Neills. He felt that he'd reached the stage where he'd have to hand in his notice at the end of the week. Initially Alice was shocked to discover that things had become so difficult for her husband. When she had time to absorb the news, she had to admit that she was not altogether surprised. She, too, had noticed how unhappy he had become of late. They talked long into the night and eventually he broached the subject of perhaps moving to Australia. To his astonishment Alice, far from objecting, seemed to actually welcome the idea. Very sensibly she pointed out that if they couldn't live in their native land it mattered very little really how near or far away they might live. She would miss London, but she would miss her home more. In the final analysis, it was her friends, the Baldwins, she would miss the most.

By the time they went to bed that night, they had reached a decision. They would make serious and immediate enquiries about the assisted passage scheme to Australia. Red would hand in his notice as soon as arrangements had been made. Letters were dispatched immediately to Nora and Frank in Brisbane and home to the Sweetmans and Gilraines in Achill outlining their plans. Over the next several weeks they got increasingly excited about the positive aspects of the proposed move.

First and most importantly, there was the longed for reunion with Frank and Nora and the chance to become part of Daisy's life. Then there was the prospect of adventure and opportunity and the expectation of an improvement in their lifestyle, not to mention the lovely climate. The only sour note was the breaking of the news of their momentous decision to

Bill and Lizzie and the Baldwin family. After all they had been through together this parting would be heart-breaking and no one wanted to think about it until the last possible moment.

Created as part of Australia's 'Populate or Perish' policy, the assisted passage scheme was designed to substantially increase the population and to supply workers for the country's booming industries. In return for subsidising the cost of travelling to Australia, adult migrants were charged only ten pounds sterling for the fare (hence the term 'Ten Pound Poms'), and children were allowed to travel free. The government promised employment prospects, housing and a generally more optimistic lifestyle. On arrival, migrants were placed in basic hostels and the expected job opportunities were not always readily available. Assisted migrants were generally obliged to remain in Australia for two years after arrival, or alternatively refund the cost of their assisted passage. If they chose to travel back to Britain, the cost of the journey was at least one hundred and twenty pounds, a large sum and one that most could not afford. Just before Christmas, all the paperwork was in order and Red had handed in his notice. The sailing had been booked for January 6th, 1948, aboard HMS Langleedene. Alice and Red had a lot to do in the intervening period. There was the packing and also decisions had to be reached regarding what they could not carry due to baggage restrictions. Within a few days of his resignation from O Neills', he was very pleasantly surprised to get a letter from his workmates containing a sizeable cheque. On hearing of his plan to emigrate, his workmates had had a whip-around. The letter suggested that he might like to use the money to visit Achill to see his own and Alice's people before their journey to the other side of the world. Red was very moved to receive such a fine token of appreciation and particularly touched by the generosity of spirit of his co-workers in thinking of the joy this visit home would mean to his parents. He couldn't wait to share the news with Alice, who was thrilled to see the restoration of his good spirits. The troubles of the past months seemed to wash away in the cascade of goodwill and consideration of his friends in his erstwhile workplace. The packing up was undertaken with increased gusto to facilitate the few days' break in Achill. The cross channel run was undertaken in a whirlwind of excitement and even the scurry from the North Wall to the train at Amiens Street in order not to miss the train to Westport didn't dampen their spirits. Four hours later they scrambled onto the bus for Achill Sound where they got a hackney car to Alice's home and surprised Danny and Maud by just appearing in Dugort.

The welcome was overwhelming and young Patrick was cooed over and passed around among his aunts Annie and Mary and his uncles Martin, Séamus and Michael. Only Dan was missing, having gone to America the previous year. After the excitement of the greetings, and poor little Patrick being kissed within an inch of his life, they set off down the road for the Gilraine home and a repeat performance. Bridie and Paddy were about to go to bed. The thrill of this unexpected arrival completely put paid to that for a notion. Breda and Rose exclaimed over their nephew and eventually even Brendan appeared to see what the furore was about. Tea was made and the fire replenished and as young Patrick drowsed in Alice's arms they had a chance to catch up on all the family news. The next few days went by in a flash while friends and relatives from all over the island came to visit at one or other of the parental homes. The culmination was a house party and dance at the Gilraines' on the eve of Red and Alice's departure for Southampton.

Bridie was busy all morning making scones and sponge cakes in the bastable oven on the open fire between bouts of inconsolable tears at the prospect of her upcoming loss. Paddy and Red had taken the horse and car to Achill Sound to collect a barrel of stout and some bottled beer as well as some sherry for the womenfolk. Clay pipes, tobacco, snuff and cigarettes had to be bought also as if for a wake. In a sense, it was akin to a wake, the bidding of a last goodbye to a loved one. In fact, in the west of Ireland the term 'an American wake' was used to describe the all too frequent farewell gatherings to emigrating youth on their departure to the United States of America. Whenever, if ever this particular group of people would meet again inevitably some of those gathered would have gone to their eternal reward. No one knew if this little family would ever again return to their native island whereas it was almost certain that their elders would never make the long and arduous journey 'down under'.

Chapter 9

Together Again

Six weeks and two days after embarking at Southampton, HMS Langleedene docked in Circular Quay, Sydney, on February 19th, 1948. All the passengers gathered on the upper deck to catch their first glimpse of the Promised Land. Among them Red stood tall and pale faced with his young son clasped to his chest and his right arm around his tiny wan and fragile wife. They had suffered a rough crossing and were considerably the worse for wear after their ordeal. Relief at having arrived safely was evident in the faces of all the new arrivals aboard, along with a mixture of excitement and residual sadness. Once they had disembarked, they were all rounded up to be led to a nearby hostel. Just as he was struggling to assemble the luggage, Red was almost upended as he was swept up into an enthusiastic bear hug by a large well-dressed gentleman. Before he could recover and see who had grabbed him he recognised Frank O Neill's inimitable chuckle.

Frank immediately took complete charge. Before they knew what was happening Alice, Patrick and Red were being settled into the back of Frank's swanky large red car. Within three months of their arrival in Australia, Frank had bought a brand new Hudson Terraplane 1946 model complete with white wall tyres and lots of chrome to set off its dark red shiny paintwork. Having greeted them with hugs and kisses Nora busied herself tucking rugs around their legs while talking nineteen to the dozen. The plan was to get started on the long journey to Brisbane as soon as possible. Frank loved driving and was confident that they'd make it as far as South Lismore by nightfall where he had booked a hotel for them all for that night. With a few comfort stops en route and all going well this part of the journey would take between eight and a half and ten hours. For the first few hours, there was plenty of chat and exchanging of news. Eventually, the heat and exhaustion overcame them one by one until only Frank and Nora were left to share a few desultory words together. At this point, Frank suggested that Nora too should take the opportunity to catch a little nap and that he would keep driving until everyone woke up. Then they would stop for a snack and to stretch their legs. The stop would be unscheduled in any case and the snacks would be selected from the generous contents of the picnic hamper in the boot. As the afternoon drew to a close, Nora re-awakened and one after the other the back-seat passengers too began to yawn and stretch themselves into wakefulness. When the chatter of conversation had resumed for some ten minutes or so, Frank began to look out for a suitably shaded place for the picnic. He was very pleased with his progress and said: "We're making great time, folks. We've been on the road for five hours and forty minutes and I calculate that we're now only about four hours from South Lismore. I, for one, am delighted that we have the back of the journey broken. Come on now, all of you, let's eat. I'm starving and I'm sure all of you are too."

Nora opened the picnic hamper and, spreading a table cloth on the grass in the shade of the stand of gum trees, she proceeded to lay out a feast of sliced ham, potato salad, cheese, olives, tomatoes, cucumber and lettuce accompanied by soft bread rolls and dry white wine. The meal ended with a selection of delicious fruits and cool fresh water from the nearby stream. Then, their hunger satisfied, they had a little walk to stretch their limbs and piled back into the Hudson for the last leg of the day's journey. By the time they arrived in South Lismore, it was quite late and they were all dog tired, so after a light supper they retired for the night and some well-earned rest.

The following morning they were all up early and after a healthy breakfast they set off again. Happy to be on the home stretch and in familiar terrain, Frank was looking forward to the four hour drive and arriving home to his own household and the joy of showing off his precious eight month old Daisy to her godparents. This final lap went by very quickly with the four way exchange of news and catching up, including constant interruptions and backtracking. The conversation was so animated as to be almost cacophonous with the result that two year old Patrick objected with some shouting of his own. The adults then took the voice levels down a few decibels and as the miles flew by the missing months vanished in their wake.

The two women now sat together with the toddler sleeping between them in the comfort of the back seat. They were able to chat away quietly so as not to disturb him while Frank and Red in the front carried on filling in the gaps since they had seen each other last. In the way of good friends, they were immediately at ease with one another and were able to pick up the conversation as if they had only spoken yesterday. On arrival in Brisbane, instead of being all talked out, they were in fact looking forward to further opportunities to spend time together. It was only on their reunion that Nora and Alice in particular realised how much they had missed each other. Frank and Red were delighted to be back together again and absolutely thrilled at the prospect of working side by side again. There was no real discussion about it, it was just taken for granted that Red would join Frank's workforce as soon as they were settled in Brisbane. The cousins were already in tacit agreement on where they should start house hunting.

Within the first week of their arrival, the Gilraines had already received an invitation to their first social outing, an afternoon barbecue party at the Kelly mansion. This had arisen from their introduction to Bob and Lisa at Nora's 'welcome to Brisbane' bash organised for them the previous Saturday. Bob and Lisa Kelly were the envy of their neighbours, the kind of successful couple who had 'everything'. Bob was one of Australia's top barristers and Lisa came from a family with 'old money'. They had come out from England after their big 'society wedding' some ten years prior and now lived in a rather pretentious large mansion in the hills about four miles from the edge of the rapidly developing city. The house, an unhappy mix of styles, was set in its own grounds consisting of five acres of manicured lawns, beautifully maintained shrubs and carefully tended flowerbeds. There was also a large outdoor swimming pool close to the house and two full size tennis courts. Red and Alice were looking forward with some trepidation to the affair, a rather splendid event in Brisbane's social calendar. Frank and Nora, being more outgoing and confident anyway, also had the advantage of having been guests of the Kellys on previous occasions, and therefore were quite comfortably anticipating a wonderful afternoon and evening. Red was happy enough knowing that he would be in the company of his beautiful wife and his best friends. Poor Alice, on the other hand, was quite apprehensive. Being rather shy, she was petrified that either she or Red would appear gauche or, heaven forbid, would make some social faux pas and thus disgrace the O Neills in front of their posh hosts. She was in a dither as to what to wear as well and was working herself into a nervous wreck when Nora came to the rescue. Although they were cousins, the two young women could not have been less alike in appearance. Tiny Alice, with her size six figure, fragile bone structure, blonde hair and fair complexion, was the perfect foil for her dark-haired, more elegant cousin who, at five feet eight inches, towered above her. As there was no possibility of their ever sharing clothes, Nora had undertaken the task of showing Alice her favourite shops and assisting her in selecting some classic pieces to see her through the season's parties. The shopping spree was prompted by not just the upcoming event but also by the necessity for Alice to acquire clothing more appropriate to the summer weather down under.

They set off in great humour and high spirits and in the hope of success. Unfortunately Alice's diminutive proportions proved to be more of a problem than they had anticipated. After several footsore and frustrating hours and visits to a plethora of shops, eventually they were forced to try the children's section of one of the larger stores. Here they finally struck gold. They found a simple drop-waisted dress in pale cream, lawn sprigged with tiny cornflowers which suited Alice to a tee. Much relieved, Nora then had the brainwave of buying some more lawn material in various colours so that they could run up some more dresses of the same pattern and cut. This plan would prove to be no great challenge to these ladies who were quite proficient seamstresses in their own right. In the end, Alice wore her own version of the dress in burnt orange, sparsely sprigged with tiny lily of the valley. The lovely shade complemented her blonde hair and fair colouring. As they were on our way over to the Kellys, Frank and Nora and Red were high in their praise of her appearance and this made her feel a little less uncomfortable.

The occasion was a great success and Bob and Lisa excellent hosts so everyone had a wonderful time. Lisa was especially solicitous of Alice and succeeded in making her feel not just welcome but at home in the big house by the simple expedient of talking to her and listening empathically to what she had to say. As young émigrés, they had a lot in common so much of the chat was about leaving their families behind. More than that they found that they genuinely liked each other and, for the moment at least, Alice had lost her fear of social encounters. Over the next few months she and Red settled down quickly in their new surroundings.

At first, they rented a small house in Emmingham not far from where the O Neills lived. Red started working almost immediately as a foreman on one of the bigger housing projects that Frank's company had undertaken. Alice wished to stay at home to look after Patrick as she was reluctant to work outside the home until her precious son would be old enough to start school. Somehow she could not bring herself to entrust him to the care of a nanny or a minder. Nora had no such qualms and had actually been looking forward to returning to work just as soon as the holidays were over. So she had started back in the local school, this time much to her satisfaction, in a permanent capacity. Little Daisy was being looked after expertly and affectionately by a lovely young woman called Maree Nolan. Maree was very much part of the family rather than an employee of the O Neills. Initially Alice found this rather odd, accustomed as she was to class conscious England where such a thing was unheard of, even in post-war London. She soon got used to the more egalitarian and easy-going ways of her new surroundings. Within a few weeks, she found that she and Maree had become fast friends and were spending a good deal of time in each other's company. They would take the children for walks in each other's company, sit in the park together and even take it in turn to prepare and eat lunch in one house or the other. Despite the disparity in their ages and backgrounds, they got on extremely well together. The younger woman brought her training and youthful enthusiasm to the relationship and Alice her experience and more sober judgement.

Maree had qualified as a mother craft nurse in Berry Street College, having secured a place there after spending two years in Flemington Girls' High. She was also a great help in terms of explaining cultural differences and easing her new friend's way socially, while Alice in turn generously shared her housekeeping skills as well as a wealth of recipes with young Maree. Alice and Red were enjoying their new life and within a few months were delighted to have found a suitable house to buy in the neighbourhood. Life was good. Red was happy in his work. Alice was thriving in the Australian climate, the friendliness of the people and the exciting social life. She was enjoying every minute of her role as mother and stay-at-home wife. Patrick was a secure and happy outgoing young fellow, already showing signs of independence and adventurousness. The O Neills were wonderful friends who had been, from the very beginning, supportive, helpful and welcoming. Best of all they felt that they were valued members of not just their Catholic community but of the broader Brisbane society.

Coming up to Christmas of 1949 Maree made a shock announcement. She had recently met and fallen in love with a roguish young Irishman from County Clare who was working at the O Neills' on a temporary contract. Shay McNamara was a carefree smiling scamp with a great sense of humour. He was uncomplicated and easy to be with, very popular with members of both sexes and all ages. He was a lovely singer and a competent fiddle player and loved to be the life and soul of a party. Until now he had managed to steer clear of commitment to any of his large coterie of female friends. As soon as he met Maree, he had become completely besotted with his Australian beauty. Now suddenly he had to return to Ireland to take up the challenge of running the home farm in Dromelton after the premature death of his father some weeks earlier. He was devastated and hugely concerned about how his widowed mother Eileen was coping with her grief and the burden of his seven lively younger siblings. He hated the thought of parting from Maree but knew that he had to return home. He hadn't taken Maree's maturity and determination into his reckoning and was both charmed and thrilled when she calmly announced, "Of course you must go home, Shay. It would be unthinkable not to. And given that you must go, then I will go with you."

And so on January 6th, 1950, a very exciting and hurriedly prepared wedding reception was hosted by the O Neills for the young couple. Maree had been brought up and received her early education from the Sisters of Mercy in St Vincent's

Orphanage in North Brisbane. The O Neills were the nearest she had to family so it was only natural that they would want to host a reception for her big day. Her guests were few and included three nuns from St Vincent's Orphanage, her two favourites, Sister Francis and Sister Anthony and a third, a Sister Joseph. The third nun had only been invited because Maree feared that the others might be refused permission to come without her. The only jarring note on her otherwise perfect day was Maree's regret that her friend Frances could not be reached and would therefore not be present. Her friends the Gilraines had also been invited. Shay had asked a few friends from work and the ceremony was performed in the large dining room of the O Neills' home by Father John Ryan, former chaplain of St Vincent's and a frequent visitor at the Gilraine house too.

The wedding guests, though not very numerous, were very stylishly turned out. Frank looked very smart in his morning suit for his role as surrogate father of the bride, and as chief hostess Nora was not about to be outdone in elegance or sophistication. As Maree's Matron of Honour, Alice was a pretty picture in her ballet length buttercup yellow frock. Four year old Patrick was a charming, if unwilling, page boy in his miniature morning suit. Little Daisy O Neill, a beautiful and rather unsteady flower girl in an even tinier version of Alice's dress, looked delectable enough to snatch up and cuddle. Within hours of the solemn ceremony and sumptuous meal, the newlyweds hurried away to begin their long journey to their new life in Ireland.

Maree's sudden departure left Nora and Frank with a problem, the solution to which was both simple and obvious. Alice immediately took over the full-time care of young Daisy which she could easily manage now that Patrick would soon be ready for school. At first, she sorely missed her friend Maree. She was getting better at adjusting to the life changes that living in Brisbane inevitably brought about. Soon she was completely absorbed in caring for Daisy and keeping up with an ever more challenging Patrick and his adventures. She saw a lot of Nora, who constantly and consistently encouraged her to consider returning to her interrupted nursing career. Alice was not ready yet and, besides, she loved her child-caring role and had no wish to give it up. The greater financial rewards of the workplace were no great inducement either as the O Neills were offering generous remuneration for her services. In fact, she loved her little god-daughter so much that Alice would have been more than willing to look after Daisy for nothing.

Chapter 10

A Surprise Gift

In September 1950, when five-year-old Patrick started at Emmingham Junior School, Alice was surprised to find that she was no less busy than she had been. Instead of organising and supervising activities for Patrick and Daisy she now found that the same amount of time was required to organise Daisy's day as she had heretofore spent on both children. Now on top of this busy schedule, she had to find the time to prepare healthy snacks and lunches for Patrick and make time for walking to and from the school, rain or shine, four times a day as well. Was it her imagination or had Daisy suddenly become much more demanding? Since when did she need Alice's constant attention and approval for her every task and utterance? Or was it simply that Daisy missed having Patrick about and that Alice had completely underestimated the advantages of the co-dependent relationship of the children? Whatever the reasons she now found herself run off her feet.

Just when she thought that things couldn't get any worse, she had a visit from Sister Francis of St Vincent's Orphanage. When Sister Francis called, Alice was a little surprised but welcomed her with delight. At first, she assumed that the good sister, whom she had enjoyed meeting at the wedding, had come to share news of Maree and her new husband. She was dying to hear how Maree was getting on with married life and how she had settled in with Shay's family in Ireland. She plied Sister Francis with question after question, barely giving her a chance to reply before she thought of some other vital query to which she must have an answer. After an hour or more of animated discussion and cup after cup of tea, it was time for Alice to go and collect Patrick from school. She popped Daisy into the pram, making sure that she was well propped up and in a position to see all around her. Then she fitted the sunshade onto the pram and set off walking at a brisk pace accompanied by the still chattering nun.

By the time they had collected Patrick and returned home, it was time to prepare the evening meal to which she felt it appropriate to invite Sister Francis. Surprisingly, the nun willingly accepted the invitation and seemed to be in no particular hurry to return to her convent. They prepared the meal in companionable conversation and had just set the table for dinner when Red arrived home from work. Over the course of the meal much of the news about Maree and Shay was rehashed for his benefit and then, as the talk turned to more general matters, Sister Francis dropped her bombshell. The real reason for her visit was slowly and carefully revealed. She had an enormous favour to ask. This proposal would change dramatically and forever the lives of at least three other people as well as the Gilraines.

Sister Francis began, "One of our girls has done extremely well for herself. After she left the orphanage she went on to drama school where she excelled. Since then she has become rather well known and extremely successful as an actress. To preserve her anonymity I will refer to her from now on as 'Miss F'. Recently she has been offered an opportunity to screen test for a Hollywood studio. The trouble is she cannot accept this wonderful offer right now because unfortunately she has fallen from grace. Her position is that she has become pregnant. If that is not bad enough, it transpires that the prospective father is a married man. Worse still, he too is a well-known figure and if this was to become public knowledge, it would ruin his family and his social standing and also destroy his political career. He now bitterly regrets his behaviour but cannot see a way he can help without exposing himself. Miss F has thought long and hard about her future and, after much heartache and discussion with her confessor, has decided that the best solution would be to put the child up for adoption. So far she has managed to conceal her condition. She is already six months gone. Now, Alice and Red, this is where you come in, if you are willing to at least listen to my proposal. As soon as I was in possession of all the facts, I immediately thought of you. What's needed now is a common sense, down to earth, loving couple of absolute discretion who would be willing to offer a good Catholic home to this little child when it is born. A couple such as you, who would be happy to adopt a blameless infant and raise him or her as their own, would be ideal. I know you will need time to think about it so now I will leave you. I will call again before the end of the month and see if we need to discuss this further at that stage. Thank you so much for your hospitality and for listening to my request. I will see you soon and meanwhile I will keep you in my prayers. May God bless you and help you make the right decision," said Sister Francis as she took her departure.

In the knowledge that they had three months of a lead-in period and after much soul searching, Alice and Red made up their minds to accept the challenge of adoption. If truth be told, neither could come up with any justifiable reason to refuse a loving home to this child being gifted to them, especially since they both feared that they would not have other children of their own in the future. They prayed that their decision was the right one for everyone concerned and when Sister Francis came to visit again they were happy to tell her that they would proceed with the adoption when the time came. A little over thirteen weeks later, just as they were finishing their Christmas dinner on Patrick's sixth birthday, a very excited Sister Francis rang to tell them the good news that a perfect and healthy baby girl had just arrived into the world weighing in at six pounds and thirteen ounces. They'd be able to see the baby next day and, all going well, they'd be signing the adoption papers the following day and taking her home. Alice, Red and young Patrick were all thrilled with this very special Christmas present and very welcome addition to the family. Patrick was probably the most outwardly excited on hearing the news. He couldn't get over the fact that he and his new sister shared the same very special birthday.

Next morning dawned a seasonably warm and sunny summer's St Stephen's Day. As far as Alice and Red were concerned, this was a good omen. The three of them set off in great anticipation to the hospital where they were allowed to catch a glimpse of the baby in the nursery. After a considerable wait Sister Francis arrived with Dr Carey in tow. "Shall we go into matron's office and go through the paperwork first?" asked Dr Carey before catching sight of the disappointment on the faces of all three of the Gilraines. Without missing a beat, he continued, "On second thoughts, let's not keep the new-comer waiting. We need to introduce you immediately to the lovely lady."

With that he ushered them straight into the nursery. Here he scooped the baby up and laid her gently in Alice's arms. Patrick, standing on tiptoe beside his diminutive mom, had a close-up view of his new sister while Red stood with a protective arm about Alice's shoulder, gazing adoringly for the first time at their beautiful daughter. Then the doctor directed Sister Francis to the door, saying over his shoulder, "We'll leave you to get acquainted. There's no rush. Take as much time as you like. Whenever you're ready you'll find us in matron's office."

They didn't feel the time slipping by as they admired and cuddled the new baby. And indeed she was a stunning looking baby. Even at a little over twenty-four hours old she was already showing signs of the outstanding beauty she would become. By the time a nurse came to give her a feed, Alice realised, with a guilty start, that they had been keeping the doctor and the nun waiting for more than twenty minutes. When they arrived at matron's office a few minutes later, they apologised most sincerely for the delay, only to find a welcome tray of refreshments awaiting them. Matron had joined the other two and immediately poured tea for all the adults and handed Patrick a soft drink. After they had all finished the tea, Dr Carey produced the adoption papers and, having read through the simple forms carefully, Red and Alice signed them. Sister Francis explained that the biological parents would sign later so that neither party would ever learn the identity of the others. In this way, the anonymity of the biological parents would be preserved and for the adoptive parents there would never be any danger that their child could be taken from them. It would also be better for the baby, who would only ever know one mom and dad and would be all the more secure for that. For now though, they must return home and tomorrow they could come to the Alexander Hotel in Quay Street at 2.00 p.m. where Sister Francis would hand over the baby. This slight delay was necessary so that all the signatures were on the forms and so the records would be in order. Neither Alice nor Red ever thought to question the legitimacy of these arrangements. After all, they were presided over by members of the medical profession and the Catholic Church.

Alice wrote to Maree, enclosing pictures of her beautiful daughter and explaining how Sister Francis had been responsible for the very happy circumstances of her adoption. When she heard back from Maree some weeks later, she had great news of her own. In a little over four months, she and Shay expected to be the proud parents themselves. The twins arrived on April 21st, 1952, to great excitement and a wonderful welcome. Shay was so thrilled with his three wonderful girls that he left the choice of names completely in Maree's hands.

Belonging was hugely important to Maree. She had always wondered about her own roots and at first had assumed that her heritage must be Irish as Nolan was obviously an Irish surname. One of the other girls in St Vincent's had scoffingly disabused her of the notion of making such assumptions with the comment, "Don't be a daft sheila. Sure, most of the nuns here are Irish and 'tis they choose the names for us foundlings and the fatherless." Maree had only had one good friend in the orphanage, a gorgeous looking girl called Frances with stunningly beautiful and unusual eyes. They suspected that she had been named for Sister Francis who was a kindly and very popular sister. Maree and Frances were inseparable from the time they were four years old until they were sixteen. Then they went their separate ways, Maree to college in Berry Street while Frances enrolled at drama school. They had corresponded for a while in the early days. Then Frances had disappeared without trace. Maree was broken-hearted, especially when she failed to get in touch so she could invite Frances to her wedding. She never forgot the friend of her youth. Now she wished to commemorate the friendship by giving one of her precious twins the fancy version of the name her friend had planned to use when she became a rich and famous actress. The other twin would be named after Shay's mother. The girls would also bear the names of Maree's two closest adult friends. She would always treasure the two Irish women who had befriended her and introduced her to the love of her life, Shay. So the McNamara twins were named Nora Eileen and Francesca Alice. Francesca loved her name and after a brief period in her teens when she flirted with the notion of being called Seska by her friends she was delighted to return to her given name in adulthood. Nora Eileen almost immediately morphed into the pet name Norella which she was delighted to answer to all her life.

Chapter 11
Lily

Alice and Red couldn't wait to show off their beautiful baby daughter. As they were equally anxious to have her baptised in the Catholic Church without delay, the christening was scheduled for New Year's Eve. This allowed them time to invite all their friends to the ceremony and back home afterwards for some party food and drinks. Those who were going out later to New Year parties would have sufficient time to get dressed up for these events while the family could enjoy the pleasures of a quiet evening of domestic bliss after all the excitement was over. Predictably the O Neills were invited to be the godparents. Nora and Frank were very pleased to accept the honour. Loving and besotted parents of a daughter themselves, even they had to admit that, pretty as Daisy was, beside the gorgeous newcomer she appeared almost homely. From the moment they had first set eyes on her Alice and Red had fallen completely and irrevocably in love with their daughter. Within minutes, by mutual agreement, they were referring to her as 'Rosebud' because of her rosy cheeks and the perfection of her little features. Already she was showing signs of being thoroughly at home as the centre of attention, the deserved cynosure of admiring eyes.

Now they had to decide on an appropriate name for the child. They might end up referring to her by the pet name

Rosebud. For her christening, she would have to have a proper and preferably Catholic name that would sound well with the surname Gilraine. Mary, Brigid, Sabina, Teresa, Cecilia and Molly were all considered and rejected before her doting dad came up with the inspired and entirely suitable suggestion that she should be called Lily. Alice was delighted and they retired for the night happy with their decision. On the morning of the christening, Patrick wondered aloud why his sister shouldn't be called Kelly and so later that day in their local church Lily Kelly Gilraine was baptised and welcomed into the Roman Catholic Church. When she grew up, she would invariably and immediately draw the eyes of everyone present towards her on entering a room. This fascination Lily exerted over males and females, young and old alike, was completely unconscious. Furthermore, she was utterly unaware that she caused such adulation wherever she went. Perhaps it was because she had never experienced any negativity in her life that she was so comfortable within her own skin. Her parents, her brother and all their friends couldn't help but love her. Her school companions and everyone else who came into contact with her were initially drawn to her by her appearance and wished to remain within her orbit because of her loving nature and the warmth of her personality. From early childhood, Lily was one of those lovely people who, despite her good looks and many enviable talents, managed never to engender jealousy in those who knew her. Instead, people once under her spell were more than content to remain within the privileged comfort of her friendship.

She was particularly close to her older brother Patrick and to her cousin Daisy, who was less than three years her senior. Because of her gentle manner and sunny disposition Lily had the happiest memories of her childhood. To all those who knew Alice, including Red, it appeared that she had been completely absorbed in mothering young Patrick. Nothing prepared him for the intensity of her besotted absorption with every nuance and detail of Lily's infancy. Everything this baby did was grist to Alice's mill and worthy of endless comment, description and repetition. Those close to the family felt that so much adulation and adoring attention might spoil the child. Lily appeared not to suffer any adverse effects. She was, without doubt, a stunningly beautiful child. She had the most intriguingly unusual eyes. They were mesmerizingly different. They were almond shaped and wide open as well as being set far apart. What was exceptional about them was their unusual colour. Most people have eyes of clearly identifiable colour, though there are variations in shade and sometimes even speckles of different pigments. Lily's irises were neatly bisected top to bottom, one half a deep, almost violet, blue and the other a speckled hazel. The effect on people was instantaneous. Their gaze was drawn to Lily's eyes which were immediately fascinating. As soon as she engaged them in conversation, the beautiful eyes became only a part of the wonderful package that was Lily. Lily attracted an undue amount of attention when she appeared in public, even as a toddler. Sometimes this could be embarrassing, particularly if Daisy was in the company and completely ignored while total strangers made a big fuss of her younger cousin. Alice genuinely tried to shield the older child from hurt as best she could but she knew that to the sensitive Daisy her own maternal pride and love for Lily shone from her like an internal illumination. Daisy, luckily for her, was a well-balanced and kindly child who loved her little cousin unreservedly and unequivocally. From very early on Lily shared everything with Daisy and soon developed her own little strategies to include her in the fussing. After Daisy went to school mother and daughter had hours each day to enjoy each other's company.

As September 1957 drew closer and the time for Lily in her turn to go to school, Alice wondered how she could possibly face the separation. When the day came at last and Lily started school, Alice grieved. Over the next few months she lost weight and became depressed. She lost interest in her own appearance, became lethargic and neglected her home and her household chores. Red was very worried about her. Meanwhile, Lily took to the new experiences and the stimulation of her new life as if school had been invented specifically for her. She was bright and vivacious and loved the challenge of learning. She was popular with her schoolmates and loved her teacher.

Soon after the Christmas break she began to notice her mother's unhappiness and her dad's constant worrying. Patrick, at eleven years of age, was also keenly aware of the situation but was keeping everything bottled up. He was very surprised, therefore, when one evening his five-year-old sister broached the subject with him. Initially he became angry and stalked off. He was tempted to tell her to mind her own business as she couldn't possibly understand what was going on. He was angry with everyone concerned. He was cross with his dad who didn't seem to know what to do. He was angry with his mom for the way she was behaving. He was mad at Lily whom in some weird way he was blaming for all this. Most of all he was angry with himself and his inability to help his family. After he had stalked off he went for a long walk in the woods near home. Here in the solitude and quietness he was able to think. He immediately regretted his abruptness towards his little sister and promised himself that he would make it up to Lily as soon as possible. Then he figured that if a five-year-old was aware that something was wrong then it was past time for action. He thought long and hard about involving others outside the family in their troubles, knowing how shy his mother was and how private Red liked to keep family business. In the end, he came to the conclusion that matters were sufficiently serious to seek outside help. He would involve the O Neills, his parents' closest friends and the soundest and most discreet people he knew. He felt that if anyone could help his mom it would be her cousin and best friend Nora and Uncle Frank always knew people who could help in any crisis.

Feeling better for having come to a decision, Patrick headed home only to be greeted by a frantic Alice, a tearful Lily and an absent Dad. Patrick had lost track of time and had no idea how much panic and concern his late return had caused. Red had been out searching for him for over an hour alone and, within the previous forty minutes as dusk approached, had enlisted five of the neighbouring men to trawl further afield for the missing boy. Luckily Nora, on hearing of Patrick's disappearance, had driven over and was therefore in a position to find Frank and call off the search. When it was clear that the lad was safe and everyone else had returned to their homes, the O Neills sat down together with Red and Alice to discuss things. Patrick was allowed to explain why he had gone missing in the first instance and, after being consoled by the relieved adults, was soon sound asleep in his bed. Lily also slept, worn out after the trauma.

Appreciating just how close to tragedy and the possibilities of the loss of a beloved child, they had come, Alice and Red were overwhelmed with gratitude. Frank and Nora shared their relief and, because they too loved Patrick and Lily, they were able to offer support and some insightful observations. Nora promised to involve Alice more in activities outside the home so she would have less time to brood. Frank reiterated his advice regarding professional counselling and promised to visit more frequently. Before the O Neills left that night Red vowed to keep a closer eye on the children and to this end was less inclined to volunteer for overtime thereafter. And as for Alice, the thought of harm befalling her beloved son, while she was distracted, was enough to shake her from her depression and refocus her attention on giving equal attention to all three members of her family.

Following the scare with Patrick, things began to improve for the Gilraines, especially after Alice had received some counselling from an excellent doctor recommended by Frank. As a result, she was careful to keep herself busy and focused on both children. She concentrated also on trying to make time for her husband and their marriage. At first, she resented Nora's attempts to involve her in activities outside the home. Later she realised that rather than interfering Nora had her best interests at heart and was genuinely looking out for her. The busier she was the less time she had for introspection and soon she discovered that she actually enjoyed helping out in the community. It had started out with a request to provide the catering for meetings of the Women's Institute every other Wednesday. Alice took on this task willingly and this led to other requests for organising afternoon teas and children's parties. She was pleased to discover that she was so very organised that she was able to provide these services as a matter of course and without any obvious disruption of her other duties. Not long afterwards she was approached by the matron of Saint Anne's Haven, a local old folks' home, to work as a carer three or four mornings a week. Miss Ingoldsby, the matron, was very persuasive and as Alice was more than qualified for the work, and for the most part free in the mornings, she could find no reasonable excuse not to oblige.

She was delighted and somewhat surprised to find that she genuinely loved being back at work. Meeting new people broadened her horizons and gave her new interests. It also had the very pleasant side effect of reducing her natural shyness. Older people seemed to have no inhibitions and loved to ask questions. Perhaps they were just lonely. Alice soon found that as she went about her work she was constantly answering a barrage of questions or being asked for her opinion on a broad variety of topics.

One particular lovely lady, Eda Hogan, aged eighty-seven, was an inveterate reader and loved to discuss her favourite books with Alice. Eda was originally from County Mayo. She and her husband Seán had emigrated from Ireland to Australia fifty five years earlier. They were newlyweds at the time. Seán was a forty-year-old childless widower and Eda a young vivacious beauty of twenty-two. Her family did not approve of the marriage, not just on age grounds but because Seán had been Eda's teacher in school. Also, she had spent two years as a live-in housekeeper in the teacher's residence in the village where she had nursed Seán's ailing wife before her death. So Seán and Eda had got married in Dublin and without a backward glance had headed for Australia, leaving behind the speculation, the gossip and the begrudgery. They had a good and happy marriage and were blessed with five children, two sons and three daughters. Seán had taught for over twenty years as principal in a little three teacher school in Rider's Crossing in New South Wales. Eda had settled down to a comfortable, if not very wealthy, rural lifestyle where she reared the children and provided a happy and intellectually stimulating home for her family. The children grew to adulthood in the respectful and nurturing care of parents who loved each other deeply and were at their best in each other's company.

One by one, as is inevitable for bright young people reared in rural areas, they moved away first to secondary school then to college and eventually to jobs in cities and faraway places. By the time her beloved Seán died peacefully in his sleep at the age of sixty-six, all five of their children had left home. Robert, the eldest, was a Catholic priest working as a missionary in the Philippines. Angela, who was married, and Mary Ellen, who was not, were both nursing in Sydney. Johnny was a marine engineer and loved his work sailing the seven seas. Susan, the youngest, was the only one to follow in her father's footsteps and become a teacher. She was now a science teacher in a large secondary school in faraway Tasmania. Widowed and alone at only forty-eight years of age, Eda had moved to Brisbane. On her arrival in the city early in 1930, she knew no one, hadn't worked outside the home since her marriage twenty-seven years earlier and was still grieving for her husband. Nothing daunted, she went in search of work. She had no wish to burden any of her children and, being of independent mind and in robust health, she was prepared for a change of direction. She had always loved books and reading, so she decided to seek work in an area where this interest would be useful. First stop therefore, was the nearest branch library to where she had chosen to live. Lady Luck smiled on this plucky and indomitable woman. Qualified librarians were in short supply in Australia and so when the Library Board advertised for a library assistant. Eda presented herself for interview. Despite her age or perhaps because of it, she outshone all of the other candidates. She was extremely well read. Not only that, she had a lovely manner, an extremely pleasant voice and her keen intelligence informed her every response. The interview board members were very impressed with her and she was immediately offered the job. Within less than a year of employing her, head office realised just what an asset she was and offered to support her in acquiring a third level qualification in librarianship.

Eda was thrilled and set off on her part time course with great enthusiasm. She absolutely loved every second of it, the mental stimulation, the practical aspects, the research, the endless reading, the tutorials, the term papers, the assignments and even the final exams. For the first time in her life, Eda was using her considerable intelligence to its full potential. She still missed her husband and her family. She was happy to have found a meaningful outlet for her substantial energy. For the next twenty-five years, she worked for the Brisbane Library service until she had to retire at the age of seventy. Even after that she continued to work part time and voluntarily organised readings for the mother and toddler groups locally. She also volunteered to read to those elderly patients in St Anne's Haven, little knowing that someday she would herself end up there and be glad to be a recipient of this invaluable service. Now in her eighties, her eyesight had begun to deteriorate and, recognising in Alice a kindred spirit, she looked forward to their daily chats. They had more in common than a shared love of reading. Both women missed their families. Also, they each had family members scattered abroad with whom they were in touch only by letter. So their conversations always contained references to distant loved ones and the sharing of interesting facts about faraway places and distant cultures.

From the beginning Eda loved to encourage Alice to broaden the range of her reading material. She recommended books to her, lent her some of her own annotated favourites and enjoyed discussing them with her. Eda particularly loved when they did not see eye to eye on a book and the arguments grew robust. At first, Alice was in awe of Eda's superior knowledge and was reticent about expressing her own opinions. Over time, with the encouragement and support of her friend, she had gained the confidence to hold her own. A bonus for Alice and the recipients of her regular and ongoing correspondence was that she now included references and opinions on her current reading which greatly added to the interest levels of her letters.

Chapter 12
The Sweetmans

The Gilraines had settled into a nice comfortable routine and their lives in Brisbane were very pleasant. Alice and Red were both content in their work and the children happy and successful in their schools. Patrick was now almost sixteen and within two years of finishing his second level education, and Lily, nearly ten, was doing very well in senior primary school when the letter from Achill arrived. Unfortunately the letter, over six weeks in transit, did not bring good news. It was ostensibly from Alice's mother Maud with the sad news that her husband Danny had passed away. Poor Alice was devastated at the loss of her beloved dad. Worse news was to follow and quite close on the heels of the first. It was now 1962 and in the fourteen years since she had last seen her parents many changes had taken place in the Sweetman household, some positive and some, alas, negative.

For starters, all six of her younger siblings had moved away from home. Three of her brothers in turn had emigrated from Achill to Rochester in the north of New York State where they now ran a very successful and busy construction company. Dan was chief executive of the company he had set up in 1943. He had worked hard in the building trade and after a couple of years had qualified as an engineer. A year later he encouraged Martin to join him and as soon as the spring term ended

Michael joined them too. They worked together through the long summer of 1945 and made a lot of money. It was agreed that Michael would join them as a permanent member of the company as soon as he had qualified the following May.

Later that same summer Annie went out to Rochester too. She did not join the family business. She worked as a nurse in the local hospital. Séamus had long since moved to Dublin to join the Civil Service. There he had met and married a German woman and they had both subsequently moved to Brussels where Gabriella still taught and Séamus worked as a representative of the Department of Foreign Affairs in NATO's European headquarters. Only Mary remained at home with her parents for another year before following her dream and joining the order of the Sisters of Mercy in a convent in County Tipperary. Alice and Red were well aware that the Sweetman parents had been living alone for the past ten years. It was not until they received another letter hot on the heels of Maud's that they realised the extreme seriousness of the situation. For more than five years before his death, Danny had been doing all the cooking, shopping, cleaning and housekeeping as well as running the little farm single-handedly. He did this quietly and uncomplainingly as he did not want his children to know that his beloved wife was suffering from senile dementia. Maud had suffered a minor stroke shortly after Mary had left home. Two years later she had suffered a much more severe one. After the first stroke Maud seemed to make a quick if not complete recovery. For the most part, she was able to cope. Sometimes, however, she was unable to remember what she had been doing. She became disoriented and forgot that she had something cooking or else she would walk off and forget where she lived. Danny watched over her carefully and did a good job covering up for her. After the second and more severe stroke Maud's quality of life was much impaired. She was in need of constant care. Danny looked after her twenty-four hours a day, seven days a week. More than that he aided and abetted her in keeping her condition a secret. He watched her like a hawk, accompanying her everywhere. When people called to the house, he ensured that Maud was comfortably ensconced by the fire where she could keep the visitors in chat while he looked after the refreshments. If, as was bound to happen on occasion, she became confused he covered for her as smoothly as he could. As time went on, it became increasingly obvious that something was wrong. Even shortly before his death, when most of his neighbours were becoming aware of just how dependent on him Maud really was, he still persisted in maintaining the myth that all was well. To this end he enlisted the aid of two friends in particular, the local curate Father Brennan and the recently retired school teacher Fergus Boland. He managed to persuade these two kind souls to explain to the neighbours the importance of keeping his secret for just a few more weeks. When he died suddenly in his sleep, something had to be done and the sooner the better.

And so Fergus undertook the sad task of informing the Sweetmans of their father's death. He thought it best to write on behalf of their mother. In some misguided sense of loyalty to Danny's wishes, he wrote the letters as if they had come from Maud herself. And so it was a huge shock to Dan Junior when he flew in to Shannon and drove to Achill for his father's funeral to discover just how ill his mother really was.

He was the only one of his siblings to attend the obsequies. His attendance had been in fact enabled through a series of opportunistic coincidences. A friend of his happened to be home in Achill for his sister's wedding and as he was about to leave for Shannon he heard of Danny Sweetman's death. On his arrival in New York, he phoned Rochester with the news, thus facilitating Dan to fly to Ireland in time.

After the burial Dan remained in Achill for a few days to get things in order. He had to make arrangements to bring his mother back to Rochester with him as there was no way she could be left alone. Then he had to pack for her and to close up the house. First of all he had to inform his siblings of the situation. So when the second letter arrived in Emmingham within a week of the first it hit Alice very hard. She had been puzzled by the letter from Maud and had finally concluded that perhaps it had been written by someone else on her behalf. Given the importance of its contents Alice was baffled by this. Eventually, she consoled herself with the thought that perhaps her mother was prostrate with grief and in the interests of expediency had delegated the task to someone else. This made sense to her as the letter would have to be copied to all the other members of the family. She was quite shocked to receive Dan's letter also posted from Achill. She opened it with some trepidation at the breakfast table. She was pleased to note that Dan had made it to the funeral and disappointed that none of the others had managed to do the same. When she came to the part of the letter describing her mother's ill health, she fainted with the shock. Luckily both Patrick and Red were present and rushed to her assistance before she fell to the floor.

Over the next several months Maud's health and welfare were the main topic of conversation between Alice and Red. Patrick and Lily were inevitably parties to the discussions on an everyday basis. Alice's constant worrying was taking its toll. Again, she was losing weight at an alarming rate. All of them were very concerned and terrified that this might signal another attack of depression. Red could never forget the drama and upset of her previous bouts, particularly that awful period after Lily started school almost six years before.

In recent weeks, Alice had been able to make telephone contact with her siblings in Rochester so she was at least spared the interminable waiting for the exchange of letters. The joy of this immediacy was unfortunately entirely overshadowed by her only conversation with her mother. Maud was completely bewildered by the telephone conversation. She had no idea who Alice was and querulously asked over and over again that the strange and frightening instrument be kept away from her. This upsetting experience proved to be the last straw for Alice. Over the previous few weeks others too were beginning to notice her distress, notably Nora O Neill and Lisa Kelly. Somehow or other she couldn't bring herself to confide in either of her friends.

At work, Eda had been aware for some time that something was bothering Alice. Being wise as well as experienced, she bided her time until the younger woman was ready to share her troubles. The more she saw of Eda's stoicism and light-hearted approach to living, the harder it was for Alice to accept that her own mother, considerably younger than Eda, had such a poor quality of life. More and more she felt that she should be sharing with her siblings the burden of Maud's care. Eda eventually got to hear the whole story and did her best to console the distraught Alice. First she reminded her of the many blessings she had already received in her life and also of the fact that Maud herself, being unaware of her condition, was probably not suffering as much as Alice imagined. She also encouraged her to share her worries with Nora and Lisa. Soon afterwards Alice made up her mind and begged Red to consider moving again. This time their destination would be Rochester where Alice would be close to her mother and most of her siblings. She had missed her family sorely over the years of living first in London and then in Australia and now hoped that she would be in a position to assist in the care of her vulnerable mother. Keeping his misgivings to himself, Red agreed with the plan to move to America. He was now forty-four years old and not in the least bit bothered about the effects of uprooting himself. Because he knew how important it was to Alice to make the move, he wasn't overly concerned about how she might cope with the upheaval. He was hugely worried about how teenage Patrick and especially young Lily would react to such a fundamental change in their circumstances.

They sat down as a family to discuss the proposal and after listing the pros and cons they all agreed to give it a try. The next thing on the agenda was to ensure that Sweetman Brothers and Company were in a position to offer Red employment. Once this was arranged, and Dan and his wife Nancy had volunteered to organise temporary accommodation for them close to where they lived, the Gilraines set about the business of moving from one continent to another and all the hassle that this would entail. By the beginning of July 1962, all was in order. Their departure date was set for the 15th when they would embark on the 'Caledonia' bound for New York. All that remained was for the family to bid farewell to their friends and colleagues. Patrick and Lily were torn between their mother's obvious excitement at the move and their own understandable reluctance to leave all they knew behind. Red tried to console them as best he could, explaining that as far as Alice was concerned she was going to be reunited with her family. All three of them were aware that Alice missed her family hugely and, because they all loved her and wanted her to be happy, they were willing to give it a go. The O Neills, especially Daisy who had a soft spot for Patrick, were still reeling from shock at the imminence of the sudden departure. The Kellys, too, were sorry to see the Gilraines go. Patrick and Lily's classmates were disappointed at losing their friends and upset that they might never meet them again. For Alice, the worst wrench of all was the severing of her ties with Eda, who had long since ceased to be a mentor and was now a dear and trusted friend. They both knew that the proposed move would mean they would never see each other again.

Cleverly, Eda had a surprise for her friend, one that she had been harbouring ever since she first heard where in the United States the family was headed. Eda's son Johnny had tired of his seafaring life and had decided to find a shore job in America. So at the age of fifty, having gone back to college to update his engineering qualifications, he had chosen Rochester of all the cities in the United States in which to settle. Like a rabbit out of a hat, Eda was thrilled to present this news to her friend, thus guaranteeing a link between them across the oceans.

Finally Alice and Red had to call to the convent and say goodbye to Sister Francis and as a matter of courtesy explain to her that they were taking Lily with them to the United States of America. Fittingly, the Kellys, as they had been the first to formally welcome them to Brisbane, wanted to throw a farewell party for them on their departure. So a little over fourteen years after their arrival in Australia they found themselves again at a fancy social occasion at the Kelly mansion. The difference was that this time they were accompanied by both of their children and furthermore they knew everyone present.

As the evening wore on, this familiarity made the experience all the more poignant. Alice, looking back at how nervous and apprehensive she had been on her first visit, now wondered at the gaucherie of her younger self. She remembered with gratitude how Lisa had tried to allay her fears and had come to her rescue when her crippling shyness overwhelmed her. She recalled a particular incident at that first social occasion when she had been cornered by a brash, rather rude guest more than slightly intoxicated who, on hearing that the Gilraines were Irish, launched into a tirade of abusive comments and questions. "Is it true that the Irish still live in mud huts? I hear that you lot live all together in one room, Granny, Granddad, Dad, Mom, along with squads of children and animals. How do ye stick the smell of pigs at such close quarters? Where do ye all sleep anyway? Bet you were glad to get away from all the filth. Oh my god, how did ye manage to keep clean with no bathroom?" Alice had been reduced to tears at this barrage when Lisa hurried over. She caught the guest by the arm and frog marched her outside where she handed her over to Nora with a whispered instruction to find the woman's husband and ensure they left quickly and quietly. Then hurrying back inside, Lisa had attached herself to Alice for the rest of the evening, drawing her out, listening to her responses and slowly introducing her to her friends and generally looking out for her.

Now Alice must not embarrass her good friends Lisa and Bob at this wonderful send off. She pulled herself together and made an effort to circulate among the guests and try not to dwell on the reason for their presence. She noticed Daisy sitting alone on the edge of the group of youngsters and the way her eyes followed Patrick's every move. Alice could empathise as well as sympathise with the young girl's anguish. It was obvious to her that Daisy had a crush on her handsome cousin. And because she was his mother and knew him so well, she also knew that Patrick saw only cousinly affection in Daisy's lovesick glances. She made her way over to her with the intention of finding some interesting chore to distract her and save her from advertising her misery. On her way, she spotted Eda also on the periphery and at this stage also without company. She introduced the pair and as a parting favour requested them to please keep an eye on each other after she had gone. She would be keeping in touch with both of them and hoped that they would become friends.

Part III
1962–1977

Chapter 13

On the Move Again

Arriving in Rochester in 1962, Alice and Red were both surprised and very pleased to see how willingly they were welcomed. Everywhere they went they discovered that Irish people were held in very high esteem. John F. Kennedy's presidency had had a hugely positive influence on attitudes to all things Irish in the US of the early 1960s. This was very evident in Rochester, a city that had a significant population of first generation, second generation and even some third generation Irish families. Their new address was Paddy Hill Drive, Rochester NY 14616, and they were soon to discover that only just around the corner lived Eda's son Johnny Hogan and his family. Johnny had been lucky enough to meet a wonderful woman called Caroline Boylan since his arrival ashore. Caroline had been widowed young and had a readymade family, a son, Chris, and a daughter, Susan, roughly the same age as Patrick and Lily. Johnny and Caroline had met at night school and fallen in love and had not wasted time on a long courtship. They were married within a year of meeting. On their marriage, they had moved in to Oakbriar Drive in Rochester.

Eda had issued instructions to both Alice before her departure and to Johnny by detailed letter that they were to meet and get to know each other for her sake. They both intended to do this as soon as they could reasonably establish the whereabouts of the other. Long before that, in fact within a mere week of their arrival, the Gilraine children were in and out of the Boylan/Hogan house. Having befriended Patrick and Lily at the local park, Chris and Susan had immediately invited their new friends to use their swimming pool. Alice and Red were pleased to accept this kind invitation on behalf of their children. First they had to call to the parents to thank them and to ensure that their youngsters would be supervised while using the pool. They were more than happy to take turns to share the chore of overseeing the pool and made their way to Oakbriar Drive to make the necessary arrangements. When they met the Hogans, they found that they got on very well and it didn't take long for them to realise that their children had, by some strange serendipity, saved them all the trouble of having to go looking for each other. Eda, when she heard it, was thrilled if typically not one bit surprised. She professed not to believe in coincidences, firmly holding to the view that such things were meant to happen. She preferred to call such occurrences 'god-incidences'.

Moving so close to her own family meant a lot to Alice and, despite the upheaval of the recent transfer from the Antipodes, she was really content, perhaps for the first time in her adult life. For all the years she had been away from Achill, she had suffered intense loneliness at the separation from her parents and siblings. Even though she loved Red with all her heart and life without her children was just unimaginable, she had always yearned for her brothers and sisters. Not a day went by that she didn't think about them and torment herself with the conviction that family life continued for the rest of the Sweetmans much as it had done in her youth, the only difference being that she was excluded. Now Maud was living in with Dan and Nancy and their three boys in Little Creek Circle less than ten-minute's drive from Paddy Hill Drive. Dan had just built on a granny flat to his house so Maud could have privacy and her own quarters complete with kitchen, living room, her own bedroom and two other bedrooms. One of the bedrooms was for Annie, who had recently moved in with her mother as her full-time carer and the other a guest room. Michael and his American born wife Linda lived only about twenty minutes' drive away with their sons Vincent and Gerard, as well as their daughter Dorothy. Martin and Maria, with their twin sons Kevin and Kieran and daughter Caitlin, lived very close to them. Alice now woke up each morning happy in the knowledge that all was right with her world. Almost all of the people she loved most in the world were now living in the Rochester area.

Six weeks later Patrick and Lily were enrolled in The Holy Rosary Middle and High Schools, separate and adjoining Catholic schools in the district of Greece, a mere two mile bus trip away. These schools were chosen after a good deal of research, not just for their excellent reputation and Catholic ethos but because Dan's sons and daughter, as well as the two Boylan children, were already attending. So too were Alice's other nephews and nieces, Martin and Michael's children, coming in by bus from the western suburbs.

Red settled down very quickly working in the construction company with his brothers-in-law, all of whom were a few years his junior. The Sweetman brothers were easy to work with. Aside from being thorough gentlemen and of pleasant disposition they all loved their older sister Alice dearly. They had been impressed with Red's references from O Neill's and appreciated his reputation for efficiency and his hardworking ethic. They also loved his old world courtesy which reminded them of their late father. His years of experience in both London and Brisbane stood him in good stead. As he was a natural leader, his work as foreman came easily to him.

Within a very short few months, Red was a valued member of the company. He was well-paid and extremely contented with their new lifestyle. He was thrilled, too, that Alice was at peace and seemed to be enjoying this new phase of their lives. Patrick and Lily loved their new schools. They fitted effortlessly into the new regimes and found that they were well capable of keeping abreast of the learning challenges of the American system. So Red slept easily each night feeling he hadn't a worry in the world. In his next letter to Frank and Nora, he shared this feeling of happiness. He reassured them that, although they all missed Brisbane and their friends, the Gilraines were in no doubt that they had made the right decision in moving to Rochester.

And then brutally and suddenly, the unthinkable happened. Before the eyes of a shocked and bewildered nation, the young, vibrant and charismatic President of the United States and leader of the free world was gunned down in Dallas, Texas, in broad daylight on Friday, November 22nd, 1963. People were numbed with shock. Men and women were overcome with emotion and wept unashamedly in the streets. Crowds gathered around television screens in store windows, watching frames of the assassination in fascinated horror. And it was not just Americans who mourned this death. Those who had so recently lined the streets to welcome him in Ireland, Germany and Iraq would always remember exactly where they were when they heard the horrendous news of the death of their idol. The Irish American communities all over the United States were heartbroken at his untimely death.

In Rochester, John F. Kennedy was mourned as if he were a neighbour's son and a member of a local family. On November 25th, the burial ceremony in Arlington was followed closely on television by a huge crowd gathered in the ballroom in the Irish Centre. Aside from their grief at the loss of the first Irish Catholic president, they were watching eagerly the guard of honour formed by the Irish cadets with whom JFK had been so impressed on his visit to Dublin earlier that year in June. The cadets had been invited by his widow Jacqueline Kennedy and travelled from Ireland in the same plane as the Irish President,

Éamon De Valera. The Sweetmans were particularly focused on the troop of twenty-six cadets as one of their number was a Gilraine cousin.

Chapter 14
Christmas in America

All the Gilraines enjoyed their first Christmas in America surrounded as they were by the Sweetman families. For Alice, it was the best Christmas ever, a dream come true. For the young people, it was unadulterated magic. Lily had never seen snow in her life and Patrick had no memory of English winters so for them the transformation of the city into a winter wonderland was very exciting indeed. For Alice and Red, it was reminiscent of their time in London and all the pleasant and enjoyable memories associated with their youth and early years of marriage there.

In marked contrast to Australian Christmases, most of the celebratory events in Rochester took place indoors. The lighting displays were spectacular. The pride taken by American householders in the decoration of their homes, both externally and internally, was nothing short of breath-taking. Because the neighbours formed a tight knit community, sharing not just an ethnic heritage and also a religious background, the celebrations were very inclusive. There was a lot of sharing of time and food and drink, lots of communal games and outings. Inevitably there was also plenty of good-natured rivalry and one-upmanship, particularly in the external lighting displays. Giant sized and miniature and all sizes in between Santas, sleighs, reindeer, snowmen, elves, Christmas trees, igloos and boxed gifts in a bewildering array of colours abounded in the most creative settings imaginable on lawns, roofs and even attached to the facades of houses throughout the neighbourhood.

For the few days immediately after Christmas in this area of Rochester, it really was genuine family time. Dads who worked so hard all year round loved this time and wanted to spend it with their children. Children, being children, wanted to spend their vacation time or at least a portion of it with their own friends. Over the years the tradition had grown for dads and their sons and mothers and their daughters to spend some time together and also to organise some group activities with their children's friends. Some of the preferred outings favoured by the 'girls', young and old, were trips to the Christmas pantomime or to the skating rink. The men and boys invariably chose a skiing trip or tobogganing in the nearby hills. As the traditions had developed, more and more families participated. By Christmas 1963, the trips to the hills required a good deal of organisation, including the hiring of buses as about forty dads and upwards of sixty teenage boys were looking forward with huge anticipation to the adventure.

Because the weather had been mild coming up to the holidays this year's event was to be tobogganing. There was a good covering of snow on the hills. The youngsters were highly excited, especially the Sweetman cousins of whom there were seven this year. Dan's three sons, Paul, aged eighteen, Shaun, seventeen and Daniel, fifteen, Michael's Vincent, nineteen and Gerard, fifteen were joined this year for the first time by Martin's fourteen-year-old twins Kevin and Kieran. Added to this group of lively lads seventeen-year-old Chris Boylan and Patrick Gilraine who, just two days earlier, had celebrated his eighteenth birthday and high jinks and mischief were guaranteed. It was therefore with huge anticipation and almost hysterical expectation that the nine youngsters, accompanied by the five dads, assembled at the school. It was a little after six o'clock on the morning of December 27th, when they met up with the rest of the group to board the three buses for the thirty-five mile drive to the chosen hillside site of the day's activities. An advance party of ten men had gone ahead in utility trucks with a great array of toboggans, homemade as well as commercially produced in a dizzying assortment of shapes, sizes and colours. Some were well constructed, some simple in design, some new, some well used, some robust, some flimsier but all were the pride and joy of their various owners.

Paul, Shaun and Daniel Sweetman had a large, battered and well used heavy sled which had been made by their dad Dan some twenty years before. Michael Sweetman's sons Vincent and Gerard were the lucky owners of a relatively new sleigh, a much appreciated Christmas present from their Uncle Dan. Kevin and Kieran Sweetman were quite happy with what their father Martin swore would give the fastest and most exhilarating rides of all the bonnet of a 1955 Buick which he had adapted by edging it with strong, rubber-covered foam. Johnny Hogan had bought a brand new, state of the art toboggan for his step-son Chris Boylan. Patrick had been invited to share in the use of this marvellous piece of equipment but because of their lack of experience this plan might not meet with the approval of the organisers.

On arrival, all the toboggans had to be hauled to the top of the slope. By the time they had reached the summit, it was bright enough for the first descent. The adults and more experienced older boys, ensuring that their younger charges were properly helmeted and harnessed, lined up all the toboggans at well-spaced intervals. Then at the agreed signal they were off to the cheers and shouts of encouragement of those left behind. The motley assortment of snow vehicles descended at breakneck speed. The heavier sleds, and perhaps the ones with the more skilled drivers, made better progress. It didn't take long until all had safely reached the bottom of the slope. As the occupants were laughing and jostling their way back uphill again, they paused to watch the next wave of fun-loving thrill seekers begin their descent. And so it continued over the next several hours until the food detail called a halt at noon.

When everybody had assembled, they lined up for an outdoor feast of barbecued burgers, sausages and turkey kebabs accompanied by baked potatoes and vegetable patties. Johnny had had the inspired notion of organising hot punch for all to ward off the cold. He had been busy chopping fruit and stoking the fire so he was in a position to serve piping hot non-alcoholic drinks to the youngsters and a special liquor-laced brew for the men.

When all was tidied up after the meal, the men organised the afternoon activities. These consisted of tobogganing over the same course with the added challenge of racing downhill while keeping within designated tracks marked by poles. Other variants of the races included the gathering of a fixed number of flags or balloons as the contestants hurtled to the finishing line. The youngsters were arranged in pairs so that there was an experienced boy leading each team. Nineteen-year-old Vincent had Kieran, one of his twin cousins, with him and they were thrilled to make it to the semi-finals. Shaun, at seventeen, with his fifteen-year-old cousin Gerard, were competing on the old Buick bonnet and they were determined to be in the winners' enclosure. Eighteen-year-old Paul in the large sled had his young cousin Kevin as his team-mate. Daniel, though only fifteen, had a good deal of experience and undertook to be the lead for seventeen-year-old Chris Boylan in his new toboggan. This left Patrick Gilraine without a team-mate until another experienced boy, Jack Connolly, who was also without a partner, asked Patrick to be teamed with him. The competitiveness added an extra fillip to the experience for all. Heats were run off and by the time the finals were on there was a high degree of excitement among the winners and runners-up and those who had been eliminated earlier and were now vociferously cheering on their favourites. Unfortunately Jack and Patrick did not make it past the first heat and Daniel and Chris were eliminated in the next round. The other Sweetman teams had done considerably better with the result that three of the six teams in the semi-final were made up of Sweetman boys. Their excitement was reaching fever pitch as they were competing for the Sweetman Cup. Dan Sweetman had offered a trophy for the winners many years earlier when he had served as Mayor. This perpetual trophy in the form of a large silver cup was much-prized and given pride of place in the homes of the winners for the whole of the following year. There were also gold, silver and bronze medals for the winning participants so that the whole event took on the trappings of a mini Olympic-style contest. Three teams were eliminated in the semi-final and one of these was Vincent and Kieran's team. That left Paul and Kevin in the big old sled and Shaun and Gerard in the Buick hood against last year's winners, the O Connor brothers Niall and Owen, in a sturdy and sleek modern toboggan. The final was hard-contested and the supporters of each team were screaming encouragement as the ultimate ordeal unfolded. Instead of competing against each other, as was the case in the earlier heats where the first three teams to cross the finishing line qualified for the next race, the final was to be a timed trial. The race this time was even more challenging. It was laid out like a slalom course so the toboggan had to be kept between the poles. Furthermore, there were eight flags to be collected at intervals on the way down. These were strategically placed so that some were more accessible to the right and some to the left. This necessitated excellent communication as well as a keen ability to anticipate which of the pair should grab each flag. This was especially problematic on the corners where the 'driver' was fully occupied steering. So the team with fewest faults and the fastest time would be declared the winner.

First to take the course were Paul and Kevin and they managed to collect only three faults, one for flattening a demarcation pole and then two more for failing to gather one of the eight flags in a fantastic time of four minutes, thirty-seven seconds. Next out were the O Connors who also accumulated three faults for similar offences. Amazingly they had finished in the slightly slower time of four minutes, thirty-nine seconds. It was now up to Shaun and Gerard on the old Buick bonnet to see if they could do better than the winning Sweetman team. Comfortable in the knowledge that the main opposition was already beaten, they set out feeling quite relaxed. They were confident that their cornering was excellent, they had practised enough and the old Buick hood was easily manoeuvred so with a bit of luck they should be able to better the times already clocked. The real challenge was to collect all eight of the flags. Riding on the tide of enthusiasm and hysterical roaring and hallooing generated by the bulk of the onlookers who as always cheered for the under-dog, they set off at a ripping pace, managed their turns in a controlled manner and calmly collected flag after flag. They crossed the finishing line with no faults and within the incredible time of four minutes and a mere twenty-five seconds, a full twelve seconds ahead of their rivals.

The presentation of the trophy and medals would be held on a separate occasion in the gym of the senior school at the weekend so that all family members could attend. For now, the victors would be toasted with some refreshments at the foot of the hill before heading towards the buses.

Most of the men and boys had gathered on the lower slopes or crowded at the finishing line to watch the finals of the races. There was a small group still at the summit organising a tidy-up before descending. It was only after the party, and as the men and senior boys were involved with getting the toboggans back on the trucks and the remaining boys were making their way to the buses, that the Sweetman youngsters got back together as a group. They were busy congratulating each other on their success and the haul of medals they had to look forward to when they noted that there were only seven of them gathered, the six finalists and Daniel. They looked around for their cousin Patrick and his friend Chris. No one had seen either of them since the heats had ended. Once they realised that no one had noticed them at either the semi-finals or the finals, they became worried. Vincent took charge and, having directed Paul to keep the cousins together, he hastened off to find his dad and uncles and report to them that the two lads were missing.

Dan, Michael and Martin Sweetman swung into action straight away, first of all reassuring the distraught Johnny and Red and then arranging for the younger boys to be sent home on the first bus. Immediately after the bus moved off the remaining men and youths were organised into search parties of five. As they made their way back uphill, it was already beginning to get dark. The men had rifled their vehicles and gathered together an assortment of torches, blankets, first aid kits and a single flare. When they reached the summit, they had a short meeting to pool whatever information they had. The last anyone had seen of the two missing lads was immediately after Daniel and Chris had been eliminated. Daniel had remained on the side-lines to cheer on his brothers and cousins in the semi-final while Chris had ostensibly made his way to leave his toboggan at the assembly point at the bottom of the hill. Patrick had last been seen accompanying Jack Connolly to the same area after the first heat was over. Jack had returned to watch the rest of the races and had not seen Patrick after that.

Almost two hours had elapsed since then. Red was immediately reminded of the horror of Patrick's previous disappearance in Brisbane all those years ago and was trying to convince himself as well as his brothers-in-law that on this occasion too there would be a happy outcome. The dread that gnawed at his stomach gave the lie to this optimism. Somewhere deep inside he feared the worst. He tried to keep focused on the search for his own sake and for the sake of poor Johnny Hogan who could hardly see in front of him, blinded as he was by tears of terror and frustration. Johnny loved young Chris as if he were his own. He couldn't get his head around how he might begin to explain to Caroline if anything untoward had happened to her son while in his care.

The searchers spread themselves out in a long line across the top of the hill. They stood almost shoulder to shoulder with their leader in the centre of each team and then, on hearing Dan's whistle set off, slowly and carefully down the slope, each person searching minutely the area immediately in front of his feet. After about forty minutes when they were about halfway down the steepest part of the incline, they heard a sound somewhere to their right and Dan shouted that all should stop instantly. On his signal, they then moved to the right of the toboggan course for about fifty yards. Here they resumed their forward progress at snail pace, crouching low so that they wouldn't miss anything. Soon they came upon a weeping Chris huddled in the snow. He had been trying to drag himself down the slope. Having fallen from the toboggan at speed Chris had sustained injuries to his legs and arms. By torchlight, the rescue team could see the blood stained trail he had left behind him in the snow. He was in severe pain and very worried that something worse might have happened to Patrick.

Instead of watching the races, the two lads had decided to slip away by themselves to have a few more goes on the new toboggan while everyone else was occupied. Emboldened by their earlier experiences, they thought that they would be safe enough having just a few more runs. So as not to interrupt the races and to avoid notice, they made their way further to the right on a parallel course. Their first few runs were exciting, particularly after the halfway mark where the more experienced Chris had to steer carefully to avoid random tree stumps and half buried rocks. It was when Patrick took over the steering that things went seriously wrong. They set off carefully enough until they hit the steeper part of the descent where the surface was littered with obstacles when Patrick lost control. In an attempt to avoid a tree stump, he swerved sharply and Chris fell off, rolling over and over until he fetched up, crashing savagely into a rocky outcrop. Patrick had tried in vain to stop the toboggan which continued careening downhill completely out of control after his team-mate had fallen off. Chris was stunned but did not lose consciousness. He knew he was badly injured. He had seen Patrick disappear at a hectic rate. Shortly afterwards he had heard a horrendous and terrified scream followed by a deathly silence. He had gritted his teeth against the pain and tried to crawl in the direction of that horrible screech.

Among the many pieces of equipment the rescuers were carrying were lightweight stretchers. Dan sent up the flare and within minutes Johnny Hogan and Martin Sweetman, accompanied by four able-bodied men carrying Chris, were making their way down to where they hoped that an ambulance would be waiting for them. The waiting ambulance took Chris and Johnny directly to Unity Hospital on Dewey Street where Alice had already driven Caroline. Chris was rushed to theatre where his fractured tibia and broken wrist were set and after some suturing he was out of danger and wheeled to a ward. Johnny, Caroline and a tearful Susan, along with Alice and Lily Gilraine, had spent the intervening time storming heaven with their prayers and pacing agitatedly up and down waiting for news. When they saw Chris safely in the ward, dopey but conscious, they were overwhelmed with relief and gratitude. The Boylan-Hogans were acutely conscious that, although their own ordeal was happily over, Alice and Lily had still no information on Patrick's whereabouts.

Back on the hillside Dan had re-organised the rest of the rescue crew to continue the search downwards from where they had found Chris. Progress was impeded at this point by the unevenness of the terrain as well as by underlying stumps of trees and rocks and crevasses. The increasing roughness of the going sapped the energy of the searchers and reduced their hopes of finding Patrick alive. The Sweetmans did their best to keep up the spirits of the team by encouraging them to continue. They were all exhausted when they reached the bottom of the hill without finding any trace of Patrick or sign of the toboggan. By now, it was approaching midnight and common sense suggested that the search should be called off until morning. Regretfully the disconsolate group of men and youths made their way back towards the buses. As they approached, they noticed that the parking area was almost full. There were several police cars and an ambulance as well as huge numbers of cars and utility trucks. The chief of police, Batt Ryan, greeted them with the news that Chris had been admitted to the hospital and that the waiting ambulance had been dispatched to remain on standby until the search was called off. He then tried to persuade the group to give up for now. Dan agreed and so the woebegone, dog-tired youths were ushered onto the waiting buses and sent home. Some of the dads went too. The Sweetmans and Red remained at the site, determined to continue with the search for as long as it would take.

From the trucks and cars men attired in warm waterproof clothing emerged and one by one joined the little group and quietly offered to assist. So they set off again from the summit. This time they moved fifty yards further right before starting the slow, painstaking descent again. At this rate, they knew that they would need only a little over an hour to reach the foot of the hill again. Somewhat encouraged by the vigour of the new team members, they made very good progress initially. As they reached the section in line with where Chris had been found, they were again slowed down due to the difficulty of the ground surface. They inched their way carefully downward, surprised and disappointed not to have found any toboggan tracks in this section. They had resigned themselves to having to do yet another sweep when, as they neared the base of the incline, the two searchers on the extreme right called out. They had spotted tracks zigzagging diagonally across the lower right hand corner. Now all they had to do was follow the trail. This they did in intense and concentrated silence until at last they reached the spot where the tracks ended abruptly. Dan called a halt and, attaching a rope around his waist, he handed the end to Michael and with great care slithered on his belly towards the edge. He peered cautiously over the ridge only to discover a vertical drop which he guessed must be at least forty feet in depth. He shone his torch downwards but was unable to see any sign of either a toboggan or the missing boy. He requested that the loudhailer be passed to him and began calling Patrick's name in the forlorn hope that if he were conscious and could reply they might yet locate him on the snowy hillside before hypothermia set in. All they could hear was the lonesome echo of Dan's call reverberating from the darkness of the abyss.

After ten minutes of futile calling, Batt approached and said that there was nothing else that could be done now. He then quietly insisted that the search be called off until daybreak and led an orderly return to the parking lot where a large group of wives and neighbours had gathered. It was obvious from the men's demeanour that they had failed to find Patrick. The waiting neighbours and friends had set up braziers and now began to serve hot soup and sandwiches to the heartsick and bone-weary searchers. Red and Dan were met by a brave-faced Nancy who had a supportive arm around her distraught and exhausted sister-in-law Alice. Hugs of comfort were exchanged and then they all returned home. Despite their obvious fatigue, they still intended to return to their heart-breaking task at dawn. Surprisingly, considering how distressed everyone was, Red managed to sleep a little.

Chapter 15

The Search

A few hours later they all assembled again at the search site as the sun came up. Once it was sufficiently bright, they set off again and gathered where the tracks ended. When they got there, the mountain rescue team was already in place. Unfortunately during the night, further snow had fallen, so if Dan hadn't had the presence of mind to mark the spot where the toboggan had gone over, the search would have been even more difficult. Men had already abseiled down the sheer sides of the drop and were preparing to search the bottom of the gorge. They agreed to accept the help of three experienced volunteers, Dan among them, who were then lowered to join them. The others, including Red, feeling a little redundant, stood about in little groups waiting for news. Within an hour, the searchers had found pieces of the smashed toboggan scattered and sticking out of the snow at the bottom of the ravine. News of progress was being filtered back to the people at the top.

Not much later news spread that they had located Patrick. He was buried in the snow and as soon as the searchers had found him it was obvious to them that there was no hope at all that he could be still alive. They dug him out carefully and as a matter of routine attempted CPR on the spot. Then with great care and tenderness they put the body on a stretcher and started to winch it to the surface. Amazingly, despite broken limbs, Patrick's handsome face was unmarked. The hood of his parka framed the beautiful clear-skinned features of an eighteen-year-old boy on the brink of manhood. Standing at the summit surrounded by his brothers-in-law, his friends and his co-workers, Red watched the stretcher appear above the lip of the drop and settle gently on the snow-covered ground. He had the weird sensation of standing outside of himself while he observed this unbelievable scene. Later he could never remember any detail of the following hour. Someone must have contacted Alice because in some 'cushioned in cotton wool' part of his brain he was aware that he was to meet with her and Lily at the hospital where they were taking the bruised body and perfect face of his only son. Someone must have driven him to Unity Hospital although he had no memory of who did. The sight of his beautiful, bereft Alice jerked him back to the horror of reality and almost unmanned him. He staggered towards her and gathered her in his arms so he didn't have to look at her shattered little face. They clung to each other in a vain attempt to offer some tiny degree of comfort with the warmth of their numbed bodies.

Chapter 16

A Last Goodbye

The next couple of days were relentlessly busy. Funeral arrangements had to be made. First, a burial plot had to be selected and paid for. The form of the service had to be chosen and agreed. Death notices had to be worded and sent to the local and international papers. People had to be contacted and the news had to be broken to friends and relatives at home and abroad. The body had to be laid out and clothing picked for the laying out. A coffin had to be selected, and so too had readings and readers for the requiem Mass. Hymns and instrumental music had also to be chosen. At least, the nuns from Holy Rosary High School were going to organise the choir for the removal and the Mass. The wake had to be arranged in the house and catering put in place. And a devastated Lily had to be consoled and included in the arrangements.

Red worried about Alice and Lily, and in turn Lily stressed about her parents and Alice fretted about the others in an endless circle of frustration and grief. They all kept themselves frenetically busy, arranging, organising and trying hard not to let the horror penetrate beneath the surface of their minds. Each in their own way was trying to help and protect the others. Lily tried to keep her mind off the tragedy by preparing enormous amounts and varieties of finger food for the huge crowds of sympathisers expected at the wake. Alice turned to her God and her Roman Catholic faith and was to be found at every moment she could spare checking arrangements, reciting the mysteries of the rosary over and over in an everlasting stream. Red was just too numbed to think. He kept himself endlessly busy looking out for everyone, when he wasn't permanently attached to the phone. Sleep was in short supply as each of them found whatever excuses they could come up with to avoid going to bed, knowing that no matter how worn out they were they'd be unlikely to get to sleep. Eventually, Red managed to persuade Alice to lie down for a while at least. He was about to get into bed beside her when she pleaded with him to let her rest alone in case her tossing and turning would keep him awake. Reluctantly, he removed himself. He couldn't face the guest room, so he returned downstairs to sit by the dying embers of the fire.

The richly decorated living room, with brightly lit tree and crib and an avalanche of Christmas cards, mocked him. He couldn't believe how hurt he was that Alice did not want him in the marital bed. His heart was already broken. This rejection knocked him even further off balance. Since they'd got married he couldn't remember a night they had ever been apart with the exception of when Patrick was born. The memories of that night eighteen years ago set him off again. He wept quietly for a while and then, looking around, realised that despite Patrick's Christmas birth date it would not be appropriate to leave the room thus decorated for the wake tomorrow. Glad of something to do, he set to and silently accumulated the boxes and cartons to stow away the decorations. Cautiously and quietly, he gathered Alice's treasured Christmas items and mementoes and boxed them carefully to be put away later. He stripped the tree of baubles, lights and tinsel and then left it carefully outside the back door to dispose of in the morning. When it came to dismantling the crib, he couldn't face it and decided that it should remain in place until January 6th as was the norm. He made a mental note that Alice should not be left alone to do it this season. The taking down of the crib was traditionally a chore for 'Women's Christmas' or, in the Irish language, 'Lá Nollag na mBan'. This feast day, bringing the Christmas holiday to an end, was also known in the old country as 'Little Christmas'.

He looked around at the suddenly bare room and noticed all the cards still on the mantelpiece and hanging on the backs of the doors. He decided to take them down and put them away in a box in case Alice asked about them later. Behind those cards arranged on the mantelpiece he came across a few small packages and a handful of birthday cards. With a jolt he realised that these were for himself for his forty-sixth birthday and had been left there in readiness for a family celebration on the evening of the twenty-seventh. As things worked out, the search for Patrick was well underway at the time. He was glad that no one had remembered the planned celebration since and hoped that it would never cross anyone's mind in the days ahead.

Now, all notions of sleep banished by recent activity, he wandered towards the kitchen with the idea of starting a pot of coffee. As he approached, he smelled the aroma of a fresh brew and knew that someone had beaten him to it. For a split second, he had the crazy illusion that life was normal and the past forty-eight hours had never happened. His wife and daughter, their heads close together, were seated at the breakfast table sipping coffee and by all appearances engaged in conversation. And then, like being hit by a runaway truck, he was struck by the realisation that the fourth member of the family would never again blow in like a whirlwind talking nineteen to the dozen to pour himself a coffee and breeze out again. The two at the table whipped around and stared at him and in unison declared, "Oh! We didn't expect you to be up so early. Did you manage to sleep at all?"

"Afraid not, I thought I'd make a start on preparing the living room for the laying out. And by the time I'd finished it was time for a coffee fix. Is that a fresh brew I smell?" As he poured himself a cup, Alice disappeared in the direction of the living room while Lily busied herself with her endless food preparation, completely ignoring her dad. He decided to take his coffee with him and set off after Alice. As he approached, he thought he heard some strange noises and hurried on. The scene before him almost took his breath away. All the work he had done during the night, all his careful stowing and packing, was ripped to shreds and scattered all over the room. It looked as if several rampaging bulls and not one tiny woman had systematically and thoroughly wrecked the place. There was an untidy mess of broken baubles, smashed ornaments, crushed boxes and torn apart sets of fairy lights strewn underfoot. Worst of all, the figures from the crib had also been destroyed. Each one in turn had been pelted with the strength of fury against the marble fireplace and now lay in a pile of shattered shards and powdered porcelain around the hearth. Alice, on her knees in the middle of the wreckage, was holding herself tightly and rocking in a paroxysm of grief.

"What's happened, a stór? I thought to clear away the Christmas decorations, that's all. I left the crib because Patrick loved it so much I couldn't bear to take it down. I'm so sorry, my love. I didn't know what else to do." When he went to help Alice to her feet, he was shocked at the expression of revulsion on her face.

"That's your trouble always, isn't it, Red? You didn't know what to do. You didn't know what to do last night. You didn't know what to do but you brought him tobogganing. You didn't know what to do but you brought my lovely boy to the hospital. You didn't know what to do but you're going to bring my darling lad back here in a box. Well, I don't know what to do either. If I could tear down the walls of this damned room about my accursed head with my bare hands, I would. Oh God, Red, what did we ever do to deserve this?" She turned towards him and, all energy spent, she collapsed into his arms. He cradled her to him. They held each other and let the tears of anguish fall for a time. Then, without a word about it, they began to put the living room to rights, sweeping and gathering in synchronised co-operation as if this were an ordinary domestic task on any ordinary day and not the day they would wake their only son.

By the time they were ready to go to the morgue to collect the body, all was in readiness at the house for the wake. Red travelled up front in the hearse and Alice and Lily, accompanied by Dan and Nancy, travelled in the first limousine. As they approached home, the nearby streets were lined with cars and all the neighbours had formed a guard of honour all the way to the house. All these people in mourning formed a strange contrast to the manically flashing coloured light displays on the houses as they passed. In stark contrast, when the hearse turned the corner Paddy Hill Drive was in darkness. The festive lights had been extinguished in all the neighbouring houses. In the gloom of the afternoon, lines of teenagers were holding lighted candles.

Patrick was laid out in the living room at 3.30 p.m. of December 29th, and from then until two o'clock the following morning sympathisers streamed past the coffin in an unbroken line. Most of them, especially the young people, touched his perfect face as they paused before offering condolences to Alice, Red and Lily as they stood stiffly beside the open casket. Uncle Dan, Uncle Michael and Uncle Martin and all the cousins took it in turn to stand shoulder to shoulder with them while in the dining room and kitchen Nancy, Annie, Linda, Maria and Caroline Hogan kept everyone supplied with food and cups of tea all through the long day and into the night. Susan spent her time in silent support and proximity to her friend Lily.

Approaching two o'clock in the morning, the crowds began to thin out somewhat and at long last the immediate family allowed themselves to be persuaded to take a seat. It was only when they got to sit down at last that they realised how weary they were and just how long they had been standing and shaking hands. Throughout the rest of the long night the extended family and neighbours and friends sat with them, prayed with them and sipped tea in solidarity with them. Towards dawn more sympathisers arrived. Most of them were out-of-town relatives and friends and there was also a surprise delegation from Achill. Red had just shaken hands with a clergyman who looked uncannily familiar when the man spoke and his accent confirmed that it was indeed none other than Father Brennan, Parish Priest of Achill. Before he could recover from the surprise and warn Alice, he felt himself enveloped in his mother Bridie's unmistakable embrace. Next in the line were his brother Brendan and Alice's Aunt Aggie, (Nora's mother) and bringing up the rear was Fergus Boland, retired schoolteacher and Red's bachelor cousin. The requiem Mass was scheduled for 12 noon the following day, the 30th at Saint Charles Borromeo Roman Catholic Parish Church, 3003 Dewey Avenue.

There was a lull around eleven o'clock, giving the family a little time to freshen up and have a chance to talk to the Achill people for a short while before they all set off for the church. The ceremony was prayerful and dignified. The choir sang beautifully a selection of funeral hymns interspersed with a few Christmas carols. The mixture was ineffably sad. The recessional hymn was 'Going Home', the first verse of which was sweetly rendered by the wonderful boy soprano voice of young Kevin Sweetman. For the second verse, he was joined by his twin Kieran and the entire choir of children and adults brought the hauntingly heart-breaking hymn to its conclusion in four-part harmony. Once outside in the crisp winter air and when the coffin had been returned to the hearse, the huge congregation piled into their cars to convey Patrick on his last journey to the graveyard a little over a mile away. By the time the cortege arrived at the cemetery, the students from the elementary school had formed a large guard of honour stretching from the main gates to the newly-opened grave. The hearse halted at the gates and Dan, Michael, Martin, Johnny Hogan, Fergus Boland and Red shouldered the coffin through the lines of solemn youngsters to the gravesite.

The priest from St Charles Borromeo church, who had officiated at the Mass, was Father Rory McMahon, a long-time friend of the Sweetman family. He had invited Father Brennan to assist at the burial service. Father McMahon gave the eulogy and said the prayers for the dead before inviting family members to toss some clay and flowers into the grave after the coffin had been lowered. Then, in accordance with Achill tradition, as the men began filling in the grave, Father Brennan led the people in five decades of the rosary. The brief ceremony over, people were reluctant to leave. The older ones stood back a little to give the family a little space to say their final farewells when the final sympathies had been expressed. The bagpiper played 'When Irish Eyes Are Smiling'.

Some of Patrick's closest friends had brought their musical instruments and when the lone piper had finished piping Patrick 'home' they intended, in turn, to play their own tributes. A strange standoff then developed. No one wanted to leave the graveyard first. Patrick's family felt they could not leave until all the others had left and the friends felt they couldn't start their tributes until they were on their own. In the end, Father Brennan intervened by asking the youngsters to leave and congregate again a little later. When everyone else had left Red, Alice and Lily had a last chance to say goodbye to a much loved son and brother. After they had gone wearily and dejectedly home at last, the young people made their farewells in ways appropriate to their age and sense of loss. The impromptu musical evening ended in a memorial singsong which continued into the wee hours. None of them would ever forget the strange circumstances under which they had seen out 1963.

Back at the house, the family sat around the fire in the living room, highly conscious of the space where just a few hours previously the coffin bearing the body of their eighteen-year-old kinsman had lain. Inevitably the discussion ranged around the events of the previous few days. All were in agreement that the ceremony paid worthy tribute to Patrick and the kind of character he was. Fulsome praise was paid to the conduct of his friends and colleagues and how they had behaved throughout the harrowing ordeal of Patrick's departure from mortal life. Positive comments were passed on the suitability of the readings and hymns chosen and their respectful delivery. Then they had a trip down memory lane, sharing their treasured reminiscences of a well-lived young life cruelly cut short too soon. Eventually, overcome with emotion and exhaustion, they retired and tried to sleep. Tomorrow they would have to face the first day of the rest of their lives without Patrick.

Chapter 17
Life Goes On

Dealing with their grief in their own separate ways, Red, Alice and Lily did their best to ease each other's pain. Because they were each suffering in different ways they found it difficult to understand each other's perspectives. Red drew on his stocks of inherited stoicism and a lifelong belief in the maxim that 'men don't cry' to help him cope with his grief. He also felt it incumbent upon him to keep a stiff upper lip and be a tower of strength for his womenfolk. Unfortunately the effect of this stance made Lily feel that her dad was unapproachable. As for Alice, she couldn't bring herself to talk about her beloved boy to a man who appeared to be so rigid and unfeeling. She was spending more and more time either in the church or locked in the spare bedroom, which she had converted into an oratory, endlessly praying. She was careful, however, not to neglect Lily. She was scrupulous in her determination to be always in the kitchen ten minutes before her daughter's arrival home, ready and waiting to offer food and drinks and spend some time with her and enquire about her day. Even when she couldn't possibly know when Lily might return she had developed a weird ability to anticipate it and be either at her post or appear within seconds. Lily appreciated her mother's concern and by some strange intuition she felt that no matter how hard Alice tried her heart wasn't really in it. Lily felt that her mother's 'concern' was ninety percent duty and only ten percent love. Since Patrick's death her heart seemed to have shrivelled to the size and consistency of a dried pea.

Red worried about Alice and watched for signs of depression. So far he could detect none. He also worried about Lily. For the life of him, he couldn't understand how he might get closer to either of them. He blamed himself for this wall of silence and uneasy toleration that had grown up between them. He did not know how it had happened or how to remedy the situation. Alice knew she had been keeping her husband at a distance. She couldn't bear to let him through the protective barrier she had built around herself for fear she would disintegrate. She blamed herself for the hurt she was causing him. There was also a part of her which also justified her actions to herself.

Lily grieved for her dead brother constantly. She also grieved for the shattered lives of her parents. She worried about the disintegration of their marriage which she was witnessing on a day to day basis. She tortured herself with the knowledge that Alice's attempts to ward off depression and her determination not to neglect her daughter were only symptoms of her love for Patrick's memory. Lily was anxious that she might inadvertently betray her understanding of her mother's fragile state and thus further add to the burden of Alice's grief. And so the three of them co-existed, in an atmosphere of polite disconnection, while living separate and parallel lives under the same roof. They ate together at the same table and at the same time even though the conversations were always trite and about surface matters. They might have been better off if they were more selfish in their misery. The fact that they could not ignore each other's wretchedness only increased the unhappy tension that inhabited the house like a separate presence. This unhealthy state of affairs prevailed until the end of March.

On the last day of the month, this sad little family gathered around the kitchen table once again. On this occasion, the task in hand was the choosing of content, layout and format of the mortuary cards. Alice, organised as ever, had accumulated a wide selection of what was available to assist them. In the end, they opted for a plain cream coloured fold-over card with an image of the dove of peace embossed on the front. They rejected the notion of the customary wide black border usual on such memorial cards as too heavy and funereal for a memento of such a young man. Instead it was to be edged with a thin gilt line. Alice and Red had selected the John Henry Newman prayer, a favourite of his mother's, for the text.

"O Lord, support us all the day long,
Until the shadows lengthen and the evening comes
And the busy world is hushed and
The fever of life is over and our work is done.
Then, Lord, in your mercy, grant us a safe lodging,
A holy rest and peace at last. Amen."

This would be printed in a clear plain font on the facing page. The choice of photograph for inside the cover was left to Lily who, after much consideration, picked an image of a happy, smiling Patrick, snapped on an Indian summer's day the previous September at the beginning-of-year garden party. She wanted everyone to remember her adored brother at the peak of his youth and as happy as a lark in the comfort of the company of his friends. Underneath the photograph was to be printed the simple legend:

Sacred Heart of Jesus
Have mercy on the soul of
Patrick Gilraine
112 Paddy Hill Drive, Rochester,
Born on 25th December, 1945
Who died tragically on
27th December, 1963

Aged 18 years.
Rest in Peace.
Fold him, O Jesus, in thine arms
And let him henceforth be a
Messenger of love between our
Human hearts and Thee

On the back cover, the family had finally agreed to place the text of an old prayer in the Irish language. Both Alice and Red had learned it as five year olds from a County Cork teacher long ago in The Valley National School. Because of the simplicity of the language and the profundity of its message it had stuck with them both throughout their lives. And they, in turn, had taught it to both Patrick and Lily. In fact, Alice had also taught it to young Daisy in Australia and hoped that the selection of it would bring some solace to the young girl when she would eventually receive the memorial card.

Dia idir mé agus tine mo dhóite
Dia idir mé agus uisce mo bháite
Dia idir mé agus taisme bóthair
Dia idir mé agus bás gan cáirde.

Which translates as:

God protect me from fire that'd burn me
God protect me from water that'd drown me
God protect me from an accident on the road
God protect me from a death without friends.

After they had agreed the details of the memorial card, Red thanked Alice and Lily for their help and as Alice was about to get up he detained her, saying, "While I have you both here I'd like to say something else. This was the last sad task for Patrick that we did today. Strangely these past few hours have been the nearest to normal we've had since we lost him. I'd like all three of us to try for his sake to get back to some kind of normality. I'd like for us to stop blaming ourselves and each other, to stop torturing ourselves and each other and to pick up loving and caring for each other as Patrick would want and expect of us. Starting now, come let me hold my two most precious girls. Then if ye wouldn't mind let us say our Irish prayer together. And now we'll ask Patrick to help us so we can support each other in our grief and also share our happy memories of him."

Chapter 18
Lily and Susan

As spring turned into summer and the weather continued to improve, inevitably spirits lifted a little. Lily was due to transfer to elementary school the following September. Due to the trauma, her grades had slipped. Alice and Red were concerned for her wellbeing but were loth to suggest that she postpone graduation for another year. In the end Red said, "I think we should have a chat with the school principal and see what she thinks. I can ring and make an appointment for us with Sister Gonzaga if that's okay with you, love?"

"I suppose you're right, Red. I've been worrying myself sick about her and that's not getting us anywhere, is it?"

As things turned out, Johnny and Caroline Hogan called over that same evening to seek their advice regarding their own daughter. Susan had always been a sickly child as she had been born with a heart defect. She had a medium-sized ventricular septal defect, or in layman's terms, 'a hole in the heart'. She was therefore prone to infection, particularly of the respiratory tract. Since she was such a bright spark, and despite bouts of ill health and consequent absences from school, she had managed to keep up with her peers until now. She had been unable to shake off a persistent cold all spring and was now considerably behind with her studies. She too had been very badly affected by Patrick's death. She was well aware that she would need to do a huge amount of work, including summer school, if she were to graduate. She was very agitated at the thought of losing her friends, particularly Lily, were she to defer transferring to middle school.

Both sets of parents agreed that repeating the year would be best for the girls in the long term. First they needed to find out what Lily and Susan wanted for themselves. The Hogans went home to have a talk with Susan while Alice and Red spoke with Lily. Susan was happy to do whatever was necessary to remain in the same group as Lily. Lily's major concern was that she might be a disappointment to her parents. So when they put it to her that there were advantages to deferring and that there was a possibility that Susan too might be postponing she happily admitted that she would prefer not to transfer until the following year. All that now remained was to seek the school's approval for the plan.

Sister Gonzaga cut straight to the chase when Alice and Red went to talk to her about Lily's future. "The strange thing about this request, Mr and Mrs Gilraine, is that I've just had a similar request from a neighbouring family of yours. Aside from the obvious problem of setting precedent here, getting sanction from the Education Board for two deferrals could prove difficult. I would therefore like to know if there is a connection between these two requests." Red explained that the two requests were indeed related but that the separate reasons for deferral were legitimate in each case. Alice added that the friendship between the girls was coincidental to their educational needs. Nonetheless, it was important for them to be supportive of each other at this difficult time. "Leave it with me and I'll see what I can do," said Sister Gonzaga.

Within a few days, permission to defer had been secured for both girls. The close relationship between Lily and Susan brought the two families even closer together and eventually helped Susan's parents to overcome their natural desire to be overprotective. For the first six months of 1964, the two girls had been pretty much confined to their own homes, Susan because of her illness and Lily because she knew that she dare not be a minute late home from school or Alice would panic. By June, she was beginning to find the constant watchfulness oppressive. Things came to a head when one day she asked for permission to go over to the Hogans' to have a swim with Susan and Alice refused, citing the peril of drowning. When Lily protested that she was a strong and experienced swimmer, Alice broke down and pleaded with her not to put herself in danger and thus visit further trauma on her jinxed little family.

When Red arrived home, he found Alice in a panic, shaking with anxiety and crying inconsolably in her bedroom. Later he discovered an equally tearful and disconsolate Lily in the sanctuary of her bedroom. Something had to be done. First he brought Alice a soothing cup of tea and then he rang Dan and told him that Lily and Susan were on their way over to visit Granny Maud. Dan understood immediately that the girls needed to be distracted so suggested that if they were to walk over he would drive them home via the ice cream parlour much later on.

Red accompanied Lily to the Boylan/Hogan's and when the two girls set off, he suggested to Johnny and Caroline that a council of war was necessary. He invited them to call over in a short while so all four of them could have a chat. Then returning home, he helped Alice to organise some snacks and iced tea on the porch in anticipation of their guests' arrival. Several hours of conversation later, they had a better understanding of what it must be like to be constantly watching over a sick child. They also had a greater appreciation of the courage that Caroline and Johnny exhibited every day in their care and love for both Susan and Chris. The two Boylan children were being reared in an atmosphere of unconditional love, being encouraged to become independent and caring people and not being smothered by overprotective constraints. As she grew older, Susan's condition was expected to improve further. Already the hole in her heart had decreased significantly and there was real hope that in time it would close completely and she would be able to live a normal adult life. The reason why Johnny and Caroline had bought that particular house on Oakbriar Drive was because of their belief that swimming would be good exercise for Susan and that having her own pool would encourage neighbouring children to befriend her and not neglect her during her bouts of illness or lassitude.

By the time the girls arrived home, Lily's parents had agreed that as swimming was such an important part of Susan's health regime and as the pool was never in use unless supervised by an adult, there really was no good reason why Lily should not enjoy using the pool too. Then all four parents further agreed to discreetly organise activities for the vacation period allowing the girls a certain amount of time to enjoy themselves without direct supervision. Thus reassured, Alice was persuaded to ease her obsessive monitoring of Lily over the coming weeks. Susan and Lily spent a good deal of that summer at the pool each day, going for walks, having picnics, cycling in the neighbourhood and mixing with their school friends.

Over the summer vacation Lily's focus had finally shifted from overwhelming grief and loss of her dear brother to a burgeoning interest in her own future. As time passed, life for the young people began to resume some semblance of normality. And because Lily's parents loved her so much they tried harder and harder to keep up the pretence of normal life in her presence. All was not plain sailing. There were always going to be milestones, days when Patrick's peers and friends would be celebrating events which he too should have been party to such as the graduation from high school and the prom the following June. Then there were the family occasions, the Christmases, the birthdays, Thanksgiving and the summer picnics. Immediately there was the upcoming first anniversary looming ahead. Alice sometimes felt that she was living in another world, a world still inhabited by her beautiful son before this strange half-life had begun. This new semi-existence belonged to someone else and she was being forced to live it until she woke up and managed to retrieve her own life. She prayed and prayed that soon she would find her way back. For now, she found herself doing everyday ordinary tasks like filling the washing machine, ironing or making dinner on automatic pilot. She was still surprised that the seasons changed largely unknown to her and that she could function so well without being aware of what she was doing. At least now, unlike the first few weeks, she frequently registered hunger and actually occasionally enjoyed the food she prepared for her daughter and her husband. She was no longer skeletal though still very much too thin.

Chapter 19

Friends Reunited

When Lily returned to school in September with her friend and classmate Susan, they were both well rested, in good health and ready for the challenges of their final year at Holy Rosary Junior School. Chris Boylan and the rest of Patrick's friends were also returning to finish their second level education at the adjoining Holy Rosary High School. Alice and Red did their utmost to keep their attention on Lily. With the best will in the world it was difficult for them not to be painfully aware of the timetable that Patrick should be following with the rest of his classmates.

Alice and Red's relationship had improved somewhat since that evening at the end of March when Red had determined that they must face their grief together. They were both heartbreakingly conscious that they might never recover the easy comfort of their early days together. Some part of their spirit had died with their son. Each of them looked out for the other but because they each wanted to spare the other pain they had locked away a part of themselves. In this private space, they mourned their dead son. Neither of them ever really understood that this deliberate withholding of part of themselves from each other would so damage the fabric of their own relationship. Their lovemaking, once such a comfort and integral part of their lives, was now practically non-existent.

Worse than that, Alice had become expert at finding excuses for not sharing the marital bed. On the odd occasion when they did share a bed, she clung to the furthest extremity of her side, barely managing not to fall out. This was very hard on Red who, while understanding her reluctance to enjoy any aspect of life while poor Patrick never would, nonetheless missed her sorely. Sometimes all he really wanted was a cuddle and the sharing of body warmth to ease his aching heart.

By mid-term it was obvious that the decision to repeat their final year in junior school had been the correct one for both Lily and Susan. Susan's health had continued to improve and her most recent check-up had revealed that her septal ventricular defect had almost completely closed. The prognosis for a normal healthy adult life was most welcome and selflessly and enthusiastically celebrated by the Boylan/Hogans' neighbours and friends. For her part, Lily had settled down to study on her return to school and was enjoying all aspects of her school life. The two girls were in friendly competition with each other. They played to each other's strengths, co-operated with their project work and supported each other when the going got tough. They were ambitious for themselves and for each other and vied with each other to get the highest class scores on assignments. They had taken to charting their successes and laying little bets with each other every time they had school tests. This form of competitiveness and incentivising kept them focused and they derived great fun from the recording of it. There was no doubt that if they continued working like this they would be sharing the honour of being top of the class and earning a good selection of the end-of -year medals and prizes.

Alice and Red were very proud of Lily and of how she had come to terms with her grief and turned her attention to succeeding at school. In their efforts to support her over the past months, they had grown closer to her and to each other. And so Red dared to hope that someday in the future they might yet regain the love and ease with one another that typified the early years of their relationship. As things were going so well on the home front, he decided on a little mid-term celebration of his own. As a reward for her excellent results, their parents arranged a treat for Lily and Susan. To this end the girls were going to a show on Saturday night with two of their friends followed by a sleepover at Susan's.

Knowing that they would have the house to themselves, Red had plans too. He was hoping to lure Alice back to the marital bed and perhaps to renewed intimacy. He suggested that, as she had some time to herself, Alice might like to go and have her hair done and perhaps spend a few leisurely hours in the city. While she was gone he had started to put his plans into effect. First he went shopping and bought all the ingredients for her favourite dishes. By the time she arrived home, he had enlisted his sister-in-law, Annie, to help him prepare a delicious dinner. He had set the table in the dining room with the best china, silver and napery. A beautiful floral centrepiece flanked by fragrant candles in silver candlesticks stood in the middle of the table. When Alice came, in she found him sitting by the fire relaxing with the newspaper. He remembered to admire her hairdo and, having solicitously helped her to remove her coat and scarf, he ushered her into the dining room. The food was delicious and they had happily shared a bottle of good Californian wine and had just settled down in front of the blazing fire in the sitting room for a chat when the front door bell rang.

"Drat, just as I was about to ravish my beautiful wife," Red half-joked as he rose to answer it. He wondered who it could possibly be at a quarter past eleven at night. He threw open the door and whooped with excitement. "Alice, Alice, Alice come here as quick as you can. I can't believe it. I just can't believe it. This has to be the best surprise ever. ALICE! Look who is here. Can you credit it? Come in! Come in, you two. You have no idea how welcome you are, Frank, and you too, Nora. Tell us how you managed this magnificent surprise. When did you arrive?"

"Easy, Red! Go easy, lad! We've only just landed. As a matter of fact, we've come directly from the airport. Our luggage is still in the cab. I'll ask the driver to wait and we'll get a hotel after we've had a chance to say hello properly," suggested Frank.

"Frank O Neill, you'll do no such thing. Nora will you tell your husband to behave himself.

"You'll stay here with us and let there be no argument about it." With that he ushered the visitors indoors, retrieved the suitcases from the trunk and paid off the taxi and hurried back inside.

Despite their exhaustion, it was several hours of animated chat later before the O Neills finally got to bed. In the ten months since Patrick's untimely death, or 'the accident' as everyone called it, this was the first time that Red had seen Alice's face light up with interest and excitement. In the course of the night, he even saw her smile and for one blissful moment heard again the sound of her laughter. Frank and Nora had been devastated when they heard about Patrick. They wanted to be there for the Gilraines. Unfortunately, by the time they had heard the tragic news it was already too late to make the long journey in time for the funeral. As Alice's letters to Nora bore testament, coping with the death of a child, especially one on the cusp of adulthood, was not easy. So with Daisy safely at boarding school in Melbourne the O Neills planned to take an extended break and spend two months in Rochester to support their lifelong friends coming up to the first anniversary of Patrick's death.

After their guests had gone to bed, Alice and Red retired, also with plenty to talk about. They were still excited at the unexpected arrival of the O Neills and, although they had asked and answered a huge number of questions, they were all looking forward to spending more time over the coming days catching up on each other's news and renewing their friendship face to face. They lay comfortably together but when Red tried to cuddle closer, Alice still shrank from him, pleading tiredness. He contented himself with holding his wife in a loose embrace while he tried not to feel the rebuff too much. It crossed his mind that he had never been lonelier in his life.

Next morning, they allowed the travellers a long lie-in followed by an extended leisurely chatter-filled brunch. Much later on, as they were enquiring about all the mutual friends in Brisbane, Alice asked about Eda Hogan. Nora explained that Eda had proven to be a huge support to Daisy in the days after the Gilraines' departure and again after the news of Patrick's death. Unfortunately she was now almost completely blind. With her indomitable spirit she was still an inspiration to all who knew and loved her. Her latest scheme, started with Daisy's help over a year ago, was a literacy programme for young adults. Despite her own loss of sight, Eda was still a brilliant teacher. She was most encouraging to the slow reader and because she had read and re-read a large number of the classics so many times she was so familiar with the text that she no longer needed to see it to be able to prompt and smooth over any little hesitancies on the part of the learners. She also loved to put them at their ease by making them feel that they were doing her an enormous favour by asking them to read her letters aloud to her. She never tired of hearing these links with her family and friends read aloud over and over. Of course she never let on to her readers if someone had already read a letter to her. To encourage them in the belief that they were obliging her she indulged in the little subterfuge of resealing the envelopes before the arrival of her new friends so that she could make a show of opening the letters as if for the first time. Because she treated them as friends rather than overgrown school children the young people grew in confidence and enthusiasm for reading. A side effect of their increased ability was that some of them joined the volunteer readers group founded by Eda all those years ago. This was an advantage for the readers and also welcomed by the residents of the nursing home who looked forward to the chance to interact with young people. Several of them visited Eda on an ongoing basis as privileged friends of this remarkable lady.

When Lily returned home from her sleepover at the Boylan/Hogan house, she was thrilled to see the O Neills again. Later in the day Red sent her back to invite the family over for the evening having sworn her to secrecy regarding their visitors. He wanted to witness the surprise and share in the excitement when he introduced the O Neills to Eda Hogan's son and family. Lily returned with the news that Johnny, Caroline, Chris and Susan would be delighted to accept the kind invitation to dinner on the strict understanding that Caroline would bring dessert. Red took Alice aside and whispered to her, "Put four more in the pot for dinner on the quiet, like a good woman. Don't say a word to Nora. I've invited the Hogans to join us and Caroline is insisting on bringing dessert. Frank and I are going for a walk now. We'll leave you women to get on with the cooking and your own catching up. We'll be back again with a half hour to spare before dinner time."

Having heard so much about each other from Eda, the meeting between the O Neills and Johnny Hogan and his family was a great success. They all sat down to dinner and by the time the main course was served they felt that they had known each other half a lifetime. The rest of the evening passed in tales of times past. Stories and anecdotes were exchanged and happy times were recalled. The two young girls were enraptured as the adults reminisced and brought to life their shared histories. They were particularly intrigued by how, as Irish people, they had managed to preserve their cultural and religious beliefs across the generations and the continents, resulting in such an easy connection among them despite the differences in the accents and experiences of this disparate group with a shared heritage. Alice and Red, now living in America, along with Nora and Frank, were first generation Irish who had lived in England and Australia. Johnny was second generation Irish, brought up in Australia and Caroline was second generation Irish brought up in the States. They all had a wealth of shared values and understandings. By the time dinner was over, they had all agreed that after hours of conversation there was still plenty to talk about.

An invitation to dinner the following Saturday night at the Boylan/Hogans' was duly issued. After their departure the chat continued unabated. The following day a lunch party had been arranged at Dan and Nancy's where Nora with Frank would meet all her Sweetman cousins and her Aunt Maud. Approaching 2.00 a.m. Alice insisted somewhat reluctantly that they should all get some sleep in preparation for the morrow. After a quick breakfast of coffee and waffles the two families set off for the 12 noon Mass at St Charles Borromeo. Immediately after Mass, all the relations met in the Church hall for a cup of tea and to meet with the parish priest, Father Rory McMahon, and other members of the congregation. Then they all followed Dan and his family back to Little Creek Circle for lunch. Nancy had plenty of experience at catering for large family gatherings. She had therefore arranged for all the youngsters to have their food and entertain themselves and each other in the games room in the basement. The adults were to be fed in the dining room with overflow in the kitchen before retiring to the large living room for coffee and conversation.

Maud was delighted with the excitement of the party. She loved family gatherings. Her senile dementia took a form that made her behaviour quite unpredictable. For prolonged periods of time, she was capable of making perfect sense. She followed the news avidly on both radio and television and could happily join in discussions on American, Irish and international events. And then quite suddenly she would wonder who her grandchildren were and even on occasion ask Nancy pettishly why she allowed that strange man in the house, pointing to her son Dan. In the previous fortnight, she had been in great form with only the tiniest glitch of memory, an occasional struggle for a word or a name. As soon as she saw Nora, something slipped and she began to address Nora as Sibby, evidently confusing Nora with her own sister who had died of consumption in her late twenties more than forty years earlier. No one could convince her otherwise, she was utterly convinced that she was talking to her long dead sibling. Alice, who vaguely remembered her Aunt Sibby, could see how the confusion occurred. Nora did indeed closely resemble their Aunt Sibby. On the other hand, later in the day when Maud noticed Frank O Neill she knew immediately who he was, that he was very successful, and that he had married her niece Nora and that they had moved to Brisbane. This led to some very peculiar moments in the course of the rest of the afternoon before Annie accompanied Maud to her room for her nap.

Over the next several weeks Maud enjoyed the company of the O Neills as much as, if not more than, everyone else. When she spoke with Nora, she still persisted in the belief that she was talking to Sibby. Things reached a head when one day she demanded of Frank why he was showing such an interest in Sibby instead of looking after his own wife whom she claimed not to have seen in ages. When she took to berating 'Sibby' for her sinful encouragement of another woman's husband, the O Neills reluctantly had to curtail their visits to Little Creek Circle.

Christmas was now fast approaching and already there were plenty of signs of external and internal decorations throughout the locality. In accordance with tradition, all the Sweetman families, in solidarity with the Gilraines, were not sending out Christmas cards as this was the first Christmas since Patrick's death. They had agreed also to refrain from erecting external lights or decorations and to confine the displays to cribs and Christmas trees internally. They had decided that the money thus saved would be donated to charity. Nora and Frank wanted to help their friends to build the kind of memorial to their son that would help both themselves and also other bereaved families. They felt strongly that remembering Patrick in a way that was both positive and helpful to others would perhaps refocus their friends' energies and maybe even help in their recovery. After much discussion they agreed to underwrite the setting up of a counselling service for bereaved parents and families and to name it after Patrick. And so the idea of The Patrick Gilraine Bereavement Counselling Service was born.

The money donated by Frank and Nora, though sizeable, would need to be well-invested if it were to employ the services of two trained counsellors in perpetuity. They had decided to keep their plans secret until Christmas when they would present the paperwork to Alice and Red as a Christmas present. Under the circumstances Christmas was a quiet affair in Paddy Hill Drive. With their house guests Nora, Frank and Daisy, who had joined them from Melbourne on the previous day, they all set off to midnight Mass. On their return, they stuck with the family tradition of opening a single present each from under the tree and because it was Lily's birthday she was allowed to open one of her birthday presents as well. This was a forceful reminder of last year and many previous years when Patrick too would be opening a birthday present. As always, Red chose the present from Alice while she chose his.

Lily was in a quandary as heretofore she and Patrick had always chosen each other's gifts for this little ceremony. So as not to have to choose between her parents' presents she selected an unmarked packet addressed to all three Gilraines. Red was pleased and touched with the hand knitted Aran sweater Alice had lovingly made for him. In her turn, Alice was gratified that he had made a gift for her rather than going out to buy something. As she stripped it of its layers of wrapping, she was thrilled to reveal a beautifully crafted cedar wood coffer, the card inside stating, 'For Your Treasures, My Love'.

Lily had deliberately waited till last to open the mystery packet. When she did, she smiled broadly and, before passing the papers to her mom and dad, she jumped up and hugged Nora, Frank and Daisy in turn. Alice and Red studied the documents for a few minutes and then, turning to Frank and Nora in amazement, Red said, "First of all, we want to thank you so much for this best of all possible gifts. Unless I'm misreading this you two have donated a phenomenal amount of money to set up a service in memory of our Patrick to help people cope with bereavement. We're completely gobsmacked at your generosity as well as your thoughtfulness in making this magnificent gesture. We really do not know how to thank you." Both Nora and Frank insisted that there was no need for thanks and then they all sat around for a long time discussing what the service could mean to Rochester. They talked about how it would need to be set up, launched and monitored. This led to a discussion as to who would be on the board, who would chair it, how counsellors would be selected, who would sit on the interview boards, where the service would be located, should they rent or buy premises and what seemed like a hundred other queries and questions. By the time they went to bed at last, very few questions had been satisfactorily answered. One thing was certain, the new service was well on the way to becoming a force for good in the lives of not just the Gilraines but lots of other people as well.

The following morning the men were up early to surprise their wives and daughters with breakfast in bed. Christmas dinner with all the trimmings would be prepared and eaten in each household. Later on all the Sweetmans, along with a few close friends, would get together as usual for mince pies, mulled wine and fruit punch. Just forty-eight hours earlier, Alice was rehearsing a list of excuses she might use to avoid having to go to Dan and Nancy's. After last night's discussion she had reconsidered and was actually looking forward to sharing the news with the rest of the family and to talking some more about it. The idea was very much welcomed by everyone and proved to be the sole topic of conversation for the entire evening. The Sweetmans wanted to help too so for starters they pledged the money they had saved from not putting up any external Christmas lights this year.

Nancy, with her years of experience as well as qualifications in management, was very excited about the proposed service. She immediately offered her time and expertise to organise a volunteer roster for the project. Further, she advocated the need for a fundraising committee to ensure its initial success and future expansion and suggested that Alice would be the ideal person to undertake the chairing of it.

Chapter 20
Fitting Memorial

After that night's discussion Alice found herself constantly thinking about the future that Frank and Nora had opened up for her. Somehow the dreaded anniversary wasn't as horrible as she'd expected it to be. It was still awful and she wondered how she would have coped without the support of the O Neills. She didn't want to think how she'd manage when they returned, as they must, to Australia in the New Year. Even during the Mass, when her mind inevitably returned to the requiem ceremony of the previous year, she found herself projecting forward to the coming year when she hoped that perhaps the service in Patrick's memory would be showing some tangible evidence of having done some good.

She and Red made their way with Lily to the cemetery to lay flowers on the grave. They were pleased to find that over the course of the half hour that they had spent at the grave site so many of Patrick's friends turned up to pay their respects too. They were surprised to find that along with the family's Christmas Day wreath several others, along with floral tributes, now adorned the grave. It was some consolation to them that Patrick still lived on in the memory of his friends. And now thanks to the O Neills Alice realised with the warm glow of gratitude his name would be forever remembered. In order that Nora, Frank and Daisy could be present it was decided to launch the project on New Year's Day, 1965. With Nancy's assistance, Alice called a press conference for noon on January 1st. The idea was to announce that the new service would be up and running by February 1st. It would be available locally and free of charge to the parents and immediate families of recently deceased young people.

Alice had spent a good deal of time and effort in preparing the press statement. She understood the need for clarity, brevity and focus in order to grab attention. She was also anxious to acknowledge the generosity of Frank and Nora O Neill for making it possible. She felt strongly that initially the people who would benefit most from the service might need to be persuaded of its value to them. In addition, she was very conscious of the necessity to recruit volunteers for her fundraising committee and to advertise the service. To cover all of these aspects in an interesting sound bite was a challenging prospect. Alice was determined to do the task justice. She toyed with the notion of dividing the task up and asking Red, Frank and either Nora or Nancy to handle different aspects of the presentation. Then she realised that splitting the presentation up would inevitably fragment the message as well. In the end, she decided that one presenter would be preferable. Because of her natural shyness it never even crossed her mind that she herself should do it. First she approached Nora who, with Frank's approval, refused point blank to undertake it, arguing that it would be inappropriate for them as donors to be focusing attention on themselves rather than on the service. Then she asked Nancy, who had plenty of experience in this area. She too refused as did Red when she asked him. Both insisted that she herself was the obvious choice. And so very reluctantly she listed the six elements she needed to address on an index card as follows:

Patrick	Clientele
O Neills	Promotion
Service	Fundraising

She ordered and reordered them until she was satisfied with the flow. Finally, she practised making the points in clear natural statements, making sure to keep it fresh and not over-rehearsed. Then she threw herself into keeping up her spirits for Lily and Red and the O Neills as they rang in the New Year. They all gathered around the Christmas tree and sang 'Auld Lang Syne'. Later they stood on the porch, well wrapped up against the cold, and listened to the church bells and the ships' sirens on Lake Ontario and watched the fireworks. Finally they made their way quietly inside where Alice prepared hot chocolate for them all. Soon after that they retired in search of sleep in preparation for what the next day might bring.

Next morning the four adults attended the 10.30 Mass before heading across the road to the offices of the local broadcasting station in time for the all-important press conference. They were welcomed by a bubbly young woman who introduced herself as Sherry as she showed them into a waiting room. She returned a few minutes later with a tray of coffee and biscuits. Alice was in no humour to add to her adrenalin levels with coffee. The others gratefully accepted while she sipped a glass of water. When the anchor man, the very popular Bill Clayton, came to escort her to the news studio she set off with a chorus of best wishes ringing in her ears. Then Nora, Red and Frank were invited to watch the broadcast through a two-way mirror from behind the sound engineer at his desk. They could see Alice seated at a desk behind a microphone. She looked beautiful and unusually relaxed. The next thing they heard was the voice of Bill Clayton introducing the item. "Here in our very own backyard is the latest breaking story. Out of a local tragic event just a little over a year ago comes a very positive project. Now here with the details is Alice Gilraine."

Looking straight ahead as if this was something she did every day Alice started to speak. In a slow, deliberate, well-modulated voice she began. "On December 27th, a little over a year ago, two days after his eighteenth birthday, Patrick Gilraine died tragically in a tobogganing accident. He was our son. Today we, his parents and his sister, thanks to the enormous generosity of Frank and Nora O Neill, our life-long friends, want to announce that in his memory a new bereavement service will be launched. This service will be located here in Rochester and will provide free of charge counselling services to the parents and families of recently deceased young people. Our hearts go out to these families and we wish to offer our sympathies and practical help through The Patrick Gilraine Memorial Bereavement Counselling Service. We appeal for volunteers to help us to make a difference. If you have even a little time to spare, you can help us to promote this worthwhile service. Perhaps you would like to join me in fundraising so we can launch the service as planned on February 1st. Thank you."

"Thank you, Mrs Gilraine. We encourage you to heed Mrs Gilraine's heartfelt appeal. You can contact us through the usual number here at Greece Local Broadcasting Station, GLBS (585)656-71449."

Immediately after the recording was over Bill Clayton reappeared with Alice in tow. He was congratulating her as they came in and turning to the others he said, "Wasn't Alice just fantastic? I've just been saying to her that her piece is flawless. It's going out exactly as is on both radio and television on the lunchtime news bulletins. Now sit for a minute and catch your breath. Sherry is on her way with fresh coffee which I'm sure you'll be ready for now. Fair play to you, Alice, I'll have to watch my job with you around. Congratulations again." Red jumped up to give her a congratulatory hug and tell her how brilliantly she had done. Nora and Frank added their words of praise and hugged her too. Then they sat down to enjoy the coffee.

As they were preparing to leave, Bill Clayton rushed in again. "Whew! I'm glad I caught you before you'd left. It's absolute bedlam out there. The switchboard is jammed with calls. Since the bulletin went out the phones haven't stopped ringing. All the lines are constantly busy. People are volunteering time, expertise and money, money and more money. I've had to set up a charity account with the bank across the road under the name 'The Patrick Gilraine Memorial Bereavement Counselling Service Fund' so that there's somewhere for the public to send their donations. All you have to do is sign these forms. Alice, they're screaming for an interview. Do you think you could do one with me today?"

"Today?" Squawked Alice in fright.

"Right now if you wouldn't mind," replied Bill calmly. "Alice, 'twill be no bother to you. It'll be just a wee conversation between the two of us. I'll ask you a few questions and you just take your time in answering them. Let the answers be long or short, it's entirely up to you. We'll do it in Studio 3 with the two armchairs facing each other. That way you can ignore everything else and just chat to me like we did earlier. Come on, you are a natural. Let's do it for Patrick's memory. Shall we give it a go, my dear?"

Within minutes, Alice found herself seated in the studio answering questions. She hadn't time to think about her appearance. She reminded herself that she had been made up professionally prior to the press conference earlier so she was probably okay. Bill, with practiced ease, was taking her through the story chronologically. He helped her through her account with great gentleness and empathy. She talked about the horrible night when Patrick was missing, the search followed by the recovery of the body, the wake, the requiem and the burial and all the hard, sad months since. Twenty minutes slipped easily by and then a further ten and they were still talking. The telephone rang in the studio and Bill answered it. Putting his hand over the mouthpiece he turned to Alice and said, "There are a number of callers on the lines who would love to have a word with you, Alice. Would you be happy to speak with one or two? Remember this segment, if you agree to do it, does not have to go out live. You will have an opportunity to edit it if necessary. Okay?"

Alice decided to go ahead with the question and answer session too. When they were eventually finished, it was after three o'clock in the afternoon and Alice was exhausted. Again, Red and the O Neills had been given access to the recording booth. They were amazed as the usually bashful Alice that they had always known blossomed before their eyes into this wonderfully warm, comfortable communicator. She was absolutely compelling to watch and to listen to. Her voice surrounded the listener like warm honey and although she was talking directly to Bill Clayton the cameras caught her candid expressions and her unwavering eye contact. Everyone who saw the interview subsequently said the same thing. Each and every one of them felt that she was talking directly to them.

There was a huge outpouring of empathy and caring for this brave, kind-hearted and above all ordinary mother and wife, who was telling her story just as it had happened to her. As she emerged from Studio 3 at last, she was surrounded by the O Neills and Red offering congratulations and also by a large group of GLBS staff and personnel who broke into spontaneous applause. By now, everyone was starving and, though high on adrenalin, even Alice was beginning to register hunger. Because of the scheduled press conference Red had decided that Alice should be spared the chore of cooking so he had booked an early evening meal for the four of them at 'The Linden Tree' for four o' clock. Later they were to join Lily and Daisy at the Hogans'. Now they made their way directly to the restaurant. When they arrived, they were greeted enthusiastically by a beaming maître d'hôtel who led them to their table. Just as they were about to sit down, the other diners spontaneously rose to give them a standing ovation. This puzzled them. When the waiter came to take their order, he explained that Alice was now a celebrity.

"We know that the press conference went down well with the public, but this kind of reaction surprises us," Red said. "Oh no, sir, it's not just the press conference which we all heard earlier. We also saw the interview which has been on the television for the past half hour at least. We're all glued to it in the kitchen. You're fantastic, Mrs Gilraine, if you don't mind my saying so. It is a great honour for me to serve you."

"Oh my God, Red, can we get out of here please?" begged Alice. "I don't think I could bear to eat in this fishbowl."

"Okay, my love, if that's what you'd like. Nora and Frank, please have your meal. I'll come back to collect you later," suggested Red.

"Not at all, we'll all go," said Frank and Nora in unison. Frank patted Alice on the shoulder sympathetically and gave her an encouraging smile.

"Don't mind me," mumbled Alice, collapsing abruptly into her chair. "Please let's all sit down. I'm not thinking straight. There isn't a bite to eat at home. I, for one, could eat the legs from under the table. I'm really sorry for making such a fuss." Nora reassured her that there was no need to be self-conscious and that people meant no harm. When she glanced around a little later, she realised that everyone was busily eating and leaving them alone. While they waited for their food they released the tension by sharing expressions describing how hungry they were. Nora said irreverently that she was so hungry she'd 'eat the leg of the Lamb of God'. Red volunteered that he was 'so hungry he'd eat a scabby dog'. Frank topped them both by declaring that he was so hungry he'd happily 'eat a child with measles and enjoy every spot'. They were laughing at the absurdity and incongruity of these statements when they were rescued from worse by the welcome arrival of their salads. The ice thus broken, they enjoyed the rest of the meal, savouring the delicious food and appreciating the good company. They even graciously accepted the congratulatory bottle of champagne which the restaurant owner insisted on bringing to the table and drank to his health as well.

Later they all adjourned to the Hogans' where the rest of the Sweetmans had gathered to fete Alice and the future of the memorial project. Everyone was full of praise for her and how she had handled the press conference and how well she had come across in the hour-long interview. They all insisted on watching the news to see if there would be any coverage on the evening and late bulletins. There was lots and lots of coverage. The news item ran to fifteen minutes, showing all of the press conference again liberally interspersed with snippets from the interview. During the advertisements a runner giving the bank account details for the memorial fund ran constantly across the bottom of the screen. The last ad promised that a further programme of Alice Gilraine, our new local celebrity, speaking with the public in a question and answer format, would air at the weekend. The excitement reached new heights and despite her earlier fatigue Alice found herself enjoying the party atmosphere and for the first time in over a year actually wanting to share an emotion with others. Afterwards she wondered if perhaps it was the unaccustomed adulation or the heady effervescence of the champagne that had caused her to feel like that. That night she felt the first stirrings of meaningful possibilities in her arid life. Later when they eventually got home, her mind in overdrive with plans for the next several days, she turned gratefully to Red and returned his embrace before settling down in the comfort of his arms at last.

Chapter 21

A New Challenge

At forty-six, Alice was a very attractive woman whose face and figure belied her years. Anyone watching her poised presentation on television could be forgiven for thinking that she was at least ten years younger. She was one of those lucky people whom the camera loves. Her tiny frame, large eyes and flyaway blonde curls combined to give her the appearance of a happy elf on screen. Instead of adding pounds to her the television cameras succeeded in making her look almost ethereal. As she matured, Alice had come into her own fashion-wise. Now instead of the tiny prints of her youth she tended to wear strong blocks of colour. She was too short for contrasting tops and skirts so tended to wear dresses with matching jackets or else pencil skirts with same colour tops and neatly waisted jackets. Her favourite outfits were bright red, emerald, teal and deepest blue. These colours were excellent for TV appearances. In the early days of January, she found herself in greater demand for appearances on GLRS radio and television. Her appeals were often carried on the cable networks also, so she very quickly became the public face of The Patrick Gilraine Memorial Bereavement Counselling Service Fund.

Because he was free and wanted to be helpful, Frank often accompanied Alice to the studios for moral support. She was busier and busier in these early days, trying to keep tabs on an increasing number of different facets of the upcoming launch. And so they were thrown together more and more. On the very first day that the fund opened, as a result of Bill Clayton's swift setting up of the bank account, radio listeners and TV viewers had pledged over twelve thousand dollars. Over the next few days a further eight thousand, three hundred and forty dollars were deposited. Things slowed down a little after that. Most weeks saw the fund grow by a couple of thousand dollars. By the end of the first week, Alice had selected, from the people who volunteered, a core group for her fundraising committee. These were mostly women, starting with her sister-in-law Nancy, her sister Annie and Caroline Hogan. Added to these stalwarts were Bethany Crow, who was a Baptist preacher, and also the wife of one of Red's co-workers along with two of Patrick's young friends Chris Boylan and Jack Connolly.

Frank had volunteered to raise some funds on his return to Australia with a view to expanding the service over there in time. In the meantime, he was hugely helpful to Alice in keeping on top of a number of tasks. He helped her to choose premises for the new service. Over three or four days they visited at least six different complexes in an effort to find a suitable location for The Patrick Gilraine Memorial Bereavement Counselling Service. They needed two decent sized rooms for the counsellors to work in. Office space for when they could afford to hire a secretary and also an archive-cum-record storage space which could be locked securely would also be necessary. Every time they found an appropriate address the premises weren't suitable or vice versa.

At first, it was innocent enough. Frank genuinely wanted to help Alice. He had always felt protective towards her. It had probably started way back when he first met and fell in love with his beloved Nora. Despite being the younger by two years, Nora was always the stronger and more robust of the cousins. Although they had always cared for each other in equal measure, it was Nora who looked out for Alice when they lived in Brisbane. There was something so appealing about Alice's vulnerability that Frank himself was hardly aware that he was a little in love with her all these years. When he heard of Patrick's tragic death, his heart went out to Red, the friend of his youth, but it was the image of the grieving Alice which haunted him. In her usual fashion, Nora agreed with Frank about what needed to be done and then went ahead and made the arrangements to achieve it. When they arrived in Rochester, Frank was overwhelmed with his first glimpse of Alice and several weeks under the same roof with her hadn't cured him of his infatuation. Little by little he found more and more reasons to be in her company whether with others or, as in recent days, increasingly on his own with her. The office hunting eventually proved too much temptation for him.

On the first day of looking, they had gone to a complex near the city centre. The location was ideal but when they got to view the property they were disappointed to discover that the building was old, badly ventilated and in a dilapidated condition. The next place they viewed that day was located at what was advertised as a shopping mall. It turned out to be a business park and an exceptionally quiet one at that. The letting agent, when they rang him, suggested that they collect the keys at the nearby gas station and go to view it by themselves. This time the accommodation was excellent and met all their requirements. However, it proved to be totally unsuitable as it was so remote and people would have huge difficulty finding it. They walked around and deplored the fact that the location was so inappropriate. They were surprised to find a note in the kitchenette suggesting that they help themselves to coffee as there was a state of the art coffee maker on the worktop and milk and cookies in the fridge.

As they were washing up Frank, standing behind her, leaned forward and kissed Alice on the nape of the neck. Startled, she turned around and he held her in a silent embrace. After a few seconds she extricated herself and protested weakly that it should never have happened. For the next while, they avoided looking at each other. By the time they arrived home several hours later, they were chatting away as comfortably as always. The following morning Nora accompanied Daisy and Lily to find suitable attire for the two girls for an upcoming social event. Red needed to call to the bank with Alice in order to record his details and register his signature as co-signatory on the Patrick Gilraine Memorial Bereavement Counselling Service Fund account. After that he had to get back to work and had asked Frank to accompany Alice to the radio station and later on to view two further premises.

The interview-cum-Q&A session went very well at GLRS. Alice emerged on a high, feeling that for the first time she hadn't been a bundle of nerves before going on air. She and Frank celebrated by having lunch together before going to view the office sites. When the maître d' asked them what they would like to drink, Frank suggested that as this was the last lunch they would share and to celebrate her morning's work they should each have a Kir Royale. In a rare moment of recklessness, Alice agreed. She liked champagne although had never tasted this concoction before. She found that she really liked the combination of rich fruity blackcurrant and bubbly champagne and so she had another one instead of coffee when she finished lunch.

In the afternoon, she and Frank took a cab to see premises in the Irondequoit district. Disappointingly this building, though suitable and in an excellent location, proved to be too small for their requirements. This left only one option, a recently built office block on Dewey Street. They had deliberately left this one to last because it was on their way home. To date only two floors of the five storey block had been fitted out. When they were shown the premises by the agent, he first brought them to view the layout that had been fitted out on the first floor by the owner occupier, a Mr Richard Waters. Richard was a lawyer who had decided to invest money he had inherited in real estate. He had commissioned the building of the five storey office block. Sweetman Brothers and Company had got the contract for the project. Richard had wanted the people who were using the premises to select how they wanted their work spaces fitted out rather than organising the space first and then have clients making alterations or living with less than ideal conditions.

Alice and Frank liked what they saw on the first floor. Richard suggested that they should see the second floor layout before looking at the empty third floor. He also offered them the plans for three alternative sample layouts that they might be interested in looking at. Ordinarily he would have been happy to go with them and discuss which of the five layouts would best suit them or which new one, combining features of several, might fit the bill. Unfortunately today he was about to have a work conference so they would have to work out for themselves what they wanted. They went up to the second level where they admired the open plan office layout which the architectural firm of Browne, Evans and Wall had selected. Then, clutching the floor plans, they made their way up to the third floor to discuss the one most suitable for the headquarters of The Patrick Gilraine Memorial Bereavement Counselling Service. It wasn't the only thing they did up there. Whether it was the second Kir Royale that Alice had imbibed that made her giggly and lowered her resistance, or the imminence of Frank's departure that was the cause, the result was that when Frank put his arms around her and started to kiss her, Alice didn't make much effort to stop him. In fact she kissed him back. Then one thing leading to another, they succumbed to temptation and mindlessly, tenderly and ecstatically they made love on the floor of what, they had agreed only a few minutes earlier, would be the ideal location for the project's headquarters.

Alice's first public fundraising event was to be a benefit dance run at the local Irish club where all the Sweetmans socialised with their friends and neighbours. The event was scheduled for January 5th, the day before the O Neills were due to fly back to Australia. Because everyone in the community knew the Gilraines, this event was expected to be hugely well attended. On the night, Alice wore a stunning evening gown of black silk with a sweetheart neckline. It hugged her tiny waistline like a second skin and had the merest suggestion of a train which, along with a pair of vertiginous black heels, added an illusion of height. Standing beside Red in his tuxedo, they made a strikingly good-looking couple. Red's auburn curls had been subdued by a liberal dressing of hair oil and he towered over his dainty little wife like the handsome prince in a fairy-tale. When the equally handsome Frank came downstairs, with the elegant Nora in a shimmering silver sheath at his side, it was the vision that was Alice that took his breath away. Frank found it difficult to tear his eyes away as he saw the colour flood her cheeks when she intercepted his besotted gaze.

Later the four of them formed a welcoming committee and greeted all the guests on arrival at the event venue. Almost all the attendees gifted items for the charity auction or the raffle. On arrival, each of the guests took an envelope into which they put donations. The envelopes were then posted into a large pillar box resembling an old fashioned post box set up in front of the bandstand. The musicians had volunteered their services free so that all monies collected in the course of the evening would go directly to the fund. The dancing was a mixture of lively Irish sets, reels and jigs interspersed with foxtrots and waltzes. Alice, who hadn't danced for ages, was finally persuaded onto the floor by Frank. "I've been waiting impatiently all day to get a chance to hold you in my arms once more," he whispered.

"Please, Frank, let's not spoil things. Promise me you'll never speak of it again. For now, let's just enjoy the dance." Watching from the side-lines, Red thought Alice looked amazing. She was enjoying the slow rhythm of the music while being gently cradled in the arms of her dance partner. He decided to sweep Nora around the floor and when the dance was over subtly ensured that they'd each dance the last dance with their own life partners. If Nora had any suspicions that there was something going on between her cousin and her husband, she never mentioned it to anyone then or later. Red could never understand what it was that made him sense a threat to his marriage as he watched his best friend dance with Alice. But something made him act as he did. When the band stopped playing, the bandleader handed the microphone to Alice. She thanked everyone for coming and started an appreciative round of applause for the musicians. All that remained then was to run the auction and the raffle and to announce the amount raised on the night.

"It is my great pleasure to introduce Mr Bill Clayton, who has very kindly agreed to act as auctioneer for us this evening. So cheque books at the ready, please, and cash of course, we may even accept IOUs for this very worthy cause," she quipped as she laughingly handed over the mike to Bill. Over the next hour the motley collection of items donated for the auction went briskly under the hammer to the accompaniment of Bill's unique style of good-humoured cajolery and hilarious raillery. Everyone entered into the spirit of the occasion and parted happily with large and generous amounts of cash for a series of diverse items. One such was a well-worn sweater auctioned by Maria Sweetman, who divulged she had been trying to get rid of it for over a decade, and for which her husband Martin now happily paid two hundred and fifty dollars. A society wife bid three hundred and eighty dollars to buy a day of her husband's time and attention and a hysterically startled woman bought back a favourite pair of her own shoes for a hundred dollars. A 'playboy' husband bid five hundred dollars to prevent his disgruntled wife from donating her engagement ring. Bill did such a good job on building up a mystery prize that he started a bidding war for which the successful gentleman bid a stunning seven hundred and fifty dollars only to discover he had bought a bottle of smoke. Afterwards some quite decent mystery prizes barely made their value. Overall the auction was an astonishing success.

The finale of the event was the raffle, after which Alice was delighted to announce, "Ladies and gentlemen, friends and family and the wonderful Bill Clayton, I am thrilled to tell you all that tonight's event has raised a sum beyond our wildest hopes. The envelope donations amounted to eight thousand five hundred and forty dollars. The auction, thanks to the inimitable Bill, netted a further seven thousand three hundred and eighty-five dollars. And Red, can you give me the total for the raffle please? Wow, another two thousand nine hundred and thirty-six dollars. Well, if my addition is correct that comes to a fabulous eighteen thousand eight hundred and sixty-one dollars. Red, I know, will round that up to a tidy twenty thousand. Very well done all of you, and thank you. Go dtéigh sibh slán abhaile anois agus arís Míle Buíochas. (Safe home now and again a thousand thanks)."

The Gilraines and O Neills were then driven home together, euphoric at the success of the evening. By the time they arrived in Paddy Hill Drive, they were all tired enough to retire immediately. Red took Alice gently in his arms and, kissing her tenderly, congratulated her on the success of the evening. Then, complimenting her on how stunning she looked, he proceeded to help her out of her beautiful evening gown. Having quickly divested himself of his tuxedo, he slipped into bed beside her. Then, slowly and gently, as if it were the most natural thing in the world, he began to make sweet love to his beloved wife. Afterwards, as they lay contentedly in each other's arms, they were transported back to the early days of their marriage when all was fresh and new and oh so thrillingly exciting. They slept.

The next day they drove to the airport. Up to the very last minute, as the O Neills were about to go through the departure gates, the four of them were still talking enthusiastically about the success of their joint venture. Thanks and kisses were exchanged as they wondered when they would all meet again. On their way back home in the car, Red reached across and, taking Alice's hand in his, raised it to his lips saying, "Welcome back, my love. Have you any idea how proud I am of you and how you've managed all this publicity recently? We'll be forever grateful to Nora and Frank for helping us to set up the project, but its success depends completely on you, my dear. I know you can do it. I hope you know it too. Now let's stop looking back and face the future together. I've always loved you. I still love you. I'll love you till the day I die." Then he drove them home. The benefit dance had been undeniably a roaring success both financially and socially. GLRS gave the event full coverage. Because it was still early January and the height of the social season, photos of the event were picked up by local and not so local papers and some of the glossy magazines. The added publicity of the twenty thousand dollars proceeds of the event itself led to an increase of a further three thousand six hundred and fifty-three dollars in bank donations. Now was no time for the organisers to rest on their laurels. There was plenty still to do starting with selecting a management committee if they were to reach the goal of setting up the service by February 1st. A public meeting was called for the night of January 12th, at which the following members were elected to the management committee of The Patrick Gilraine Memorial Bereavement Counselling Service: Alice Gilraine, chairperson; Nancy Sweetman, treasurer; Bethany Crow, event co-ordinator; Red Gilraine, assistant event coordinator and Jack Connolly, secretary.

By January 16th, interviews had been set up. First on the basis of the applicants' résumés and their years of experience the committee narrowed down the forty-two applicants to a more manageable fourteen. These were then invited to present themselves for interview at forty-five minute intervals over the next two days. As there were only two positions to fill, ideally the board would have liked to employ one female and one male counsellor. As chairperson, Alice was anxious to select the very best people for the jobs so she impressed on the others that bearing gender balance in mind they must still make sure that the best possible candidates were selected.

The committee was unanimous in offering the jobs to an older woman with twenty-five years' experience of bereavement counselling, most of it in inner city New York and a forward looking young man in his late twenties. Marina Fox and David Donaldson proved to be inspired choices, not only complementing each other's skills but working together harmoniously as an extremely professional team until Marina's retirement some twenty years later. They were at the core of the service from the very beginning and presided over an ever growing team of counsellors in ever expanding offices in Rochester and other venues over the following years.

No sooner had she finished with the interviewing than Alice had to rush off to Dewey Street to oversee the fit out of the office premises. After that she had a committee meeting in the Park Hotel on East Avenue and immediately after that a meeting of the fundraising committee, luckily at the same venue. She was pleased to be so exhaustingly busy. It meant she had no time to dwell on things like Frank, her own appalling behaviour and the possible consequences of the previous Thursday and Friday. Part of her regretted it bitterly and a part of her felt no remorse at all. Most of her conscious mind just did not want to either acknowledge it or deal with it. So she threw herself fully and whole-heartedly into the work.

The project had really taken off and was snowballing towards launch day at breakneck speed. She knew that as soon as the launch was over she would have to start taking driving lessons. Her current crisscrossing of the city by taxi was not only costing a fortune it was also unsustainable in the long run. Despite her deep seated terror of driving, part of her was looking forward to the challenge. Sometimes she no longer recognised this new person that she had become. The old Alice would never have considered taking driving lessons. Neither would she have had the courage to do radio and television interviews. And the old Alice would never in a million years have conceived of the notion of allowing herself to be kissed by a man other than her husband. Again, her mind veered away from what this new Alice had not only countenanced but had actually indulged in and, if truth be told, enjoyed. Briefly it flashed across her mind that she might be going crazy. Right now she hadn't time to think about that or anything else.

In the ten days left before the official launch, she still had to do a dizzying amount of preparatory tasks. She had to organise a press statement as well as prepare her own speech for the launch and speaking notes for the mayor. She had already chosen the colour schemes for the offices and arranged for the painting of the walls and the carpeting of the different areas. She had yet to consult with Marina Fox and David Donaldson about the layout and furniture for their individual workspaces. She wanted to do the job right and felt strongly that in order to function at their best the counsellors should be comfortable in their rooms so that they could make their clients feel welcome and at ease. She knew that colour was important and also that the spaces should flow smoothly one into another. It was important, therefore, that all three of them should agree on the choice of soft furnishings and drapes for the communal areas. Then she had to organise the catering for the event as well as prepare the list of invited guests and select the invitation cards and ensure they were posted on time. At some point, she needed to have her hair cut and styled and find an outfit for the launch. As well as all that, she must design some advertisements for the newspapers as well as for radio and television. Should they do a poster or flyer campaign too? It was vital that as many people as possible knew about the service if it was to hit the ground running. She added the poster/flyer question to her list of agenda items as she sat in the back of the taxi. Then, opening her diary, she made an entry for the next day to remind her to book the driving lessons. When she arrived home, shattered and happy with what she had achieved, her brain was still buzzing with all the details of what needed to be done the next day. She found Lily and Red in the living room comfortably ensconced in two armchairs either side of a blazing fire companionably reading. Red immediately left the room only to return minutes later with a tray of homemade cookies and three mugs of hot chocolate. "Oh, Red, you dear man, you spoil me so," she said.

"Don't thank me, my love, I only made the hot chocolate. It was your wonderful daughter who insisted on making the cookies," he protested. After they had enjoyed the suppertime snack Alice thanked her daughter and husband by kissing them both goodnight before heading to bed.

Next morning she booked the driving lessons and, despite the hectic schedule, managed to squeeze in her first lesson even before the launch date. With her usual efficiency she had succeeded in getting all the details organised in time. Marina and David were delighted with their working environment and were living proof that, when like-minded people are working towards a common goal, agreements about minor details such as decorating schemes can be reached with the minimum of fuss or delay.

On January 31st, Alice made the press statement at GLRS and was pleased that everything ran smoothly. She drew attention to all the adverts for the event and reminded the public to look out for the posters locally. Everybody would be getting flyers delivered with their milk next morning with the details of the new services available along with the address, phone numbers and hours of opening. She encouraged all those who had been invited to be sure to turn up to the launch and reminded the general public that they would be able to tune in to full live coverage of the event on both radio and television.

She had already written her own speech as well as the speaking notes for the mayor. As soon as she was finished at the radio and TV station, she brought the notes personally to the mayor's office where, over a cup of coffee, she briefed him on the order of events for the morrow. Then as she was about to call a taxi the mayor insisted that his driver would take her wherever she wished to go. She accepted the kind offer as her hair salon was en route to the mayor's next appointment.

Just a few days earlier, she had spotted the ideal outfit in a little boutique in her local shopping mall. It was a poster red suit, with a long slim-line pencil skirt and a fitted jacket slightly flared below its cinched waistline. To wear with it she had selected a silk blouse with a softly ruffled neckline in exactly the same shade of red. She intended to wear her most elegant killer heels with it and instinctively knew that she would cut a striking figure for the launch. Now as her hair stylist, having washed, cut and styled her hair, put her under the dryer, Alice took out her speech and the index cards to which she had earlier transcribed her main points and proceeded to rehearse her presentation. By the time she arrived home, she was well prepared for the following day and had time to relax with Lily and Red.

The morning of February 1st dawned fine and mild. The launch was scheduled for 2.00 in the afternoon. When Alice arrived around 10.30, she found that Marina and David had been there already for a couple of hours before her. They had been answering the phones, taking messages and even making appointments which they agreed was a great indicator of things to come. Alice had a number of last-minute details to see to so she had brought her outfit with her as she did not intend to return home before the launch. She had learned early on to leave nothing to chance. She had always believed that failing to plan was only part of the problem. First she needed to plan and then she had to follow up on the plan and most importantly she had to check in time that everything was going to plan. And so she was on the premises with plenty of time to spare. First she checked with the caterers and went over the time schedule with them. Then she rang Bill Clayton to make sure the cameramen and television crews knew where the venue was and where and when they would need to set up. Finally, before leaving her temporary office she rang the mayor's office to check that he would be on time. Then she checked that things were set up as she requested for the platform party before thanking the young Sweetman lads who had been hanging banners and balloons in a welcoming display throughout the space. Like a lot of very successful people Alice adhered to a few simple common-sense rules. Later in life when she was asked over and over again to what she attributed her success and from where she had acquired her business acumen, she always answered that there was no great mystery to it. There was no false modesty about it either; Alice sincerely felt that all she had was common sense, hard work and a belief that the service she was promoting was a force for good. The fact that it would turn out to be a million dollar business in the end was neither here nor there.

At 12.45, she hustled all the team to the neighbourhood delicatessen so that they would have some sustenance before everything kicked off at 2.00. Then she acknowledged their efforts and hurried back to headquarters to, as she put it, 'get into her canonicals' and to be ready to welcome her guests. It was extremely important for the project to maintain momentum so in the immediate aftermath of the successful launch Alice called a meeting of The Patrick Gilraine Memorial Bereavement Counselling Service Fund. There was only one item on the agenda and that was to list the upcoming fundraising events in order of priority. Once that decision had been made, all that remained was to select a date for each event so that they could plan and organise it. The meeting was taking place in the waiting room of the headquarters on Dewey Avenue at 7.30 on the evening of February 2nd after the first day's work had been completed. After welcoming the other members, Alice called the meeting to order and suggested that they'd brainstorm for a few minutes first. Each member was asked to suggest the first promotional activity that came into their heads. Alice charted each one, including her own, without comment or judgement. Among them they had come up with eleven ideas for raising money out of which they selected four to be run over the next months and then one each for September, Halloween and Christmas. Because ensuring publicity for the service was as important as the collection of funds, they had decided to run a whist drive in March, a charity walk in April, a garden party in May and in late June, they intended to run a jamboree camping event for teenagers. This would be organised as an extension of the Sweetmans' summer event and would include girls as well as boys. Then in September there would be a golf classic, for Halloween a fancy dress ball and just before Christmas another gala charity auction.

As this was a demanding schedule, Alice asked for assistance in the organisation of the events. Bethany would still be the main organiser for each event. From now on there would be a named co-organiser too. At this point in the meeting, Alice called on Bethany as events co-ordinator to take over. Her first suggestion was that it was timely to now recruit subcommittee members to assist in the organisation and smooth running of the ambitious programme of upcoming events. Meanwhile, the whist drive was to be run by Bethany and Alice, the charity walk by Bethany and Red, and the garden party by Alice and Nancy. Alice and Red, with Dan Sweetman's assistance, would organise the jamboree. After this meeting Bethany would draw up a list of people to invite to join the subcommittee. She would select people who had particular skills and expertise suitable to the particular events and bring this list to the next meeting for approval. First she proposed that it might be a good idea to send a letter to all those who had signed on as volunteers, updating them on progress and inviting them to become friends of the Patrick Gilraine Memorial Fund. In this way, there would be a ready-made list of people who could be called upon to form subcommittees. Thus, with very little fuss, a well-oiled machine came into being. Little did Alice know in these early days that running this steadily growing service would prove to be her full-time, all-absorbing, extremely busy and satisfying career for the next twenty-five years.

Chapter 22

Change of Direction

Whether it was that Alice was so fully occupied with her new role that he no longer needed to constantly worry about her, or that his own involvement in the organisation of events gave him new energy, or whether it was the fact that Alice made the whole thing look so easy that gave Red a new impetus, he could never tell. By the end of the summer of 1965, when the hugely successful jamboree was over and he was up to his tonsils in co-ordinating the golf classic arrangements, he had come to a decision about his own business life. He had always harboured an ambition to run his own business. Because he was naturally shy and self-effacing, up to now he had always just gone with the flow. Also because he was known to be hard-working, well-organised and efficient everyone he had ever worked for had paid him well to manage and oversee jobs and staff.

Suddenly, now in his late forties, he finally recognised in himself for the first time the qualities that others knew he possessed. He also recognised as he watched the monies flow in for the memorial service named for his son that the skills required to run a successful company were well within his capabilities. Without cutting back on his voluntary work he could put some of his extra energies into improving his own financial status and making life more comfortable for his wife and daughter in the short-term and maybe even provide a decent retirement fund. He had an enormous amount of experience in the construction trade. Where he really came into his own was in his absolute insistence on the perfect finish. He could literally turn his hand to any building task so he was ideally suited for what he had in mind. In Rochester at this time, there was a growing market for good quality stand-alone suburban homes. Those who could afford sites and had acquired them in the previous decade were now in a position to build their dream homes in their already landscaped gardens. What most of them needed was a good builder who would undertake the supervision of the whole operation and guarantee a good quality finish. From working with the Sweetman brothers over the last couple of years Red knew that this kind of work was plentiful and actually on the increase. Up until now if he ever thought about working for himself he had allowed himself to be distracted by some real or perceived family crisis. Or else he let himself be dissuaded by his inner voice on the basis that he'd be letting down his current employer or maybe the time was not right or else it was just too risky for someone such as him. Now he felt confident that he could handle the challenge. He recognised that there would never be the right time. Now was a good time for him to take the plunge.

He had been putting out feelers for a while and knew exactly the kind of project which would best suit his talents, provide him with the greatest satisfaction and challenge and at the same time pay well. If such a project by some miracle were to come up in the neighbourhood, that really would be the icing on the cake. He had made up his mind that he would accept anything that combined a number of these elements as the sound of his mother's voice echoed in his ears declaiming, "Red, my son, don't forget that procrastination is the thief of time."

One day in early August when construction work traditionally slowed and Sweetman Brothers had practically closed down while most of the workers were on vacation, he arranged to meet up with Dan at the golf club. They were going to meet with Hank Henshaw, the captain, and Hal Porter, the president of Tall Trees Golf Club to thrash out some of the details for the upcoming golf classic. When they had finished their business, they were having a quick sandwich and coffee prior to playing a round together when Hank was called away on some emergency. He apologised and returned within minutes with a gentleman who had agreed to substitute for him. He introduced Chuck Mallon to Dan and Red before hurrying away. The four of them set off for the first tee and on the way Chuck said to Red, "I don't know whether you believe in fate or not but I have heard a lot about you and have been hoping to run into you for weeks now. Could you spare a few minutes to chat with me after the game? I think that you might be interested in a proposal I have for you." Red's curiosity was piqued and he readily agreed to spare some time after the round.

After they had finished they returned to the clubhouse where Chuck outlined his proposal. Next day he collected Red and drove him a little over two miles away, to where he showed him what he wanted him to undertake. Chuck's elderly uncle had died and left him a property out on Shore Road. It was a lovely old stone cottage with a coach house and in a very poor state of repair. He wished to preserve the stone structure and have it re-pointed. He was flexible about the conversion of the interior of both buildings into suitable accommodation for himself and his wife as a retirement home. His only requirement was that the integrity of the building, including the arched doorway to the coach house, be preserved.

Chuck had had architectural plans and drawings prepared some years earlier. He had been waiting to find the right man to convert them to an appropriate reality. He hoped that Red was that man. After a couple of hours of measuring and calculating and discussion Red was delighted to accept the contract. He had requested that he would be paid by the hour for the work and Chuck had readily agreed. For his part, Red had agreed to keep within what he considered to be a rather generous budget. The work would begin in September and he would undertake most of it himself. If from time to time he needed to employ an assistant, he could arrange this himself as necessary to keep within timeframe.

First they'd have to sit down with Chuck's wife Diana to discuss the proposed layout and get her opinion on the amendments to the drawings that Red had suggested. For example, the ever pragmatic Red thought that having steps up to the kitchen and down to the living room and having the dining area on a different level to the kitchen area was probably less than ideal for a retiring couple. He also felt that the bathroom area, as designed, was far too big and it might be more practical to include a utility room-cum-walk-in airing cupboard in a third of the allocated space. Upstairs he suggested that rather than opting for a large and wasteful landing some of the space could be used to fit an en suite bathroom in the master bedroom. He also had some creative ideas around how to fill the arch and design original handmade units for the kitchen. He was delighted to find that Diana agreed with all his suggested changes and had added some very good ideas of her own which he could easily incorporate into the improved renovation plan.

So before August was out, Red had handed in his notice at Sweetman Brothers in order to set up his own company. Now every morning instead of rising at the crack of dawn and making his way to some distant building site and running himself ragged from sunrise to sunset he could set off cheerfully for his day's work a mere ten minutes from home. He knew exactly what had to be done and how much he could do in a day. Being in total charge of the work was immensely satisfying as was the pride he could take in a job well done. There was joy for him too in picking up each day precisely where he had left off the day before so that the finish was always seamless. He loved the variety of tasks he was involved in and the knowledge that because he was so experienced at sourcing materials he was never delayed or idle waiting for deliveries. The first thing he did was ensure that the site was secure so from the outset he wasn't worried about pilfering. Being organised, he rotated his tasks so he didn't need to waste time waiting for concrete to set or paint to dry as there was always some other task he could turn to. If truth be told, he absolutely loved working with wood and he knew he was a brilliant cabinet maker. Red was one of those rare people equally skilled and comfortable at plumbing, block laying, plastering, building and repairing stone work, pointing, electrical work, painting, varnishing, hanging doors and laying wooden floors. He also derived immense satisfaction from working methodically through a wide variety of tasks while watching a project progress and develop like a living organism. Furthermore, he'd always loved working alone as he was perfectly content in his own company and was always happy to return to a task knowing no one had interfered with it in his absence.

Chuck and Diana were his only visitors and they only came occasionally, not so much to check up on him as that they couldn't keep themselves away. Red actually looked forward to when they dropped in, either together or individually, as they were invariably thrilled with the progress he was making and the finish he was achieving. And because they were also fulsome in their praise of his work he found their visits very rewarding. On one of her visits, Diana said to him, "Now that I have a little time to spare I'd like to become a friend of the Patrick Gilraine Memorial Fund. My problem is I'm not at all sure how much help I could be."

Red explained that Alice never turned down any offer of help. She was an absolute genius at establishing how people's skills and aptitudes could best be utilised for the good of the service. "Why don't you and Chuck drop over to see us in Paddy Hill Drive tomorrow evening? He knows where we live, and we could all get to know each other better and you could quiz Alice to your heart's content." Diana was delighted at the prospect and Alice welcomed the idea when Red mentioned it that night. As two couples, they got on very well and over an informal supper they had a long and enjoyable discussion. The upshot of all the talk was that Alice found herself with two volunteers as Chuck was so enthused that he too wanted to offer his services. Alice, having listened to and talked with Diana, was delighted that she was willing to join her on the fundraising committee, as she had a wealth of experience in event organisation. And since Chuck was just about to retire from his own business as a stockbroker he was now in a position to undertake voluntary charitable work.

Alice had shared her concern that the project needed advice on how best to manage the money. To date the bulk of the donations was sitting in the bank in a current account where it was easily accessible for current expenditure. The Gilraines felt that as the fund was increasing exponentially it didn't make economic sense not to have the money working, gaining a good rate of interest or being invested where it would grow at a faster rate. They didn't have enough know-how or confidence in themselves to be sure what exactly to do. Chuck was more than willing to contribute his time, expertise and energies to managing the fund.

Over the next several years Alice and Red lived parallel lives of frenetic busyness. Alice had made a fantastic success of The Patrick Gilraine Memorial Bereavement Counselling Service. It was completely self-sufficient financially and over the years had expanded hugely. The service now had fifty-four offices in total in the US. Of these, thirty-one were spread all over New York State with three in Boston, five in Chicago and five more in Cleveland, Ohio. Fittingly, demand for the service invariably came from locations where significant numbers of people of Irish extraction lived and worked. Thanks to Frank's efforts there were now also offices in Australia. He and Nora had set up the first one in Brisbane and later after opening the second one they had expanded the service to Sydney and to Melbourne. Now there were three practices in Brisbane, three more in Melbourne and four in Sydney.

Meanwhile, Red's company had gone from strength to strength. That very first conversion he had done for Chuck and Diana Mallon was a huge success and brought in its wake a flood of enquiries. He only had the luxury of completing one other project on his own after that. He'd managed to do one completely new build before he got so busy that he had to start employing help. Soon he had three separate work teams of five. He could now devote himself to doing only the unique elements of the wood work for which his firm had become justifiably renowned. He was as busy as ever. Now he was loving the fact that he was leaving his own individual stamp on the projects he undertook. Better still, money was flowing in steadily. By the summer of 1978, through hard work and wise investments, the Gilraines were now as well-to-do as the Sweetmans and many of their wealthy neighbours. Family life had been good in recent years. The starting up of The Patrick Gilraine Memorial Bereavement Counselling Service Fund had actually proven to be the turning point in their marriage. In January of 1965, immediately after the return of the O Neills to Brisbane, Red had determined to banish from his mind once and forever any suspicions he may have fleetingly had about Frank and Alice. He vowed to love and cherish her for the rest of her life and never allow her for a single moment to feel alone and open to temptation.

For her part, Alice felt so relieved that her lapse had left no permanent mark on her marriage that she was eventually able to put it behind her and in time forgive herself for it. Unfortunately it had changed the tenor of her correspondence with Nora which, at least in the first months after their visit, became stilted and infrequent. With the passage of the years that too had improved though it still lacked some of the warmth and spontaneity of their earliest eagerly-awaited exchanges. Conscious of how much of their time and energy the project was absorbing, Lily's parents were both very anxious to ensure that she would not be neglected. So arrangements were put in place that she remain at school for homework club. Thus all three of them would arrive home within minutes of each other, free to relax for the remainder of the evening. They managed to eat together most evenings though meetings occasionally disturbed this schedule. Preparing dinner became a family chore with each of them mucking in. Red was hopelessly old fashioned when it came to food and as far as cooking was concerned the plainer the better was his motto. He'd happily wash and peel potatoes, shell peas, trim and carve meat and prepare, boil and mash veggies till the cows came home so long as no one asked him to do anything fancy. Alice and Lily took it in turn to take the lead as far as the shopping and cooking were concerned. This led to great variety and also to some hilarious concoctions if, as happened from time to time, the 'lead' person forgot to check supplies before starting the meal.

Because Red was such a traditional eater and loved the kind of food he had grown up with Alice tended to stick with his favourites. Lily, on the other hand, was much more familiar with American, Italian and even oriental food. She had learned to make some wonderfully tasty dishes from time spent at Uncle Martin's whose wife Maria had Italian ancestry. All of the other Sweetman wives cooked American dishes. As the school canteen often served oriental dishes, Lily had been taught to make some in home economics classes. So when it was up to her she chose to serve anything other than Irish cooking. In the immediate aftermath of Patrick's death, his name was never mentioned. Later they had gone through a phase where barely an hour passed without some mention of him followed by upset and grief, usually on Alice's part. Since the setting up of the memorial service things had improved greatly and they were now much better at remembering him as he was and as he deserved to be, a much loved member of the family.

In September of 1965, Lily and Susan had happily and successfully transferred to Holy Rosary High School at the age of fourteen. Over the next five years they had worked hard and by the time they graduated in the summer of 1970 they had each secured a place in the university of their choice. Susan was bound for Stanford to study medicine and Lily had chosen Harvard where she intended to study law. They remained close despite their challenging courses and even when they worked through their summer vacations they always managed to get a few days together for a break every year. These days were sacrosanct, no one else was welcome to join them at this time, not even their beloved parents. If it happened that they were in Rochester at the same time, then they reverted to youthful habits and were in and out of each other's homes as comfortably as ever. They both appreciated their time together as the gift it was for two girls without sisters to have such a close bond. Susan had now been enjoying robust good health since her mid-teens and her parents, relatives and friends were very relieved.

Part of the reason she had been drawn towards medicine as a career, she always thought, was because of the amount of time she had spent in hospitals when she was young. From a very early age she had been fascinated with hospital life. She had great memories of confident and good humoured, busy adults who always patiently answered her questions. The doctors and the nurses treated her seriously. If they had time, they showed her how procedures worked and if they were too busy they would tell her so and come back to her later. She could never remember being patronised in hospital in contrast to the way she often felt in old Dr Hatton's surgery or on home visits. All through her high schooling her interest in medicine never waned. She worked extremely hard to ensure that her results would be sufficiently high to guarantee her a college place.

Lily worked hard too and was equally determined to do well to earn her place at Harvard Law School. Lily's motivation was different from Susan's in that her main focus was on doing well so that her parents would be proud of her. She was obsessed with the notion of being as successful as Patrick would undoubtedly have been. She wanted to return to them what they had been so cruelly robbed of in the only way she knew how. She had decided very early on to follow the career that Patrick had chosen for himself. In spite of that, she had sailed through all her exams and graduated summa cum laude from the jurist doctor program in 1974. She took the LLM programme, qualifying as a Master in Law in the top three of the Class of 1975. She spent a little over a year at a top law firm in Boston before returning to Rochester to become a junior partner in the large and very successful firm of Ross and Hamill. By the summer of 1978, she had a number of successful and high profile cases already to her credit and was well on her way to a flourishing and lucrative career.

Susan too was qualified and was currently a valued member of Unity Hospital's oncology team locally. Chris Boylan had been ordained a priest in the Catholic Archdiocese of Rochester in 1970 and was currently in a city centre parish in charge of Youth Services. The Sweetman boys and all their friends, who had been in the toboggan races with Patrick seven years earlier, were all grown men now in their mid to late twenties. Many of the second generation Sweetmans, both male and female, were now working at what used to be Sweetman Brothers, now named 'Sweetman Construction Ltd.' All three of Dan's sons, Paul, Shaun and Daniel, had joined the family firm. Paul had qualified as a civil engineer, Shaun as a draughtsman and Daniel, the youngest, had joined Sweetman on the administrative side as an accountant. Michael's son, Vincent, and his sister, Dorothy, both qualified quantity surveyors, had also joined their dad in the company. Young Gerard who was as passionate about woodwork as his uncle had joined Red in his business and was now leading his own team. Only Martin's boys, the twins Kevin and Kieran, showed no interest whatsoever in the family business. Kieran ran away to join the Marines and when his tour of duty was over joined the CIA and was very happy with his adventurous life. Kevin did what he had always wanted to do and became a junior school teacher. Their older sister, Caitlin, who was one of the first women to qualify locally as a plumber, couldn't wait to join the Sweetmans and her dad at work.

Now in the summer of 1978 it was time for change. The old order needed to cede its place to the new. The older Sweetmans were all in their late fifties now and some were looking towards retirement. Red was over sixty and Alice had just celebrated her fifty-ninth birthday. Next summer they would celebrate their ruby wedding anniversary. They could hardly believe that forty years had elapsed since that glorious June morning in Tooting when they had exchanged their wedding vows. It had been a good forty years and overall it had been a good marriage. They still loved each other and above all else each wanted what was best for the other. They had survived the death of their only son and they had weathered a potentially fatal glitch not so long afterwards. They had also been very lucky in other aspects of their lives and were extremely proud of their beloved Lily.

Lily was most anxious that her parents would make an effort to celebrate appropriately this milestone anniversary. She had taken to ringing her mother every couple of days and would talk to her dad at least twice a week, pressing them for progress on the plan. So they sat down one evening and decided what they would most like to do. They both agreed that there were good people who could take over from them for a month to six weeks without any ill effects to either the memorial project or Red's business. Since they hadn't had a vacation in years and hadn't travelled anywhere outside of the US since their arrival from Australia in 1962, they decided that an overseas trip was long overdue. Would they take a trip back home to the Emerald Isle or more specifically the island of their birth, the unique and scenic Achill? Or should they make the longer journey and visit the O Neills who were always asking when they'd visit Brisbane? The choice was an easy one in the end. They'd go to Australia and who knows, they might even get to Ireland the following year.

Happy now that the decision had been reached they rang their daughter to inform her of the plan and to invite her to accompany them. Lily immediately kicked to touch, claiming that she couldn't afford the time so early in her career. Sensing how disappointed they were she then promised that she'd try her best to make it up to them at some future date. With this they had to be content. The only shadow on their otherwise sunny horizon was that despite her stunning looks and warm personality Lily never seemed able to sustain a long term relationship. She had no trouble in attracting men and even occasionally women showed an unrequited interest. So far, no matter how suitable in her parents' view or how keen they were, Lily tired of all her suitors in short order.

Chapter 23

A Questionable Quest

From the night they had first announced their plan to Lily eleven months earlier the days and weeks had just galloped by and before they knew it June 9th, 1979 had arrived. The celebrations for the ruby wedding anniversary planned by Lily were kicking off with a big family get-together at the house in Paddy Hill Drive. She had insisted that this party would be her treat to her parents to make up for the fact that she was unable to travel with them. What she didn't tell them, nor intend to reveal, was that she had already booked a two week break and intended to join them for the final fortnight of their stay in Brisbane. Meanwhile, she had reserved a marquee, caterers and pulled out all the stops to ensure that this would be an anniversary to remember for her parents and the extended family. Maud was now a very frail old lady and pretty much housebound. Tonight they had planned for her to attend the party for the first half hour or so. At ninety-seven, she was quite healthy, ate and slept well and still loved to talk. Strangely her mental state had deteriorated very little over the past twenty years and luckily for her she had no sense of being a burden to anyone. Her large brood of grandchildren loved her unreservedly and visited her regularly and willingly, giving Annie a break and allowing her to enjoy what little free time she had.

The family party on the day would serve also as a farewell do for Alice and Red who would be away for a full eight weeks, all summer in effect. Alice was thrilled to see her mother at the get-together. Maud was in her Sunday best and delighted to be at the centre of things. She was under the impression that the party was for her and wondered aloud several times, "Where exactly am I going for my birthday, Annie?"

"We're at Alice's, Mam, it's her birthday and also she and Red have been married for forty years so it's their anniversary as well."

"Yerra Annie a stór, don't I know well when Alice's birthday is? Sure, wasn't I there for all of it? Well, I remember all the palaver that she mightn't be so bright seeing as I was so young and she had arrived so early. Sure, what did they know about any of it when in the end weren't the pair of us as healthy as trout? I'd be well able for another one even now, so I would, only I can't seem to find my poor Danny. Where is your dad, Annie? When was the last time you saw him? I swear I haven't seen him in over a week. Is he at home in Achill do you think? That's it, I'm off to Achill, ain't I?" She said, gleefully clapping her hands. After they had cut the cake and offered some to Maud, Dan and Annie were ready to drive her home to put her to bed. On her way out, she grasped Alice and Red by the hands and thanked them with tears in her eyes for their kindness in arranging to bring her home to Achill to meet up again with her Danny. Red tried to console Alice, saying that by the time they were on their way to the airport next day Maud would have forgotten all about it. And of course he was right. When Dan and Annie returned a little later, they were able to reassure everyone that Maud had gone happily to her night's rest having completely forgotten where she had just been. The party was a lovely mix of good food, great company, a few drinks, reminiscences, stories and yarns all rounded off by a great singsong. Looking about the crowded marquee Alice and Red were intrigued to see just how well their relatives and friends jelled. There was no one in the large group who was not in some way connected through The Patrick Gilraine Memorial Bereavement Counselling Service. Looking around now at the gathering they noticed that some of those present, though no doubt touched by the tragedy of Patrick's death, had never actually known him. It was, after all, fifteen years since the accident. For now, they should really be circulating among their guests and this they did, not separately as they were used to doing at functions, but as a couple as befitted the occasion.

Part IV
1978–1988

Chapter 24

Back to Brisbane

Dan had insisted on leaving them to the airport with all their bags and baggage. They were flying to New York in time to make their first transfer to Qantas Airways which would fly them direct to Darwin. From Darwin they would have to change again for the short hop to Brisbane. All in all they would be over thirty hours in the air including the two smaller journeys and the long haul flight. When they arrived in JFK airport, they went to the transfer lounge and discovered that they had only a short wait before boarding the Qantas flight. All of their baggage, with the exception of one small bag each, was stowed away, and then even their in-flight bags were spirited away to the lockers overhead their allocated seats. Red whispered to Alice that they were being treated like celebrities and better still were actually enjoying all the spoiling and the attention. Immediately on boarding they were brought glasses of champagne and nibbles. They toasted each other and felt like they were teenagers on honeymoon with the added advantage of having the maturity to fully appreciate it. At the outset of the journey, as it was approaching nightfall, the air hostesses encouraged everyone to try to sleep for a few hours. First they offered everyone a choice of drinks: cocoa, hot chocolate, consommé, tea or a range of alcoholic drinks to help them relax. Then blankets and pillows were distributed and after a while the cabin lights were doused. They were shown how to recline their seats and then, other than the sound of the engines, silence reigned. Most of the travellers managed to sleep even if not very soundly.

Later they were brought hot towels to refresh themselves with and served a delicious hot breakfast with tea or coffee. They chatted away easily for a while and then Alice tried to read her book for a bit while Red dozed off. Later on the cabin crew served dinner with a choice of wines after which most people napped again. They made their way in turns to the toilets and enjoyed the opportunity to stretch their legs. By now, they were all very tired of sitting. The remaining four hours eventually passed in anticipation of arrival, the monotony interrupted once again by yet another in-flight meal. When they landed in Darwin, they were pleased to discover that transfer for Brisbane was achieved with the minimum of fuss. All the discomfort and boredom of the journey was completely banished in the excitement of seeing friends for the first time in fourteen years. It had crossed Alice's mind that there might be some awkwardness when she'd meet Frank. She hoped that time would have buried the memory for him as it had for her.

To her relief the reunion was almost a replica of their greeting on their arrival in Brisbane all those years ago. Frank grabbed Red in a bear hug and she and Nora threw themselves into each other's arms in the warmest of embraces. Then, having greeted each other's spouses, they stood back to get a proper look at each other. Time had been kind to all of them while money and artifice had lent a helping hand to the women. Alice, despite the jet lag, was fashionably dressed and beautifully made up. Nora was as elegant as ever and, having retained her slim figure and poise, could have passed for a much younger woman. Alice, oozing sophistication and glamour, carried herself like the successful ambassador of a hugely successful organisation that she was. Red's crowning glory was as thick and luxuriant as ever though it had darkened with the years and had recently acquired a light dusting of grey. In the harsh lighting of the airport concourse, Frank appeared to have changed least of all. His wavy blond mane, his one vanity, was perfectly styled as always. It wasn't until they were outside in the bright sunlight heading towards the car that Alice realised with a pang that what she had taken to be golden locks were now in fact silver. Somehow this sign of aging caused her to see Frank more clearly and recognise the weak, vain, spoiled and insecure abandoned little boy at his core. With that realisation she was at last able to get closure on what had happened in Dewey Street on that crazy January day. She was relieved and a little chagrined that Frank appeared to have completely forgotten the incident. Now at last she could forgive him as well as herself for what could have been the ruination of them all.

As they made their way from the airport to the O Neills' home in Emmingham, the conversation was brisk and lively with constant interruptions so they could admire the myriad changes in the cityscape since they'd last seen Brisbane. It was hard to believe that what was no bigger than a large provincial town in 1962 had flourished and developed into a bustling city in the intervening years. For their first day, the O Neills had kindly arranged a light meal for just Red, Alice and themselves and Daisy. So they had plenty of time to catch up in a relaxed and easy fashion. Alice and Red were thrilled to meet up again with their god-daughter and were delighted that they had the luxury of meeting her in her own home. They agreed later in the privacy of their bedroom that both of them would have passed her by in the street without recognising her. Nothing, not their frequent correspondence with her parents, not their constant exchanges by letter and by phone with herself, not even the letters from dear Eda until her death, could have prepared them for the beauty who right now was sitting across from them at the lunch table.

Daisy had blossomed from an ordinary, somewhat gangly, seventeen year old into an attractive, poised young woman with quiet confidence. Since she had first entered into her friendship with Eda Hogan, Daisy had fallen in love with books. To begin with reading was just a refuge for her. It proved a most effective escape from her unrequited love for Patrick and also from the loneliness of losing her cousin and best friend Lily when the Gilraines moved to America. After Patrick had died so tragically even reading proved poor consolation for Daisy in her desolation. She could sit for hours on end staring at the same page of text and not absorb one word of it. Eventually, Eda came to her rescue by persuading her to help her set up the young adults' literacy programme and with reading to the residents at St Anne's Haven. They both appreciated Alice's gift to them on her departure, the beginnings of a mutually beneficial, deep and lasting friendship. Eda's love of literature had influenced Daisy from the start. Following her example and devoting her life to the library service, did not manifest itself for quite a few years. When she outlined her plan to her parents in her final year at school, neither Nora nor Frank knew what advice to offer. In the end, after discussion with Alice and Red, they agreed that Daisy was probably best placed to decide her own future and should be encouraged to follow her dream. Having qualified with a degree in librarianship she had gone on to do her Master's before returning to become Head of Library Studies at the University of Brisbane. As part of her very busy and satisfying job, she occasionally did radio and television lectures and had become quite a celebrity locally. Her parents were very proud of her achievements but it was not in their nature to boast about her success. Her godparents had no such reservations and made no secret of their pride in her.

Well refreshed after a good night's sleep, they sat over a late breakfast discussing the plans for the next few days. They were anxious at some point in their eight week stay to undertake three projects. One was to take a trip to the Gold

Coast to see the sights and the second was to make their way to either Melbourne or Sydney and visit The Patrick Gilraine Memorial Bereavement Counselling Service offices there. First they wanted to visit the last resting place of Eda Hogan. Other than that they were not overly concerned about travelling and were happy to leave the organisation of such matters to their friends. The O Neills were delighted to help with their itinerary and advised leaving the Gold Coast trip to closer to the end of their stay as the weather would be more suitable then, or so they said. The trip to the cemetery could be done at any time as it was actually within walking distance of the house.

In a strange manifestation of déjà vu, Red and Alice found themselves the following Saturday night at a formal dinner in, of all places, the Kelly mansion in Emmingham. Here it was, in the home of Bob and Lisa, that they had been welcomed to Brisbane in 1948. It was the Kellys who had hosted a farewell party for them fourteen years later. On this occasion, it was a fundraising dinner for a charity dear to the hearts of the Kellys and their friends the O Neills, The Patrick Gilraine Memorial Bereavement Counselling Service. Frank and Nora had deliberately kept secret the identity of the friends who were to accompany them to the fundraiser and needless to mention the Gilraines were also kept in the dark regarding the details of the event. Daisy insisted on driving them over and as she had dropped them at the imposing gateway it wasn't until they had walked up the tree-lined driveway that Red and Alice realised where they were.

The ugly house had aged well and looked more imposing and less in-your-face now that the landscaping had matured around it. Meeting Bob and Lisa was a bit of a shock, however. The Kellys had aged badly to put it mildly. Bob had let himself go and the man who greeted Red and Alice now was completely unrecognisable. Except for the voice and perhaps something residual in the eyes he could have been an absolute stranger. He appeared shorter or maybe it was his huge girth that dwarfed his height. He was almost grotesquely obese, his shiny bald head emerging from his thick, short, wrinkled and bull-like neck. For some reason, he had chosen a white tuxedo rather than the more flattering black. To Alice he looked like a pallid, swollen toad. Lisa, in contrast, was thin to the point of emaciation. Her beautiful fashionable ball gown hung shroud-like from her bony shoulders. Her gaunt face was cadaverous and deeply scored from too much exposure to the sun and the ravages of anorexia nervosa. Now was not the time for asking questions.

After the excitement of the greetings and a little chatter they had to move down the reception line towards the dining room. Word had been swiftly passed to the organisers and immediately Alice and Red were shown to the head table as guests of honour. Nora and Frank were discreetly guided towards the bar and invited to have a pre-prandial cocktail while extra places were set for them also at the top table. The dinner was very well attended and Alice made a very professional, enthusiastic and motivational speech when requested. The local organisers were thrilled to meet the founders as well as the sponsors of the charity and were very pleased with the success of the event and the amount of money raised.

Chapter 25

Lily

Dust motes danced in the ray of sunshine that illuminated the otherwise darkened office of Attorney Lily Gilraine. She had been sitting at her large, oak antique kneehole director's desk nursing a severe headache for at least an hour. Through the waves of pain she was vaguely aware of muffled sounds penetrating the plush and luxurious silence of her professional cocoon. It took a few moments for her to understand exactly where she was. She had never viewed her sanctuary from this particular angle before. She was on her side, her face pressed into the deep pile of her very expensive mushroom coloured carpet without any idea of how she had got there or even how long she had been lying there. The stiletto ray of sunlight she was staring at had infiltrated the space through the tiniest of slits at the edge of the tight fitting black-out blinds she had had fitted to her office window. Over the past year and a half she had been suffering with infrequent, savagely painful migraine attacks from which her only relief was deep impenetrable darkness.

When she felt able to, she got slowly to her feet and went to investigate how the light had managed to creep in. She was relieved to find that it was not a question of shoddy workmanship. The blind had just temporarily snagged on the cord. She released the cord and the room was immediately plunged into perfect blackness. She felt her way back to her desk and, closing her eyes, switched on her angle-poise reading lamp. Slowly she opened her eyelids, allowing her eyes to adjust to the muted light. When she had managed this feat without too much pain, she knew she was ready to face the rest of her busy day. When she first started to get these cripplingly debilitating headaches, she worried about cerebral haemorrhaging. Despite the agony and the worry, she couldn't face the notion of being poked and prodded at the hospital. Worse, she shrank from the invasive questions she knew she would be subjected to. When it came to her medical history, she had none. Of her birth parents she knew absolutely nothing and she was well aware that her adoptive parents knew nothing either. She hated the idea of strangers involving themselves in her private business. She wanted also to spare her parents being quizzed about the circumstances of her adoption on another continent more than a quarter of a century earlier and half a world away.

After a couple of months when there didn't seem to be much chance of the headaches disappearing of their own accord she decided to confide in Susan. When all was said and done other than her parents Susan was the closest to family Lily had ever known. Not only were they best friends, Susan was also best qualified to reassure her. Professional as always, Susan declined to diagnose. She did recommend, however, a good neurological expert to whom she referred Lily. These health concerns and the subsequent introspection brought all of Lily's insecurities to the surface again. Adopting her usual strategy when faced with any problem of a personal nature, she threw herself headlong into her work. She worked longer hours and added pro bono work to her already overloaded schedule. Her excuse for this frenetic busyness was that she had planned a two week trip to Australia at the end of August. The reality was she was running away from her own thoughts.

Focusing on pleasing her parents had always been the central tenet of her existence. Her self-image, her self-esteem, indeed her very sense of self, was bound up in being the successful lawyer who would make Red and Alice proud. She couldn't countenance any sign of failure or weakness in herself as this would inevitably threaten her sense of well-being. The fear that some manifestation of less than perfect health would emerge from her less than perfect Australian bloodlines did not bear thinking about. The combination of over-stretching herself and the underlying worry was not conducive to a stress free existence and certainly was not likely to reduce the frequency or severity of her migraines. Watching out for her friend, Susan feared that at the last minute Lily would pull out of the trip down under. She was determined not to let this happen even if it meant having to physically put her on the plane. It didn't quite come to that. Susan did end up driving her to the airport.

By the time Lily arrived in Brisbane, she had had plenty of opportunity to clear her mind and leave all her work cares and problems behind. She fairly bounced off the flight and was thrilled to be met at the arrivals area by her parents and her cousin Daisy as well. She was over-awed at the changes in the city. In the way of young people, she welcomed all these changes as signs of positive progress. She ate a light meal with her mum and dad and the O Neills and they filled her in on the planned trip to the Gold Coast.

Afterwards the two young women felt that they could do with a walk and killing several birds with the one stone they walked to the cemetery so Lily could pay her respects to Eda. Then, as it was such a balmy evening, they walked a little further to Quay Street where they joined some of Daisy's friends for a few drinks outside a friendly little pub frequented by young professionals. The pub was comfortably busy on this summery Thursday evening so they spent a while in good company before walking home.

A few days later the three Gilraines and the three O Neills were seated around a table in the shade of a parasol on the beach sipping cool cocktails and enjoying the afternoon sunshine in Southport. Earlier that day they had driven down the sixty miles or so from Brisbane to Rainbow Bay. The elders were driven by Frank while Daisy was delighted to drive her cousin. They had booked into one of the beautiful beachside hotels. Rainbow Bay nestles between Greenmount Hill and Snapper Rocks and sports arguably the most spectacular of the Gold Coast's best beaches. The beach is shaded from the worst excesses of the sun by stands of pine and pandanus trees. It is a popular resort for young and old, families and children, sun lovers and swimmers and surfers of every sort from the raw beginner to the competitively successful adventurer. The two families were delighted to be here for a number of reasons, chief of which was the opportunity to take in some whale watching. The O Neills had enjoyed the awesome sight of humpback whales frolicking close to them in the white waters of the bay on several occasions in previous years. They never tired of the sight. They equally loved the ambiance of the resort, the flawless weather, the swimming and the surfing as well as the chance to soak up the rays on the soft and shimmering sand. They couldn't resist the idea of sharing this holiday idyll with their oldest friends. They had every confidence that the two young women would also enjoy themselves enormously with the variety of activities and the gathering of so many people of their own age.

Chapter 26
The Quest Begins

On the return journey to Brisbane, Alice decided to travel with Daisy and Lily. In the course of the journey, while Daisy was busily occupied at petrol pumps Lily asked her mother if she or Red would have any objection to her seeking information on her birth parents over their remaining few days in Brisbane. Alice was taken aback but did her best to respond in an even tone which belied her immediate agitation. "No problem, Lily, as far as I'm concerned. I'll have a word with your dad tonight. I'm not hugely hopeful, love, that you'll find out very much. Try not to be too disappointed if that is the case, darling. As far as your dad and I are concerned, you are our one and only best loved daughter and we couldn't be more proud of you."

Later that night Red took Lily aside and in similar words gave her his blessing to begin her search. Starting the very next morning Lily, accompanied by Alice, made her way to Jacaranda Street where they expected to find St Michael's Orphanage. Their errand was to enquire after Sister Francis and perhaps check birth records for Christmas Day 1951. When they arrived in Jacaranda Street, they were surprised to find no trace of an orphanage. What they did find was a large red brick building which had the appearance that it might have perhaps been a convent in a previous existence. They entered by the main door and approached the reception desk of what was now obviously a suite of offices where Lily, feeling rather foolish, asked the receptionist if the building had once been a convent or maybe an orphanage. The twenty-something receptionist looked blankly at Lily. Then, shrugging her shoulders, said nonchalantly, "I'm only here a few months so how in heaven's name would I know and anyway I'm not even from around here."

At this point, Alice approached the desk and asked politely if she might use the phone. She returned a few minutes later and said to Lily, "Come on, love, let's go." Then, smiling her thanks to the receptionist, she made for the door. Once outside, she explained that they really should have told Nora what they had planned for the day. "I've just rung her now and she's on her way to the Alexander Hotel to meet us. I should have remembered that Nora was the one who introduced us to Sister Francis in the first instance. And if we were thinking straight, she or Daisy are also the obvious people to talk to about buildings in Brisbane." A little while later they arrived at the hotel to find Nora waiting for them. The first thing Nora said was that Daisy had gone into her office to see what information she could dig up on the building in Jacaranda Street. She would pick them up in half an hour and drive them out to Nudgee Beach to St Vincent's Orphanage in the Northgate ward of north Brisbane. Meanwhile, she suggested that they should have coffee while they waited and draw up a sensible list of what else they might do should their visit to Nudgee prove unsuccessful.

Not long afterwards they heard the toot of a car horn and they joined Daisy. On the drive out to Nudgee, she was able to tell them that the building on Jacaranda Street had indeed been a convent in earlier years. It had closed in the early 1950s when the Sisters of Mercy resident there had moved out either to St Vincent's or else to a smaller house recently set up in the inner city. She had no information as to the identity of the sisters who moved at the time. Her best guess was that Sister Francis would have gone back to St Vincent's. When they arrived in Nudgee, unfortunately they hit a snag. Sister Francis had indeed moved back to Nudgee but not until 1965. Where she had lived after leaving Jacaranda Street and before turning up again in St Vincent's was unclear.

The women were welcomed and ushered into a carpeted and austerely furnished parlour where they were soon joined by a tall middle aged nun who introduced herself as mother superior of the complex. Her initial reception was reasonably warm and she seemed happy enough to talk about Sister Francis who she described as a saintly and deeply devout woman. She then explained that the dear sister had passed to her eternal reward the previous October and even offered to show them the final resting place of the dear departed. When Lily raised the question of viewing the records of the orphanage, things cooled dramatically. Suddenly Reverend Mother was extremely busy and needed to rush off to deal with an urgent matter. She excused herself and hurried off, leaving the four women looking at each other and wondering what had just happened. They waited a while and when it became obvious that the nun had no intention of returning they eventually rang the bell for attention. This time two formidable older nuns appeared and explained that no such records existed. Whatever information Sister Francis may or may not have had that would be of interest or relevance to the four women would have died with her, they insisted. When they asked about visiting Sr. Francis' grave, the two nuns expressed absolute horror at the idea. It was unheard of for lay people to enter a convent graveyard. Such a thing would be utterly impossible. Ever the pragmatist, Nora moved them away as quickly as possible; after all, there was nothing to be learned here.

Back in the car Nora said, "There has to be some other way of accessing the information we need. It is obvious that the nuns are following instructions from somewhere so asking questions of them is a waste of time. First we need to establish who is issuing the orders and why. I suggest we start at Bishop's House. Let's go there right now. Surprise is always a good idea when you want answers to tricky questions or even if you want to ask questions of tricky people. Do you mind if just Lily and I go into the lion's den? We don't want to frighten the dear old man now, do we?" Alice and Daisy sat in the car and waited while the others went inside the bishop's palace. They were relieved at first and pleased that at least Nora and Lily had been invited in. As time passed, they began to wonder what was going on. After they had been sitting in the car for three quarters of an hour they decided to take a walk and stretch their legs. So they paced the roadway opposite the bishop's palatial residence up and down for twenty minutes or more. When they tired of walking in the sun, they moved the car to a spot in the shade and continued to wait.

Eventually, Nora and Lily reappeared. They too had spent a good deal of time waiting before his Lordship Bishop Murphy agreed to grace them with his presence. Then he had insisted on having them join him in an elegant afternoon tea in the course of which he entertained them most graciously. When they got around to their errand, he smilingly told them that unfortunately details of orphanage records were completely outside of his remit and that he couldn't access information even if he had wanted to. Nora persisted and, using their earlier experience at St Vincent's as an illustration, pressed His Lordship to explain why the nuns were being deliberately unhelpful and indeed downright obstructive. His Lordship objected to Nora's choice of language and a heated exchange ensued. Eventually, having turned on the charm again, he told them that they were wasting their time as it was the policy of Catholic orphanages worldwide not to keep detailed birth records. When Lily asked if she should try to trace her parentage through State of Queensland birth certification records, he latched onto the idea with obvious relief. What he must have known and had chosen not to share with them was that in the absence of all relevant detail this task would prove impossible.

He knew, too, that the church's policy was specifically designed to prevent people such as Lily from tracing their parents. How could you search the records without the names of either parent? They did not have even the mother's forename, never mind her surname. As for the father, they had no details whatsoever. The sum total of the information they had was Lily's own date of birth and the fact that her birth mother had been brought up in St Vincent's Orphanage. Bishop Murphy was quite comfortable in the knowledge that the anonymity of the couple who had given their daughter away would continue to be preserved. He had no conscience whatsoever that he had sent Lily on what he knew to be a wild goose chase. He never gave a second thought to her side of the story. He had no idea and, worse still, no care for the fact that Lily and thousands like her had been deprived of their heritage, their cultural background, their health history, their extended family or even their sense of identity. What the good bishop, in his blinkered and self-righteous view, hadn't bargained for was the determination to get to the truth of the women he had so cavalierly fobbed off. And so he had set them on an arduous and agonisingly frustrating journey which would last for years and years and extend long past the date of his own demise. In the car on their way back to the O Neills', the women were not unhappy with their day's work. Lily, with Daisy's assistance, would take it from here and see what they could uncover before the Gilraines' return to Rochester at the end of the week. Over the next couple of days the two young women were very busy. They spent a number of hours in the library researching. In different combinations, all four women traipsed around to all the Mercy convents in the Brisbane area trying to find either Sister Joseph or Sister Anthony. They felt that if these good ladies could be located they might be able to cast some light on the story. They might even remember some vital piece of new information or be able to recall some salient detail to set Lily on the right track. Unfortunately, by the time Thursday came they had had no luck in locating either of the nuns and the Gilraines were already on their way back to the States by nightfall of the same day. Their abrupt and early departure was not by choice but sadly necessitated by the death of Maud Sweetman. She had been in perfectly good health and great form when she bade farewell to Lily less than two weeks earlier. The previous weekend her ninety-seven-year-old body had finally let her down and she had slipped into a coma. She had passed peacefully away on Tuesday night. They were lucky enough to get flights home a few days early in order to be in time for the removal and funeral of Alice's mother.

Despite her longevity, the death of Maud Sweetman signalled the end of an era for her children, her surviving grandchildren and her great grandchildren. All of her sons and daughters, with the exception of Mary (Sister Consilio), were able to attend her funeral. The passing of their mother brought home to them all just how old they had become. Suddenly they were aware that as they were all now in their late fifties they were no longer young, indeed they were well past middle age. It was a matter of some surprise and a good deal of comment among them how much Maud had influenced all their lives since she had moved to America sixteen years earlier. After all, she had already been suffering from senile dementia even then. Strangely her condition had not worsened significantly over the years. There was no doubt that she had used her formidable intelligence to overcome the stroke damage. What vocabulary she had lost she strove to recover and when that failed she patiently learned alternative ways of saying things rather than wasting time on what she recognised were words forever lost to what the medics referred to in their fancy terminology as 'nominal aphasia'. She had also learned very early on to make the most of the hand of cards she had been dealt and to face forward with positivity and good humour. Her strong Catholic faith was also a huge support to her in adjusting to her new life in America. Apart from an occasional lapse, such as when she mistook her niece Nora for her sister Sibby, Maud had led an almost normal life in her latter years. She had been a wonderful grandmother and a much-loved great grandmother. She had been part of all their lives for so long that it was only when she was gone that they realised just how much they would miss her.

As soon as the burial was over and everyone was back at work, Lily returned to the task of trying to trace her roots with a vengeance. She was obsessed with her need to find out all she could and as soon as humanly possible. Every waking hour was occupied in researching, making phone calls and writing letters. She was also spending a fortune on sometimes daily international phone calls to check on progress with Daisy.

After all this time and disappointment after disappointment with still no trace of either Sister Joseph or Sister Anthony emerging in Brisbane, there was finally a small glimmer of possible light. Something in the newspaper one day resulted in a conversation where someone mentioned in Frank O Neill's presence that of late changes in the rules in convents had resulted in some elderly Irish nuns being allowed to retire to the land of their birth. That evening during supper he said, "Nora and Daisy, did ye ever think of checking whether either of the nuns ye are looking for might no longer be in Australia? As they're both Irish, maybe they were allowed to go back to Ireland. Sister Anthony would be retired by now but Sister Joseph could be young enough to be still teaching. It might be worth a try anyway, don't you think?"

Nora was excited at the thought and immediately got on the phone to Alice. After talking it over Alice had the brainwave that rather than having to write to every Mercy convent in Ireland she could short circuit the process by writing to her sister Mary Sweetman, now Sister Consilio, currently domiciled in the convent at Ivymount a few miles from Nenagh in County Tipperary. In one of those odd twists of fate that causes people to declare 'truth is stranger than fiction', a few days after Alice had dispatched her letter to the Mercy convent in Ivymount, she had a welcome phone call. A very excited Sister Consilio was on the line with the great news that not only had Sister Joseph returned to Ireland she was actually resident in the convent in Ivymount. Right now she was still at school. If Alice cared to ring back in a few hours, she would be able to talk directly to Sister Joseph herself.

Later, having spoken with the nun, Alice had to share the heart-breaking news to Lily that they were no further ahead with their search. Sister Joseph had absolutely nothing to offer. It was now 1981 and three years into the search Lily was as far away as ever from the information she needed. By now, she had become so absorbed in her obsessive need to pursue her search that she couldn't give up even had she wanted to. Besides, unknown to anyone else, she now had an even more pressing reason than ever for pursuing her quest.

Then after a further eighteen months of frustration and several more dead ends and false alarms, out of the blue one day Nora had a phone call. "Hello, Nora, I don't suppose you can guess who this is? Maree McNamara here, Maree Nolan that was."

"Oh my God, Maree, I'd know that voice anywhere. How wonderful to hear you. How's Shay? And how are the girls? Tell me all your news. By the way, where are you ringing from?"

It transpired that she was ringing from Brisbane and was delighted to meet up with Nora even for a quick cup of coffee, preferably today. They had not met in over thirty years. They had kept in touch especially at Christmas over all that time. Maree had settled very well in County Clare surrounded by Shay's family who had taken to her immediately and loved her for her outgoing and warm personality and especially for her obvious devotion to their Shay. She and Shay had never been back to Australia until now. One of the reasons for the trip now was a celebration of their thirty-fourth wedding anniversary and a more relevant one was to visit their younger daughter. Francesca was anxious for her parents and her twin sister Norella to meet her Aussie fiancé, Peter Armstrong. Francesca had moved to Melbourne about four years prior and despite Maree's repeated suggestions that she look up the O Neills if she ever got to Brisbane this hadn't happened to date. Even though Peter's people were from Salisbury only a twenty minute drive from Emmingham this was Francesca's first visit to these parts. After they had met up and had copious amounts of coffee Nora insisted on returning with Maree to the hotel and collecting Shay and Norella and bringing them back to Emmingham where they would have a meal together with Frank and Daisy and catch up on the rest of the news. Later they would all go to meet Francesca and Peter for drinks.

The evening was a great success. As is the way with strong friendships, Nora and Maree slipped comfortably into conversation as if the interruption were a matter of a mere number of hours instead of decades. Frank and Shay were equally comfortable in each other's company and Daisy immediately took Norella under her wing. While the older couples were busy chatting Daisy took Norella on a tour of the house, pointing out where her parents' wedding had taken place and ending up in what used to be the play room when Daisy was young. In recent years, Frank had made over the bulk of the basement area as a self-contained apartment where Daisy now lived. Here she could entertain her friends and have her privacy while still living in the parental home. She had her own study, a kitchen/dining room, bathroom, bedroom and guest bedroom. The play room had been tastefully converted to a generous living room. It was here that Nora and Maree found the two young women poring over old photograph albums when it was time for them to go out. The meeting with Peter went very well and before the night was out the McNamaras' holiday plans included all four of them staying with the O Neills for the next few days.

In the course of the following days, the subject of the Gilraines' visit a few years previously came up. This led, among other things, to an overnight visit to Southport on the Gold Coast being organised. While relaxing by the shore after a most enjoyable shellfish dinner the conversation turned to the last occasion the O Neills had been here in the company of Red, Alice and Lily. Inevitably the question of Lily's as yet unsuccessful quest came up. Maree was fascinated and straight away got stuck in asking dozens of questions and tripping over herself in her eagerness to understand what precisely had been found out to date. "Where did ye start? Did ye track down Sister Francis? Sister Anthony? What about Sister Joseph? What was the name of the doctor? Did ye find him? Come on, Nora, bring us up to date as quickly as you can."

They sat late into the night as Nora, with occasional help from Daisy, told Maree and the rest of the McNamaras all about the ups and downs of the saga to the present day. The following morning, despite the fact that she had hardly slept a wink, Maree was still full of enthusiastic ideas about how to move the quest on. She had been mulling over the details all night and dredging her memory. The only straw worth grasping at was a memory she had that Sister Francis and Sister Anthony had been very close. If there was any chance of Sister Francis ever confiding in anyone, that someone would have been Sister Anthony? When Nora reminded her that they had failed to find any trace of her in either Australia or in Ireland, she asked for the sources of their information. When she heard that Sister Joseph was the main source in Ireland, she became thoughtful.

Eventually, she said, "In view of the fact that Sister Joseph is our only source and the fact that I never altogether trusted that woman, I think that perhaps a visit to her convent might be in order. I'll bet my bottom dollar that she knows something about Sister Anthony that she's not telling you. And Sister

Anthony is the only possible link to Lily's past now that Sister Francis is dead. By the way, what does Lily look like now? Her mother always talked about her as if she were Grace Kelly, Elizabeth Taylor and the Virgin Mary all rolled into one."

"Maree, have you never seen an adult photo of Lily? Alice was not exaggerating, Lily is stunningly gorgeous. She really is the most breathtakingly beautiful, young woman you have ever seen. Anyway, as soon as we get back home you can see for yourself. I've loads of photos from their visit." Later that night, after looking at a wide range of both professional photographs and amateur snapshots of Lily taken over the thirty years of her life, Maree made a selection of four particular poses. She asked Nora if she could hold on to them for a while so she could study them more closely. She was stunned at the rush of memories occasioned by the familiarity of the face in the photos, especially the arresting eyes. The images were not really clear enough for her to be sure she wanted to raise anyone's hopes on what was, after all, only an unproven speculation. Nora and Maree wasted no time in filling Norella and Daisy in on what they thought the next steps should be.

Chapter 27

The Quest Continues

Before leaving Australia Maree had talked a lot to Nora and quizzed her in particular about Lily's unusual eyes. From Nora's description Maree was convinced that she herself had seen such eyes before. She did not share with anyone then her hope that she might hold the key to a possible connection between her memory and Lily which could lead them closer to a solution of the conundrum of Lily's heritage. So, hugging the possibility to herself, she prayed for a successful ending to the story.

As soon as Maree arrived home in Dromelton, in County Clare, she rang Alice to try to persuade her that she should arrange for herself and Lily to come to Ireland as soon as possible. Alice was happy to confirm that all three of the Gilraines had already made the necessary arrangements and would be flying into Shannon Airport in a little over three weeks. They were scheduled to arrive at 07.30 a.m. of June 3rd, 1984. It was agreed that Maree would meet them off the flight and that they would stay with the McNamaras for at least a week, during which it was to be hoped they would manage to get some information from the reticent Sister Joseph.

Alice had been in contact with Sister Consilio before leaving Rochester but no firm time or date had been agreed. There was an expectation that they would be visiting the convent in Ivymount during the course of their visit. Maree was adamant that it would be best if they could manage to meet with Sister Joseph without any prior warning. She was convinced that the element of surprise would be a useful ally in any dealings they would have with the nun. Maree explained that when they were in St Vincent's all those years ago, the two older nuns, Sister Francis and Sister Anthony, were very popular with all the girls. This was no accident as each nun in her own way had a heart of gold. In a system, that of its very nature was overly strict and unnecessarily severe, these two were the only ones who showed any humanity to the children in their care. They modelled loving behaviour and understanding and encouraged the older girls to behave sympathetically to the younger ones. While Maree and her friend Frances appreciated how lucky they were to have the good sisters in their lives it was not until their latter years that they realised just how lucky they had been. It was only much later that they realised that the two nuns were not as popular with their sisters in religion as they were with the children. The older nuns did not approve of their kindness and some of the younger ones were, believe it or not, jealous of them and the esteem and love in which they were held by the girls. To begin with when the younger Sister Joseph started to follow them about, simpering and hanging on their every word, the girls thought that she too loved the older nuns. It took Maree and Frances quite a while to realise that the constant presence of Sister Joseph wherever the other two were was perhaps not as innocent as they had at first thought. Eventually, they came to the conclusion that Sister Joseph had been sent to spy on her colleagues. They had discovered for a fact that she was reporting back to her superiors any tiny deviations from the rules that either sister turned a blind eye to. She also eavesdropped shamelessly on them when they thought they were alone and their conversations too were reported back.

More and more often as time went by Sister Francis and Sister Anthony seemed to be in trouble with their mother superior.

Certainly, they appeared to be involved in an inordinate number of punishing and menial tasks. These tasks were to be undertaken alone and never together. It looked like they were doing a lot of penance too. They didn't complain. It was part of their vocation after all. They had taken vows of obedience, poverty and chastity in good faith. As caring human beings, they had always tried to bring solace to the afflicted, comfort to the lonely and loving care to the abandoned. They had also undertaken not to have what were called 'exclusive friendships' with any other nun. Both were genuinely shocked when they were accused of breaking this rule. As far as they were concerned, the fact that they worked together necessitated a good deal of discussion. They never spoke of their own feelings or worries; their focus was entirely and rightly on the children in their care. Their reactions to the shock of the accusation were poles apart, however.

Sister Francis, in her innocence, did not understand what the big deal was. She apologised immediately and tried to see it from her superiors' viewpoint. She tried to justify their perception to Sister Anthony by saying that from the outside looking in no one could possibly know what they talked about and after all they did work together an awful lot.

Sister Anthony, being more streetwise, was perfectly well aware of what they were really being accused. She burned at the injustice of the accusation and hated the idea that some twisted mind could harbour suspicions of misconduct on the part of the blameless Sister Francis. She had been aware for some time that they were being watched and was disgusted that such underhand tricks could be used in a convent and, worse, were approved of from on high. It had never ever crossed her mind that there was or could be anything inappropriate in her relationship with Sister Francis. Now all she wanted to do was to protect her from the taint of evil attaching to the accusation.

It rocked her to the very core of her being and caused her for the first time in her twenty-three years of religious life to doubt her own vocation. Here she was at forty-one years of age seriously considering bailing out. First she prayed about it long and hard. Then she willingly undertook all the punishments, not because she was guilty of anything but out of solidarity with Sister Francis. Besides, she needed time to think through her next move; after all, twenty-three years was not just a long time, it also represented a huge level of commitment to being a bride of Christ.

Around this time two of the older girls were about to leave St Vincent's, the only home they had ever known. Maree Nolan was taking up a place on a mother craft course in Berry Street College and Frances Brennan was going to enrol in drama school in the city centre. They were sixteen years old and setting out to realise their dreams. Sister Francis had made all the arrangements for Maree, having recognised her obvious suitability for such work. Sister Anthony, recognising in Frances the combination of ambition and talent coupled with stunning good looks which would guarantee her success on the stage, reluctantly helped her on her way into this precarious world. She hoped and prayed that she would be safe and find her niche and thought that with proper training Frances would stand a better chance of success.

At first, they all kept in touch regularly and frequently. As the young women got more absorbed in their busy lives, their letters to the nuns grew more sporadic. By the time the girls were nearing twenty, the correspondence had dwindled to occasional exchanges at Christmas, feast days and birthdays.

Then suddenly Frances disappeared without a trace. When Maree wanted to share with her best friend that she had met the love of her life and failed to get any information from her friend's last address, she made her way to Nudgee at the first possible opportunity. On arrival at the orphanage, Maree was shown into the parlour where she awaited impatiently the arrival of Sister Francis and Sister Anthony. After what seemed ages the door opened and Sister Francis was ushered in by Sister Joseph. When Maree enquired, she was told by Sister Joseph that Sister Anthony no longer lived there. When she asked for an address, this request was coldly refused. Her enquiries regarding the whereabouts of Frances were equally futile.

Maree left the orphanage for the last time feeling sad and upset and more than a little suspicious that she had been lied to. She was also concerned that Sister Francis was imprisoned there. When she wrote to her, subsequently she was very circumspect as she suspected that her letters were being censored before being delivered to her friend. She wondered if some of the letters were ever delivered at all.

She was understandably thrilled therefore when they both turned up at her wedding even if they were chaperoned by the inimical Sister Joseph. Despite the frenetic nature of her big day, Maree had managed to have a private word with Sister Anthony who whispered that unfortunately she would be leaving the order in the near future and would more than likely be forbidden to keep in touch with Maree. Her only possibility of keeping in touch with Sister Francis after her departure would be through Sister Joseph. They were both aware that this arrangement was far from ideal but accepted that it was better than the alternative which was no communication at all.

Now over thirty-three years later, Maree divulged this information for the first time. She shared it with Alice, Lily and Red in the comfort of her country kitchen on the farm in Dromelton. What she kept to herself at this point was her growing conviction that Sister Francis would have come to the aid of Frances Brennan and most probably did if Frances had got herself 'in trouble'.

The former Sister Anthony, if she were still alive, would now be seventy-five years old. Sister Joseph, whom they would meet in the next few days, would be sixty or maybe sixty-one.

That night they decided that there was no point in delaying any longer and as the weather was glorious and school holidays just beginning they would head for Ivymount the following morning, June 5th. Alice had a little bit of a conscience about not giving her sister Mary/Sister Consilio some notice but agreed that it was for the best. They left early in the hope of finding both nuns at home. When they arrived in the village, the church bells were ringing for Mass so they slipped into the back pew from where they were able to watch unobserved as both Sister Consilio and Sister Joseph worshipped close to the altar.

As soon as Mass was over and they emerged into the sunny morning, Alice ran to hug her sister whom she had not seen in nearly forty years. Maree greeted Sister Joseph and then Red introduced Lily to her aunt and the other nun. Sister Joseph tried to slip away, saying this should be family time. Maree was not about to be shaken off so easily. The compromise was that all six of them withdrew to the nearby convent garden. Sister Consilio sat with her family around a picnic table and Maree went for a walk with Sister Joseph. After a short while, as planned, Lily went to join the other two in their perambulations. She was just in time to hear the nun say, "I've no idea where Sister Anthony is; I haven't seen nor heard from her in nearly forty years."

Maree took issue with this statement, reminding her that they had both attended her marriage to Shay in January 1951 thirty-four years ago. At this, Sister Joseph objected and said she had no intention of remaining in Maree's company one second longer to be harangued and argued with. Maree apologised immediately and tried to placate the angry nun by drawing Lily into the conversation. Turning to Sister Joseph, Lily said, "Sister, it is extremely important for us to try to contact Sister Anthony. We have tried every other avenue and she is our only possible link with the history of my birth. It is not on an idle whim or to satisfy my curiosity that I need this information. This could turn out to be a matter of life or death for me. I'm sorry to have to put it so baldly, Sister, but I am very, very ill. The doctors cannot seem to be able to identify what is the matter with me. Of one thing they are certain and that is that without a medical history they are seeking the proverbial needle in a haystack. This search was never about causing upset to either the Sisters of Mercy or the people whose identity they were trying to protect. Looking for any detail of my birth parents is relevant only in the context of prolonging my life. My adoptive parents are not aware of how ill I am and are only helping me in my quest because I have told them that it is important to me. If there is anything at all you could tell us, that would help us to trace Sister Anthony I beg of you please let us know before it is too late."

Shortly after this conversation Sister Consilio went to organise some tea and refreshments. At this point, Maree rejoined Alice and Red at the table, leaving Lily alone with Sister Joseph. When Sister Consilio returned with a laden tray, the other nun went indoors. Lily returned to the group in a very despondent state. Though Sister Joseph appeared to have softened somewhat Lily wasn't hopeful. She couldn't help feeling that the nun was being economical with the truth and, having maintained her story for so long, was unlikely to change it now.

After the morning tea Sister Consilio cleared it with her sister superior that she could take her visitors out and show them some of the local sights. They drove out of the village a short distance and parked the car. They started to climb through a woodland area, emerging halfway up a ridge with the beautiful valley stretching below. They could see Keeper Hill rising majestically behind them. Sister Consilio loved this area and was delighted to point out its beauties and fill her relations in on some of the local lore and history of this wonderful place. She told them all about Patrick Sarsfield and how he had saved Limerick city from being sacked when he had intercepted the siege train of the Williamite army in 1690. Returning to the car an hour and a half later, she was still talking excitedly about the beauty of the area which she admitted had been a great consolation to her when she was lonely for her native Achill in the early days of her convent life.

When Red proposed finding some place nice for lunch, no one argued. At Sister's suggestion, they followed Sarsfield's Ride for a bit heading for Portroe where they turned onto lakeshore drive to the lookout point above Lough Derg. Here they enjoyed the breath-taking views over the lake with Holy Island and its ruined churches and round tower. They could see occasional anglers standing on the lake's eastern shore below and others on the opposite edge in County Clare. They watched the mixture of lake craft on the lake, small row boats with fishermen aboard and sailboats and some yachts with elegant sails of different colours gliding gracefully in either direction. At the height of the tourist season, there were plenty of lake cruisers of various sizes making their way in and out of the marina in Killaloe to their left. Later they drove down to Garrykennedy where they had a delicious seafood lunch on the veranda of a wonderfully welcoming and well run restaurant. On their way back to Ivymount, all agreed that it had been a wonderfully enjoyable day out.

On her arrival, as Sister Consilio was getting out of the car, Sister Joseph rushed towards her with a letter in her hand. She spoke hurriedly, "Sister, will you please give this letter to your niece? Tell her and all of them that it contains all that I can tell about the matter. I have no further information. I do not ever want to hear another word about it. Please make them understand that I will never refer to it again and make them promise not to ask anything further of me. As far as I am concerned, this is the end of the matter." Everyone was surprised at this turn of events and wanted to thank Sister Joseph for changing her mind. "Just read the letter and leave me alone," said the nun brusquely before hurrying away. Lily couldn't contain herself and immediately opened the missive which read as follows:

Ivymount
June 5 1982

Sister Anthony left the convent and the congregation of the Sisters of Mercy under something of a cloud in April of 1952. She and another sister were discovered to have been involved in making arrangements for a private adoption of a child in secret and in direct contravention of their vows of obedience. When confronted, her intransigence proved to her superiors that Sister Anthony was unsuitable to religious life and she was asked to leave. Her name, on entering the convent, which she resumed on departure from Saint Vincent's Orphanage, was Margaret Nolan. For a few years afterwards, she was allowed to correspond quarterly with the other nun. These letters came through me and were postmarked Melbourne for the most part. Then the monitoring of the other sister's letters ceased. Other than the fact that Margaret Nolan originally came from the townland of Enagh North outside the village of Kilkishen in County Clare that is all the information I have that could possibly be of any relevance.

I hope this is of some use and beseech you please not to contact me again.

Yours in Jesus Christ,
Sister Joseph.

Back in Dromelton later that evening after the Gilraines and the McNamaras had all pored over the letter, Maree wondered and marvelled at the fact that within less than ten miles of where they were sitting was the home-place of Sister Anthony Nolan. Better still, Shay was able to confirm that the Nolans still lived in Kilkishen. Energised by the new information and the proximity of the village, it was agreed that they would repair to Donnellon's pub where, it being Friday, they would be able to enjoy live music, a singsong and possibly even a Clare set or two.

Shay intended to add somewhat to their store of knowledge by making a few harmless enquiries of his own at the bar. He was in luck because before the night was out he had run into P.J. Murphy, a nephew of the lady they were looking for who was happy to confirm that his aunt was indeed still alive and actually currently visiting in Kilkishen. When he heard that visitors from America and Shay's own Aussie wife had known his aunt in Brisbane and were very anxious to meet her, he suggested that they call to his mother Kate in the old Nolan home the following day.

Next morning they were all up early and excitedly looking forward to the reunion with Sister Anthony. Maree was busy making a batch of queen cakes to bring with them to the Nolan/Murphys later in the morning. Alice and Red had slipped in to Ennis to do some shopping and to get a present for Sister Anthony. Lily, in the company of Norella McNamara, was plundering Maree's garden for flowers. True to his word, P.J. had warned his mother to expect visitors for Margaret so when they arrived in Kilkishen Kate was prepared to entertain them all. She warmly welcomed everyone into the homely kitchen and graciously accepted the flowers and not quite cool queen cakes before ushering them to the already laden table. Emerging from the scullery, wiping her hands on a towel appeared a slim, lively, grey haired woman neatly dressed in a white blouse, plain skirt and a summer cardigan. Her tentative smile now blossomed into a broad beam when she saw first Alice and then Maree. It was unmistakably Sister Anthony looking exactly as they remembered her, just missing the habit and veil. Despite it being only a little after 11.00 a.m. they sat in to the table and over the next half hour sampled Kate's lovely scones and drank gallons of tea.

Then Red went off with Pat and P.J. Murphy on their farming chores while Maree, Alice and Lily went to sit in the garden to continue their chat with the former Sister Anthony. As soon as they were seated, Maree excitedly asked, "Do you see what I see, Sister?"

"Indeed I do, Maree, and please call me Margaret; it's really nearly half a lifetime since anyone has called me Sister. We'll start with the answer to Maree's question before she combusts with excitement. As soon as I met Lily, I knew I had seen such hypnotically beautiful eyes before. From the way Maree was watching me and waiting for my reaction I guessed that the same thought had crossed her mind too. Aside from being stunningly beautiful, Lily, our contention is that you have inherited those gorgeous and unusual eyes directly from your mother. I am convinced, and I'm sure Maree agrees, that we know who Lily's birth mother is or perhaps was as neither of us has seen her in a very long time. When I was in St Vincent's in the nineteen thirties and forties, Maree's best friend was a girl called Frances Brennan."

"Oh my goodness, Maree," interrupted Alice gleefully, "wasn't it after her that you named one of your twin daughters Francesca?" Lily handed Margaret the letter from Sister Joseph. After reading it and marvelling at the coincidence of ending up geographically so close to her nemesis after all these years, Margaret continued with her story.

"I remember like it was yesterday the morning I first laid eyes on Frances as a new-born baby. She was only a tiny mite a few hours old and Sister Francis had found her abandoned in the church porch when she went to unlock it. The new-born was wrapped in a little pink blanket that had been lovingly, if not expertly, knitted for her. It was on an early June morning in the cool of dawn in 1930 and Sister Francis was concerned that the child might die of hypothermia. Needless to mention, there was no sign of the mother: she had made her way deliberately to Nudgee and left her baby at the orphanage.

"Abandoning foundlings was now less common than in earlier times though still not too unusual. For some reason,

Sister Francis was convinced that this little creature was very special. It was a tradition in the house that the person who had found the baby was allowed to choose a name for it: it was therefore up to Sister Francis to name this child. She was very happy to bestow her own surname, Brennan, on the wee mite. She was stymied when it came to a first name. Eventually, she suggested Marianna or Marina. Sister Superior was having none of it and insisted that the baby must have a saint's name. She suggested that they'd call her Frances with an 'e'. So understandably there was always a bond between the two, not that there was any favouritism. Sister Francis was meticulous about that."

In order to move on, Margaret needed to start with Sister Joseph's letter and fill in the blanks from her standpoint. She did not want to burden her listeners with the details of her own story. They were entitled to know about her part in the saga of Sister Francis and Frances Brennan insofar as it might be helpful. "First of all, the content of the letter is factually correct. I am grateful to Sister Joseph for providing the information that brought us together after all this time. The 'under a cloud' reference is more than a little disingenuous of her in that she was largely responsible for my decision to leave. She is right about the date too even though my departure had been decided almost a full year earlier. I had remained to support the nun she is referring to who was Sister Francis. That was a terrible time for both of us.

"I chose to leave and Sister Francis chose to stay. We were both profoundly damaged by the experience and Sister Joseph must face her God for her part in it. The reason I delayed my leaving was I genuinely feared for Sister Francis' health as well as for my own sanity. Enough said on all of that. When she adverts to the 'secret' adoption, it is an unnecessarily cruel and inaccurate reference to the circumstances surrounding Lily's adoption. When Frances came to us for help, we couldn't refuse her. In earlier years, we would have done exactly what we did, now our every move was being scrutinised. You remember how Sister Francis sought you out, Alice? Well, that was our plan. We were both under very strict surveillance at the time and I had acted as decoy that day so Sister Francis could spend time with you.

Any and every action on our part was being used to build a case against us and we feared that Frances' trouble would become another weapon. Ruining Frances would serve no purpose and making arrangements for private adoptions was the way things had been done for decades in orphanages such as ours. Maree, you will remember coming to visit at Saint Vincent's the year before and being told I was not there. I was there all right, locked in my cell for three weeks as punishment at that time. We were so thrilled that you managed to ensure we were able to attend your wedding some weeks later. Your inspired idea to invite Sister Joseph was what made all the difference.

"Lily, my dear, it is my firm belief that you are the child born to Frances Brennan. I do not know the identity of your father though I suspect Sister Francis probably did. All I know is that he was a public figure and a married man. Frances had just begun to make a name for herself on the stage. The scandal of a pregnancy would have destroyed him and ruined her chances of an acting career. It was their decision to keep their alliance a secret and Frances' own decision to sever all ties with him. He was never told the sex of his child nor even if the pregnancy had reached full term nor was he ever given any details of the adoption. Frances went to Hollywood after you were born. She promised to keep in touch with Sister Francis. For some months afterwards, postcards arrived regularly from Hollywood but then suddenly stopped. Nothing was heard from her after that. And in the thirty years since, still nothing. Now, while you three digest all of that, this old lady is going to lie down for a nap. I'll see you in an hour for dinner, okay?"

With that Margaret excused herself, leaving Alice, Maree and a stunned Lily agape in her wake. All of this information, coming as it did in one fell swoop, was indeed difficult for them to absorb. It was also an immense relief to know the facts. Lily, in particular, was mightily relieved that after all the setbacks and the years of searching they were now nearing the end of their quest. At last, they had a name and a little history for her birth mother. All they had to do now was find Frances Brennan who would be able to provide them with details of Lily's father. If luck were on their side at last, then Lily might yet get relevant details of her medical history in time for it to make a difference.

Chapter 28
Back to Achill

Next day they were heading to Achill for a few days before returning to Rochester. Alice and Red hadn't been back home, as they still referred to Achill, since 1948. In their early days in Rochester, they had planned to bring the children to Achill at the first opportunity. After Patrick's death they just kept putting it off. In the end, they just stopped talking about it. Lily was aware of the plans and thought that if she just gave them enough time her parents would eventually get around to taking her on this long planned trip. When it didn't happen, she was hurt at first. Eventually, she understood and forgave them. Sometimes when she was younger she had cried herself to sleep. She missed her brother but perhaps her tears were as much for herself and the idea that her parents had loved Patrick more than they could possibly love her.

Now at last the longed for trip was within reach. Having left Dromelton early in the morning they had stopped for refreshments in Castlebar midmorning. They drove through Newport in glorious sunshine and, as they approached Mulranny with its spectacular views of sea and sand on their left and the heather clothed slopes to the right, Lily begged them to stop so she could absorb it and perhaps capture some images on camera. Like Turner before her she was enormously impressed with the unusual blues of the sky reflected in the waters of the bay and around the islands in the ocean beyond. It was one of those perfect June days when the sun poured down from an almost cloudless sky. What clouds there were, were almost transparent wisps of the finest filaments of cobwebby lace being lazily woven by the merest puffs of a breeze drifting around the headland.

By now, Lily was so busy taking picture after picture that Red had to threaten to leave without her before they could inveigle her back into the car. Lily was absolutely overwhelmed with the beauty of the island of her parents' birth. In her view, it had to be the most scenically stunning place on earth. She had seen the Grand Canyon, Niagara Falls and Victoria Falls and she had visited most of the Seven Wonders of the World, both ancient and modern. As far as she was concerned, nothing compared to the majesty and the wonder of this gem on the west coast of Ireland. Alice and Red were looking forward eagerly to showing her around the island.

They arrived in Achill Sound just in time for lunch. As they drove across the bridge which joined Achill to the mainland, Red explained that its construction in 1888 had dramatically changed the lives of the islanders forever. For the first time, they were in a position to face outwards and consider the possibilities of travel. "In a way, I suppose we can blame the Victorians for making Achill folk emigrants and happy wanderers of the earth. That's why anywhere you go in the world you'll find people of Achill origin and their descendants. Now in God's name, women, let's have a bite to eat, my poor belly thinks my throat is cut."

After lunch in the hotel at the Sound Red took their luggage to their rooms before setting off to follow the Atlantic Drive. Driving along this scenic route their first stop was at the graveyard in Kildomnet where he told Lily the story and Alice pointed out the gravestones of the youngsters who had died in the drowning accident in Westport in 1890. As they resumed their journey, Red revelled in telling her all about Gráinne

Mhaol, Grace O Malley the Pirate Queen before showing her one of Gráinne's many castles close to Darby's Point. Further on they came to Ashleam Bay where they admired the might of the Atlantic as it crashed against the rocky outcroppings and carved caves and caverns in the cliff face and left sea arches and sea stacks behind.

Avoiding the village for the moment they made their way along the cliff edged route which then meandered up and down before it reached the village of Doeega perched above its sheltered beach. Here they stopped again to admire the views in all directions. First, looking out to sea with Clare Island enticingly close at hand in the foreground, they noted the sun shining on its green fields and grassy knolls with the tip of Achill Beg visible to the left. Facing in the opposite direction their eyes were drawn the length of the rift valley towards Mweelaun. The steep mountain slopes on either side were dotted with hundreds of horny Achill sheep. There were lots of cottages clustered together in the village with now very few on the lower folds of the uplands. After that the steeper faces boasted no signs of human habitation as far as the eye could reach.

They motored inland for a while through moor land covered in purple heathers and golden furze and bogs awash with fluffy white bog cotton. At last, they arrived in the village of Dugort East. Then, leaving the car parked at the Golden Strand, they got out and looked seawards again. Standing at the edge of the road the view was breath-taking. Directly across from them in the foreground the fertile sandy soil of Dohooma, famous for early potatoes, basked in the evening sun. Peeping over its shoulder was the jagged shoreline at Belmullet. Following the view to the left, the dark blue seascape was speckled with white caps or seahorses until the eye was drawn upwards to the majestic sweep of two thousand two hundred and twelve feet tall Slievemore Mountain, towering above the roadway to Dugort Pier.

Turning to look to the right the first thing to attract the gaze was a rivulet flowing slowly seawards and taking a meandering route across the strand and spreading delta-like before entering the ocean at last. Beyond the marram grass holding the sand dunes from the ever present threat of erosion stretched the Valley sandy banks where generations of youngsters had played football. And closer to the edge of the waters was a serene and lonely spot on the headland called Cawrawn where unbaptised children have been buried for centuries stretching back so far they are lost in the mists of time. Further to the right beyond the Cockle Lake lay the village of the Valley and the pier at Bullsmouth. Having admired the view for some time while Red pointed out the sights, they set off walking uphill with their backs to the sea in the direction of Dugort East.

The early afternoon sun beat down on them as they made their way past Kate's until they reached the Sweetman home, now unfortunately abandoned and in a very derelict condition. The thatched roof was sagging and moss covered, the whitewashed walls discoloured with mould and the paint cracked and peeling on door and windows. Lily was intrigued, especially when her dad agreed to open the door and check whether it might be safe to go inside.

From the stories Alice had told over the years Lily had made her own pictures of the house in her imagination. Now she could match her images to reality. They spent the next half hour exploring the house which no one seemed to have entered since Dan, by removing Maud, had virtually abandoned it in November, 1961. The ashes were still scattered on the hearth of the open fire having been joined over the decades by clods of soot along with twigs and sticks, the residual debris of nesting crows. The jugs and platters were still on display on the open dresser in the kitchen and the neatly dressed beds with their lacy pillowcases and hand-woven bawneen coverlets, just as they had been on that long ago morning, were now swathed in a grey film of dust and cobwebs. The lovingly hand-crocheted lace curtains, long since devoured by generations of undisturbed moths, now hung in tatters at the tiny windows. Still, the rooms retained a sense of comfort despite being frozen in time.

When they emerged from the house, they looked back the way they had come to the sun setting over Dohooma, turning the sea blood red and painting the sky fabulous shades of scarlet, pink and coral. Then, turning again, they continued upwards the last half a mile to the end of the road and the Gilraine home. As they approached, they saw Red's bachelor brother Brendan leaning on the gate. He hurried towards them and welcomed them in. The house was exactly as they remembered it with just a few modern touches. The same stove stood in the kitchen and there was an open fire still in the living room. Now there was a central heating burner in the scullery as well as a fridge freezer. The kitchen floor was covered with linoleum as of old. Now the living room was tastefully carpeted. Bridie, his long-dead mother, would have been proud of how her youngest son kept his home.

After a welcome supper they walked the little over a mile back downhill to the pub near the beach where they had a few drinks and enjoyed the company of locals and visitors alike. The next few days were spent in exploring the rest of the island.

They climbed up to the megalithic tomb, made the ascent to the Star on Slievemore and walked through the Deserted Village. Lily and Red, braving the chill, swam in Keem Bay after they had climbed to the abandoned coastguard station at the top of Mautshogue Mountain. Another memorable day they took a boat trip from Purteen Harbour out towards the Bill's Rock. Then, heading northwards towards the traditional shark fishing grounds and across Keem Bay, they enjoyed viewing where they had climbed the previous day. Rounding the head, they travelled parallel to the shore for the seldom seen uplifting view of the spectacular Cathedral Cliffs, the highest cliffs in Ireland. "Many people, even in Ireland, are still under the mistaken impression that this designation belongs to the Cliffs of Moher in County Clare," Red explained before proudly stating, "we know better."

Next they followed the famine road up over Minaun Mountain and skirting along the edge of the cliffs. Red even managed to squeeze in a game of golf on the pretty course at Keel while the two ladies had a chance to shop at the pottery and gallery in the village and have a snack and leisurely chat in the tearooms. While there they wrote their postcards and posted them in the post office before driving back to collect Red. When they had to leave for Shannon Airport the following morning, Lily couldn't stop talking about Achill, the island of dreams. All the way there and half way across the Atlantic she raved on and on about the beauty of the place until eventually she fell into an exhausted slumber.

Chapter 29

Lily's Search Ends

On her return to Rochester, Lily immediately threw herself back into her frenetic life of work. Even while in Ireland and thoroughly enjoying every minute of her holiday Lily was experiencing bouts of inertia and extreme tiredness which she was at pains to keep hidden from her parents. In the short term, Alice and Red returned to their work too. Somehow the visit to Ireland, more than their sense of aging, seemed to help them to ease back on their busyness and concentrate on the two really important things in their lives, Lily's quest and the memorial project. They set about extricating themselves from the day in, day out involvement with their work commitments. Red sold on the company to Alice's nephew Gerard and immediately retired.

Alice decided that since Bethany had so effectively deputised for her in her absence she would be a safe person to take over the duties of chairperson of the Patrick Gilraine Memorial Counselling Service on a more permanent basis. Diane Mallon, too, offered her services to support Alice's retirement. Bethany happily agreed to take on the challenge, allowing Alice the freedom to join Red in assisting Lily in her continuing search on a full-time basis. Lily was delighted with her parents' one hundred percent commitment to her search, particularly as her own health was on a downward trajectory.

Her energy levels were at an all-time low so if the next phase of the quest, as it undoubtedly would, involved travelling then having the support of her parents and their company would be a great help. And if worse came to worst and her health deteriorated to the extent that she became unable to make journeys Alice or Red would be free and willing to fill in for her. Meanwhile, she had to get on with her busy work schedule as her doctors were no nearer to understanding her condition or providing her with either relief for her pain or much hope of recovery.

The logical place to begin the search for Francesca Brennan was either the last place she was known to reside, Hollywood, or her last movements before leaving Australia. It made sense to try to find out as much as possible before heading out to California on what, at this stage, could easily be a wild goose chase. Alice, with her excellent organisational skills, set about mobilising assistance. Susan, as always, was very supportive of Lily both as friend and medic and was now increasingly anxious that Lily share her health worries with her mom and dad.

Daisy was Alice's first port of call when it came to starting a computer search because of her undoubted expertise and also because her personal interest made it impossible to side-line her without causing huge and unnecessary offence. Preliminary enquiries could also be made from Rochester. Alice would leave this to Red as he had already lined up his own coterie of friends and helpers to call on.

Buoyed up by the breakthrough in Ireland, things seemed to be going well at first. Within a few days, Daisy had been able to find that a Francesca Brennan had embarked from Sydney aboard the Castelblanca bound for California on 11th February, 1952. This was welcome proof that the information gleaned earlier was accurate. Unfortunately, at this point their luck turned again. When they got to check out the arrival of the Castelblanca in California, the records of disembarkation at the

Port of Los Angeles revealed no information on Francesca Brennan. Then they tried the records from the Port of San Francisco and Hunter's Point with no better results. To all intents and purposes Francesca Brennan had vanished between the time she joined the ship in Sydney and its arrival in the United States.

There were a number of possibilities which needed to be explored. Had she disembarked at one of the stops en route, and if so, which one? Had she got married aboard ship and thus changed her name? Had she simply assumed another name under which to disembark and thus leave no trail? Again, if so, what name did she then choose? And what other possibilities were there that the Gilraines had not even thought of? Over the next months all of these scenarios had to be investigated. Each one was queried in turn and as they came up against a blank wall time after time, then other possibilities had to be considered and followed up on.

Eventually, they agreed as a family that perhaps it would be best to start at the other end and see if they could establish whether or not Francesca was still alive. If they found a death certificate, then they would at least know for certain that the search was over. So now they turned their attention in this direction. Here again they ran into a dead end straight away. A computer search revealed that no death certificate was available for Francesca Brennan in Hollywood, Los Angeles or in San Francisco. Later on, they would have to do the search the hard way. Initially they tried lots of other avenues including trying to find if, by any chance, Francesca might have died aboard the Castelblanca or perhaps if there was any information at all available about that voyage which might help them.

Again, they ran into problems. The Castelblanca had run aground and broken her back during a storm off the coast of Africa in 1963 and had sunk. Her log and all the information it held now rested at the bottom of the sea. What secrets regarding

Francesca Brennan, if any, it contained were now residing safely in 'Davy Jones' locker'. Once over the disappointment of yet another door closed in their faces, Lily and Alice realised that their options had narrowed significantly. They would have to go to Hollywood in person.

On their first trip, they spent three full eight-hour days searching the death records for the Hollywood area painstakingly for women with the forename Francesca or Frances in the hope of finding anyone with the birth date June 10th, 1930. For some reason, they had opted to start from the current year and work backwards rather than the other way around so after three days of scrutinising the records for the years 1984 back to 1971 they had found no match. Before leaving California they visited a number of film studios. They also went to Universal Studios in Burbank, Los Angeles, in the hope that they might be able to find some trace of a young Australian actress from 1951 there.

Although they had no concrete results, they had sown some seeds and felt that they were at least doing something that might yet lead somewhere. So they returned to Rochester exhausted but not too despondent. Lily's deteriorating health left her vulnerable to infection and unfortunately on the return flight from Los Angeles she fell prey to a serious cold. As a result, she was unable to return to work the following day. Although rather tired herself, Alice spent the next couple of days playing nursemaid to her daughter and to her husband as well.

In their absence, Red had gone out as a volunteer on a search and rescue mission and caught a chill. After a few days of tender loving care and homemade chicken broth and spoiling Lily was back on her feet and back at work. Unusually Red was still lingering about the house feeling under the weather, lacking in energy and crawling back into bed after a few hours of hanging about listlessly. Alice was worried about him and sent for the doctor. As luck would have it, while she was waiting for the arrival of Dr Robertson the family physician, Susan called to see Lily who was due home. In the course of conversation, Alice mentioned that she was concerned about Red and waiting for the doctor.

Watching Susan's reaction as she did a cursory examination of her husband Alice was not at all reassured. In the kitchen a few minutes later, as she made a pot of tea for Susan and herself, she tried to press Susan on what she was concerned about. All Susan would say was that she was pleased that Alice had sent for the doctor and that this was a good decision. Later still, after Dr Robertson had left, a whey-faced Alice came to speak to Lily and Susan. "Doc Robertson wants Red to be admitted immediately to hospital. He thinks that he has pneumonia. He's taken some blood and urine samples. He's sent for the ambulance and has gone ahead to be there for the admission. What's going on, Susan? What do you think is the matter with him? Please don't lie to us."

"Alice, you know he's not my patient and I really shouldn't be second guessing my colleague. As Dr Robertson has admitted him, ostensibly because of the pneumonia, which I think is only a symptom, he'll want to get to the root cause as quickly as possible. I'd recommend that you travel in the ambulance with Red. Lily and I will follow immediately and meet you there. You know that as soon as the results of the tests are back Doc Robs will fill you in," Susan said as both she and Lily tried to reassure Alice. On arrival at the hospital, Red was brought directly to a private room where Alice, Lily and Susan were allowed to visit him almost immediately. They didn't have too long to wait before Dr Robertson arrived.

"Hello, Red, I see you have brought your harem with you, you lucky devil. Anyone else would be fortunate to have one bedside beauty. Trust you to have three. Nice to see you all again, ladies, and each of you looking so lovely. I'm sure you're all anxious to know what my preliminary tests show. Well, let's have the good news first. As for the pneumonia, with a little medication and rest you should be right as rain, Red, and in short order too. Something odd is showing up in the blood work, however, and I won't be able to tell you any more until I run more comprehensive tests. As we'll be keeping you here anyway, we can do that over the next few days so there's no need to worry. Goodnight all, I'll see you tomorrow."

Within minutes, a nurse appeared and gave Red some antibiotic tablets to take. Next she checked his blood pressure and warned his visitors not to tire him out. She smiled at the patient and, after promising to return soon, she left. Susan drove Alice and Lily home after wishing Red goodnight. Within minutes of their coming home, Susan's parents Johnny and Caroline arrived. Johnny had brought with him a bottle of good Irish Bushmills Whiskey called 'Black Bush' by way of a gift and in the hope that it would keep the cold out and perhaps help the ill Lily and the over-tired Alice get a good night's sleep. While the women were gathered around the fire Johnny made for the kitchen to make up hot whiskeys for them all. He had just handed them around to the ladies and was on his way back to the kitchen for his own tumbler when the phone in the hall rang. "Shall I answer that, Alice?" He called.

"Please do if it's not too much bother." When he did, he found it was from the hospital, requesting the immediate return of the Gilraine family as Red's condition had suddenly deteriorated. Poor Johnny then had to break this unwelcome news to his friends. Luckily he hadn't drunk any alcohol, so he was in a position to drive them to Unity Hospital. As the journey took no more than ten minutes, imagine the shock when on their arrival, they were ushered not into the private room rather into a waiting area designated 'Family Room'. Here they were joined by Dr Robertson who had the unenviable task of breaking it to them that they were too late. Red Gilraine had suffered a massive heart attack and died within the last few minutes. Repeated attempts to revive him had failed. He was a little over sixty-six years of age and had never been sick a day in his life. A post mortem examination carried out the next day revealed that Red had had a very large adenocarcinoma. In other words, he had pancreatic cancer at a very advanced stage. It also revealed that Red's heart had indeed given out. Whether he suspected that he had cancer and the stress of keeping this suspicion to himself had caused the heart attack, they would never know. One way or another, his days had been numbered. Accepting this knowledge after the event in no way lessened the shock and trauma suffered by his loved ones at his sudden death. In fact, both Alice and Lily were extremely distressed and disturbed as a result of the suddenness of their loss. They had had no inkling that there was anything wrong with Red and were completely and utterly unprepared for the abruptness and finality of his unexpected departure. Each in her own way missed him and had soul-destroying regrets about not giving him more of her time and attention, particularly in recent months since their return from their shared magical idyll in Achill the previous summer. What they were afraid to voice for fear of further hurting each other was the question of how much strain and stress Red had suffered as a direct result of his part in the search for Lily's birth mother.

Lily in particular blamed herself for allowing her search to become a family obsession. Alice, having already suffered the demise of a treasured son, now felt bereft at the sudden and irrevocable loss of her soul- mate, her much-loved husband and her dearest friend. She honestly wondered how she would cope without having a total breakdown. She was stronger than she gave herself credit for, a fact that was forcibly brought home to her when she saw how weak and wretched Lily looked. So, like any mother who worries about her child, she drew on her reserves of maternal strength to come to the aid of her wounded and suffering daughter. They survived the funeral and burial somehow in mutual support of each other. In the immediate aftermath of the funeral and even before the month's end, Alice and Lily talked of continuing the search. They consoled each other with the thought of planning the next phase and it also helped to distract them from the hurtful reality of life without a beloved husband and father. It was only after his passing that they began to realise fully just how much work Red had always undertaken to keep them comfortable. Even in their home they kept discovering task after necessary task that neither of them had ever had to do. Red had always done such chores as laying fires, cleaning out the ashes, putting out the garbage, chopping wood, ordering coal and oil as well as everything to do with gardening. Alice and Lily, living in their sheltered bubble, had forgotten that these jobs didn't just happen and that someone had to do them. It was Red, too, who had always done the shopping. From the dim recesses of her mind, Alice dredged a memory of occasionally doing the shopping with Red. She seemed to remember that there was a time when she used to draw up the shopping list. That was all such a long time ago. Now she found that between looking after Lily, who was increasingly unwell, and all the extra jobs to be done about the place she had very little time to brood. It was extremely frustrating for her that there was nothing that she could do except worry about Lily's debilitating illness. Until such time as the doctors had isolated precisely what was her condition there was still no possibility of a cure. Finding out more of her medical history was still the surest route to a solution.

Alice vowed to return to Hollywood as soon as possible. She would have to go on her own as Lily was far too frail to undertake such a journey. In fact, Alice was so concerned that she feared to leave her and had determined to seek another medical opinion before making her travel arrangements. Meanwhile, the best she could do was to prepare a decent meal to cheer up Lily and perhaps invite Susan and the Hogans to join them. The dinner was planned for the very next day. Alice was busy in the kitchen most of the day with trips to and from her daughter's bedroom where Lily had opted to remain in order to conserve her energy. Just as she was about to bring a cup of tea to Lily, the phone rang.

Finally there was a breakthrough and the hospital wanted to share the good news that they had at last been able to make a definitive diagnosis. Lily was suffering from a very rare blood disorder called Paroxysmal Nocturnal Haemoglobin IA. This disease starts with the mutation of stem cells in the bone marrow which then causes red blood cells to break down as they pass through. In addition, platelets are no longer developing at a normal rate. The good news was that recent advances in medicine meant that bone marrow transplants could now be undertaken successfully, provided of course that a match could be found with a family member willing to become a donor. This diagnosis made the search for Francesca ever more urgent. The dinner party had suddenly turned into an occasion for celebration. In the course of the evening, the mood swung from elation to sadness, nostalgia to excitement and back again as well as the full gamut of emotions in between. Fleetingly the thought crossed Alice's mind that Red had been spared the worry of their beloved daughter's deterioration.

The plan for Alice to go to Hollywood was accelerated and she was to be accompanied by a willing Caroline. Susan would organise some leave so she could move in and look after Lily for the few days their mothers would be away. A few days later, Alice and Caroline were seated in front of the record books wearing white cotton gloves and again searching for any death record for a Frances or a Francesca Brennan or indeed any other surname matched to a June 10th, 1930, birth date from 1970 back to 1951. After two and a half days of systematic and careful scrutiny they had again come up with nothing. With what time they had left before their return flight they went back to the film studios and, believe it or not, at Universal Studios in Burbank they had an amazing piece of luck.

One of the props guys remembered Alice from her previous visit and better still had been doing some amateur detective work in the interim. He had actually managed to establish that for a short period in the early summer of 1951 there had been an Australian starlet who had worked for the studio under the name of Francesca Brennan. She had got a few bit parts and suddenly disappeared after only a few months. Seeing the obvious disappointment engendered by this news, he hastened to add that he had managed to track down a photo of the girl taken shortly after her arrival. He duly produced a copy of the photo which he offered to Alice to keep, explaining that the other lady in the picture was Francesca's mother who insisted on accompanying her daughter each day to the studios. In fact, according to their informant, it was the overbearing and unreasonable nature of this indomitable lady which had put paid to her daughter's chances at the studio. She couldn't resist interfering until at last no director would hire Francesca, whose little talent could not compensate for the handicap of her domineering and pompous parent. They thanked the man for all his help and Alice gave him some money for his time and trouble. On their way to the airport, Caroline said, "Alice, I thought that we had at last made a breakthrough but you don't seem too happy. What's troubling you?"

"Oh, Caroline, I'm so sorry. You're absolutely right: at first I was really excited. Now I can't help thinking there's something not quite right about the photo. As for that whole saga about the mother, it just doesn't fit. From everything I've ever heard about Frances I can't imagine where this woman has come from. The girl in the photo bears no resemblance whatsoever to Maree's description of her friend, nor to my memory of Sister Francis' description of her to me. And I've always believed that, even aside from their remarkable eyes, Lily bore a striking resemblance to her mother. The girl in the photo couldn't be less like Lily than an apple is to an orange. Every detail is wrong. Hair colour, eye shape, height, build, everything in fact. The girl in the photo has clear round monochromatic eyes that appear to be pale blue or grey. I can only conclude she is not our Francesca."

On the flight back home, they had plenty of time to talk about their experiences and decide what to share with Lily. Alice would send the photo to Maree to confirm her suspicions. Now that they had had time to think about it, if the girl in the photo was not, in fact, Francesca but pretending to be, then they must have met aboard the Castelblanca and maybe it was she who had posted the cards from Hollywood. This suggested to them that Francesca may have disembarked before the ship reached the United States. It reopened an avenue of enquiry earlier considered and from which they had already established that the ship had called at only two ports on the voyage in question, Cape Town, South Africa, and the Cape Verde Islands.

This time they would start with the more likely of the two. If a person wanted to start a new life in the fifties, optimising job opportunities and minimising chances of discovery would suggest Cape Town rather than Cape Verde. With this planned next step they arrived in Rochester in a reasonably upbeat frame of mind. As expected, Johnny came to meet them. Instead of driving directly home he headed for Dewey Street. En route he told them that Susan had recommended hospital care for Lily as her condition had continued to worsen. At Unity Hospital, she would get whatever treatment would keep her alive until a bone marrow match could be found. Alice was very worried and also grateful for Susan's expertise and prompt action as well as her loving care for her friend.

They were shocked to see how emaciated Lily looked and how much she had deteriorated in the five days since they had last seen her. Her current environment in the intensive care unit, surrounded by bleeping machines and tubes and equipment, made her look even more vulnerable. Alice and Caroline did their best to keep the mood light and make the most of the positives they had gleaned from their trip. Alice intended to visit Lily as soon as she'd be allowed the following morning and after she'd posted on the photo to Maree for identification. She'd also speak with Maree, Sister Consilio and Daisy to fill them in on the latest developments. She wanted to enlist their help in the tracing of Frances to Cape Town.

She also intended on having a chat with Sister Joseph to see if she could shake loose any further information which she felt convinced this cunning lady had withheld to date. Later that night she rang Sister Consilio first and told her the news. Then, fearing she'd lose her nerve, she asked to speak with Sister Joseph. Wisely Mary asked no questions, just rang the internal code which summoned her sister in religion and handed over the phone to her when she came.

Alice explained about Lily's deteriorating health, about the possibility of tracing her birth mother to Cape Town and about the urgency of finding a bone marrow match. Then she asked for prayers and appealed to the nun to rack her brains to see if she could dredge up any memory which might lead them to Lily's paternal family. Then, crossing her fingers that she hadn't oversold her plea, she rang off, not before leaving her number so Sister Joseph could get back to her. Then she had a chat with Nora and brought her and Daisy up to date. Daisy immediately promised to start a computer search through her contacts in the library service in South Africa and to get back to Alice as soon as possible. After that she thought she'd be as well to try and get some sleep but first she must talk to Maree and maybe Margaret Nolan as well. As it was now approaching one o clock in the morning and still too early to ring Ireland, she made a pot of tea for herself and started to write an account of all her concerns to put with the photo she intended to post to Maree in the morning. By the time she had finished, she had a better idea, she'd copy both the photo and the account and get them off to both Maree and Margaret in the morning. When she awoke, she was surprised that it was after nine so she dressed quickly and hurried to the post office, got her copying done and posted her two packages. Then, grabbing some magazines, she went to visit her daughter. She made her way to the Intensive Care Unit. When she got there, she was told that the ICU was off limits to visitors. She took a seat in the corridor and waited, knowing that someone was being attended to on the other side of the wall. She had no idea that the patient needing attention was Lily. So she was surprised when, well over an hour later, she was approached by a white coated young woman whom she took a few seconds to recognise as Susan. Taking her hand between both of her own, Susan whispered, "She's out of danger now, Alice, and you can see her in a short while. Meanwhile, come with me and we'll have a cup of coffee in my office." In a bit of a daze, she followed Susan, her feet as well as her brain frozen with trepidation. Susan showed her to a seat and hurried off to get the coffees. She returned a few minutes later accompanied by two other specialists also bearing coffees. They took it in turns to explain what had happened and to reassure Alice that Lily was over the worst. She had had a bad reaction to some element of her treatment and had gone into shock. Now that they had isolated the responsible element they would continue to treat her safely. They were hopeful that there would be no recurrence of the problem as it was unlikely she would survive another episode in her current weakened condition. Poor Alice was aghast at the seriousness of Lily's state and at how close they had come to losing her. When at last she got to see her beloved Lily, Alice decided that she would remain with her until she would be forcibly removed if that's what it took. She knew that Lily was being monitored remotely and that if anything moved in the room it would be picked up on camera and appear on the television screen on the desk in the nurse's station. It was her maternal duty, as well as her wish, to offer what comfort she could to her very ill daughter. When Susan was finished her shift, she came and sat with them for a while. Alice was grateful that she did not try to persuade her to leave. Nor was she surprised when her brother

Dan and her sister Annie slipped in later on to share her vigil. Typical of Annie, she had come well provisioned. Her commodious handbag contained a selection of dainty sandwiches, home baking and biscuits as well as a vacuum flask of boiling water. She had also packed four picnic beakers, three small covered bowls containing coffee, sugar and milk and a handful of teabags. Within minutes of her arrival, she had laid out a tempting array of food and a choice of tea or coffee in front of Alice. Not even feeling hungry, Alice realised that she hadn't eaten all day and with the exception of the half cup of coffee she had tasted in Susan's office earlier she had had nothing to drink either. She gratefully ate some of what Annie had put before her and even managed to persuade Lily to try a morsel. A while after they had left Lily fell asleep and Alice, too, nodded off.

She woke up when a night nurse slipped in and offered her a chair bed for the few remaining hours. She turned down the kind offer quietly and firmly on the basis that moving furniture would wake Lily. In reality, she feared that Lily might slip away while she slept. Alice kept watch and prayed. Just as dawn broke, the door opened silently and seconds later Caroline appeared at her side. They sat there in silence and prayed. At 6.30 a.m. Lily woke up and when she saw them both she smiled at each of them in turn.

Then, turning to her mother, she whispered falteringly, "Mom…thanks…Dad's…waiting…for…me…I'm…so…sorry."

Then the machine began to bleep. By the time help arrived, Lily was gone. For the second time in six weeks, Alice was back at the Church of Saint Charles Borromeo at a funeral Mass after which she followed the hearse containing her daughter to the cemetery to be interred above her brother and beside her father. In the fullness of time, the headstone would bear the legend recording Lily's death at age thirty-three and Red's at sixty-six.

Chapter 30

Home at Last

It was less than nine months since Alice had given up full-time involvement in her own personal project which had occupied a huge amount of her waking hours for fifteen years. It was hard to believe that a mere six months ago she had been on the holiday of a lifetime in her favourite place on earth. Since then she had been very busy while she concentrated on the hunt for Lily's cure. And now within six weeks she had lost the two people who were the focus of her life. It was no surprise then that she felt that her life had become meaningless.

Worse still, she found time hanging very heavily on her hands. Coping with bereavement was enough of a challenge, not to mention the crushing loneliness of being the sole occupant of a family home echoing with memories. Remembering her bout of depression so long ago, Alice was determined to keep herself occupied. Annie and Caroline were equally anxious to ensure that she was not spending too much time alone. So they took it in turn to accompany her to the cemetery, initially each day and later a little less frequently.

Slowly they encouraged her to make at least some of these visits on foot. First one of them would walk there with her while the other collected and drove them home. As the weather improved, they walked in both directions for their health's sake, a round-trip of almost six miles. Now that they were fit they began to take part in charity walks which inevitably drew Alice back into attending events associated with her son Patrick's memorial counselling service. This set her thinking about what kind of memorial she might organise for Lily. Over a few weeks in early summer of 1986 she made a point of meeting members of the family and friends for coffee or for lunch to discuss a fitting memorial for Lily. She also wanted to sow the seeds of her planned abandonment of Rochester. Her June round of discussions had yielded a number of good suggestions, one of which was the renaming of The Patrick Gilraine Bereavement Counselling Service to include Lily's name.

In the end, Alice chose to remember her daughter in a different manner. She wanted to find a way that paid tribute to her character, in particular Lily's strength, her love of family and her single-minded determination to succeed in whatever she set her mind to. She planned to set up a bursary in Lily's name for a medical research student to concentrate on developing medical interventions to prolong patient lives while sourcing suitable bone marrow donors. The Lily Gilraine Memorial Bursary would be awarded for three year periods on a competitive basis to deserving medical students who showed an interest in the area.

Once this was set up, Alice intended to retire to Achill. First she would move there in July and supervise the refurbishment of the old Sweetman home. She would return to Rochester to spend Christmas with her siblings' families and visit her own family in the cemetery. She would return to Achill in the spring when she hoped her new home would be ready for fitting out and furnishing.

Everything worked according to plan and work was going ahead nicely under the stewardship of a younger generation Sweetman cousin, fittingly named Redmond. He would be assisted by his brothers Paddy and James. Brendan Gilraine had begun to make a habit of strolling by to watch the progress of the work and chat to the Sweetman lads about the importance of building to the highest standards.

One lovely September afternoon, as Alice was at the site in her hard hat and wellington boots, a hired car pulled up. Out hopped her brothers Dan and Michael and then her sister Annie and sister-in-law Nancy. They planned to stay for two weeks during which the two older men intended showing these Irish youngsters how real builders worked. The two women would accompany Alice to Castlebar and Westport and maybe even further afield to see about choosing fittings and soft furnishings. In the course of the next few days, as they rummaged in hardware stores and furniture shops, Annie asked Alice if she would consider having a companion to share her retirement home. "Annie, Annie, don't tell me you're thinking of leaving Rochester? Would you really consider moving back to Achill? I never even thought to ask you as I never dreamed you'd want to do it. Get me out of my misery please; please tell me that's what you were thinking."

Annie laughed heartily at Alice's excitement before replying, "I guess I've got my answer and there was me worrying that you wouldn't like the idea. Now, Alice, if we are going to do this we need to do it right. First I must insist on paying my own way whether that is by way of room rental or contributing up front to the costs of the renovation is entirely up to you. I must put it on the record that I'm not looking for a freebie here or wanting to cramp your style if you'd prefer to preserve your privacy. We need to be entirely sure that it's what we both want and that the arrangement will work well for both of us. Let's have a think about it and we can talk about it again in a day or two."

Then, throwing their arms about each other, they hugged and, re-joining Nancy, they returned to the business of shopping. When the fortnight was up, two very tired but deeply satisfied brothers were ready to return home. They had achieved a huge amount of work and thoroughly enjoyed themselves working with their young relatives on the family home. They had forgotten how pleasant it was to be working outdoors in warm weather with no humidity. When they finished in the evenings, all they had to do was wander down the hill for seafood and creamy pints of Guinness with the young lads before the women came to collect them. Dan and Michael were very pleased with the progress of the work achieved over the two weeks of their stay and were in confident agreement with young Redmond that the building would be sealed by the end of October and that all the plastering, both external and internal, would be completed before Christmas. When the party left for Shannon the following morning, it comprised only Dan, Nancy and Michael. Annie would stay on with Alice until her return for Christmas.

Chapter 31

Island of Dreams

One beautiful sunny day in July, 2000, Alice and Annie were sitting in their garden behind their cottage looking down over the stretch of the Golden Strand and out to sea. There was hardly a puff of wind and the sun was warm on their straw-hatted heads. They were sipping tea from china mugs at a little table halfway up the terraced garden. They were reluctant to disturb the silence which surrounded them. The only sounds were the humming of bees gathering nectar in the fuchsia hedge or among the summer colour of the flower beds at their feet. In the years since they had moved here, they'd been great companions, best friends and devoted sisters. They had enjoyed a lovely retirement, sharing a love of reading, crosswords and scrabble while pursuing their individual interests undisturbed by the other. Annie had always loved the old crafts so she spent hours spinning, carding and hand dyeing wool in the old traditional ways using only natural dyes. She then used her yarns to knit and crochet fabulous garments which were much sought after in the fashion houses of Dublin, Paris and New York. Shortly after settling in Alice decided to write her memoir. She had undertaken the task more as an exercise in coping with bereavement than for any other reason. When she had finished, she circulated typed copies to her siblings and a few friends who were particularly interested in reading it. All were impressed with her story and before she knew it she had been approached by a publishing house to have it published. The first edition was understandably a small one. Word of mouth made it popular and it sold out in a very short time as did the second larger edition. Later there was an American edition and then an Australian one. Alice was very surprised and pleased with the interest her book had generated.

One unexpected spin off from the publication was the number of letters, many of them containing money and cheques from people who wished to contribute to research on the condition of paroxysmal nocturnal haemoglobin IA. Alice immediately opened a special fund account, details of which appeared in subsequent editions. From time to time she still received letters from readers which she treasured. She still wrote occasional articles for the newsletters of both The Patrick Gilraine Bereavement Counselling Service and The Lily Gilraine Memorial Bursary. She and Annie loved their life in Achill, especially the summers when they could entertain family and friends from all over the world.

As they sat in the garden on this June evening, the silence was broken by footsteps on the roadway below accompanied by tuneful whistling. Their attention drawn in that direction, the two ladies noticed a good looking well-dressed gentleman of indeterminate age breasting the uphill climb. They did not recognise him so were a bit surprised when he paused at the cottage and then made his way around the side and, leaning on the picket gate, called up to where he could see them in the garden. "Is either of you two lovely ladies the author Alice Gilraine?" A little taken aback by such seeming effrontery, it took a moment for their innate good manners to reassert themselves. Then they invited him to come and join them. He strolled boldly toward them with his hand outstretched.

As he shook hands with each of them in turn, he introduced himself. "My name is Jonathon Wyatt and I've been looking for you since I read your book last year. Mind you, it took me a while to track you down. And when I did finally I found your island people were rather coy about your whereabouts. Oh my God, I hope I haven't scared you, I'm so sorry. Let me start again?" With that he reached into his inside pocket and produced a little pack of photographs which he spread out on the table. The first one was a tiny snapshot of a baby which Alice recognised with a start as Lily, taken within hours of her birth. The second was a classic photographer's portrait probably taken in the 1950s of a strikingly beautiful young woman in her late teens who Alice guessed was Frances/Francesca Brennan. Next was what appeared to be a wedding picture of Francesca and her groom who was undoubtedly a younger version of the man before them. The other four photos were of a girl at approximately age three, age eight, age sixteen and then the same young woman in a wheelchair obviously close to death at perhaps age twenty or so. The girl looked scarily like Lily. When Alice recovered, her equilibrium and her breath she invited Jonathon to sit down and tell his story from the beginning.

Jonathon began. "Alice, let me start by sympathising with you on the loss of Lily. As you've already figured out, Frances was Lily's birth mother. And you have probably gathered by now I was her birth father. In 1950, I was introduced to Francesca Brennan and fell instantly in love with her and she with me. We met at an after-show political fundraising party. I was in cabinet at the time and Francesca was in her very first show, having been plucked from the obscurity of her drama class to star as the young second wife in Noel Coward's 'Blithe Spirit'. We established a rapport immediately at that first meeting and I knew that I never wanted to let her out of my sight again.

"In my defence, I did warn her off me by telling her straight up that I was married. Fate threw us together again within a few weeks and I tried very hard to steel myself against her on that occasion. I won't bore you with the details. Before the month was out we had started writing to each other. For some reason, it has been reported over and over again in the media that I was a family man. This was not entirely accurate.

"I had made a precipitate, ill-advised and unfortunately unhappy marriage in my early twenties. Martina Scott Phelps was a very attractive and very popular wealthy socialite with political ambitions. She was very knowledgeable and encouraged me in my early days. By the time I realised that Martina's interest in me was only as a puppet for her own ambition, we were already married. Martina was also making it abundantly clear that she held all the winning cards. She had the money, the ambition, the contacts and all the bed partners she could handle. As far as she was concerned, my role was to be her stalking horse politically and her tame escort socially. She never really understood that this arrangement did not gel with my idea of marriage. In fact, she could not accept that I could possibly be unhappy given that she had 'bought and paid for me' as she so crudely put it. Anyway, Francesca and I began to see more and more of each other and eventually, against our better judgement, consummated our relationship. Wouldn't you know it, Francesca immediately became pregnant. We stopped seeing each other straight away to avoid scandal. I pleaded with Martina to release me. As the timing was not right for her, she was having none of it. She threatened to ruin us both and to bring down the government if that's what it took to keep me in line. By now, Francesca was distraught and feeling that she had let down the good nuns who had reared her. She begged me to return to Martina and not have the break-up of my marriage on her conscience as well as her own shameful condition.

"In the end, to my shame, I gave in, provided she would at least keep in touch by letter. This she promised to do and I lived for her letters. Then at the beginning of December she suddenly stopped writing. When she failed to reply to my third letter, I got concerned and, going against her express wishes, decided to call around to the address I had for her. I found she had moved five days prior, leaving no forwarding address.

"I searched frantically for weeks on end. By now, I didn't care who knew or what the political consequences might be, I just wanted to find her. Seeing how distraught I was, Martina relented somewhat so, provided I resigned and left the country, she declared herself happy to divorce me quietly later on the grounds of desertion. By the time we had worked out this agreement and I had resigned, it was mid-January, 1951. My search for Francesca was proving fruitless.

"Then one day this little photo arrived. No letter, not even a note, just the little snapshot carefully wrapped in tissue paper. I knew it had to be our daughter and that Francesca must have sent it. Sadly I had no idea from where. She had had the baby and the obvious place for her to turn had to be the orphanage where she had been brought up. I made my way to Nudgee and St Vincent's Orphanage. I had heard the names Sister Francis and Sister Anthony several times from Francesca so when I arrived I intended to ask to see them both.

"When Mother Superior ushered me into the parlour, some instinct made me ask for Sister Anthony only. Straight away I was told that the nun was not available. Reverend Mother stonewalled at every turn. She obviously knew who I was and made sure I knew that. I had run out of questions to which no answers were forthcoming. I gambled on tradition. No refreshment had been offered. If I were bold enough to ask, could the Reverend Mother refuse me? So I plastered on my best smile and, referring to the heat of the day and the long walk, begged for a refreshing cup of tea.

"Reverend Mother rang her bell and seconds later a nun appeared. Tea and light refreshments were reluctantly ordered. Five minutes later, to the senior nun's obvious dismay, the tray was carried in by a different nun. 'Please put it on the table and leave immediately, Sister Francis. Where is Sister Damian and why did she not bring the tray as requested?' Before turning around to answer her superior's question, Sister Francis pointed to the underside of the cup in front of me. Then, while she explained that Sister Damian had had a spillage in the kitchen necessitating a change of habit, I lifted the cup and secreted up my sleeve the tiny piece of paper I found there. As expected, I got no information whatsoever from the Reverend Mother who couldn't wait to get rid of me. Once clear of the premises, I opened the scrap of paper Sister Francis had gone to such trouble to give me. In tiny writing, I read the legend 'F. going to USA. Baby safe. Adopted. Good family.'

"Over the next days and weeks, I searched and searched but could find no trace of Francesca. Then I had a brainwave: if she were planning on going to the United States I should check the shipping lists. Within twenty-four hours, I had found that she was booked on the Castelblanca from Sydney on February 11th, only two days hence. I booked a ticket for myself as far as Cape Town and went aboard. I watched her sad figure as she came aboard and as soon as we put to sea I sought her out. I explained that soon I would be free as Martina had agreed to a quiet divorce. If she would only agree to come with me, I was on my way to a new life in Cape Town. She was as pleased to see me as I was to see her. Not so long afterwards she agreed to my proposal. We found a young woman aboard whose obnoxious mother wanted her to go to Hollywood. Francesca decided to hand over her introductory letter to Universal Studios if the girl agreed to post the handful of postcards Francesca gave her at the intervals specified when she got to Hollywood.

"When my divorce papers came through the following year, Francesca and I married. We tried and tried to trace the baby but to no avail. As Sister Francis' note had so concisely put it, she had been safely adopted by a good family and was no longer ours. Francesca never got over her regret at parting with her baby.

"Two years later our gorgeous Francine was born. When she was only eight years old, we lost her mother to Paroxysmal

271

Nocturnal Haemoglobin IA. Twelve years later, I watched my beloved daughter die of the same accursed disease. I wasn't a match, you see. When I read your book, I prayed that I might be a match for Lily. Then I heard that she too had lost her battle long ago. I'm so sorry to dredge it all up again, Alice, but thought perhaps it might bring you closure."

"Thank you, Jonathon, for filling in the gaps. Let's go inside; it's getting late."